It was ironic, after all the promises of worldwide nuclear destruction and such, that the world had actually died with a whimper after all. All the prosaic, predictable things, but reinforcing each other, had come to a head at once.

First there had come the large breakdowns—of the international economy, then of the national economy, then of local economies. Then, following economic systems into chaos, had gone the systems of world trade, of food production and other necessary supplies. Law and order had struggled for a while and gone down in the maelstrom. Cities became battlefields of the dead left by riot and revolution. Isolated communities developed into small, primitive, self-fortified territories. And the Four Horsemen of the Apocalypse were abroad once more.

It was a time of bloodletting, of a paring down of the population to those with the patterns for survival under fang-and-claw conditions. A new medievalism was upon the globe. *The iron years had come again . . .*

Nine fine stories from the creator
of the Dorsai . . . Gordon R. Dickson

GORDON R. DICKSON

IN IRON YEARS

SF
ace books
A Division of Charter Communications Inc.
A GROSSET & DUNLAP COMPANY
51 Madison Avenue
New York, New York 10010

IN IRON YEARS
Copyright © 1980 by Gordon R. Dickson

An ACE Book

Published by arrangement
with Doubleday & Company, Inc.

First Ace printing: December 1981
Published Simultaneously in Canada

2 4 6 8 0 9 7 5 3 1
Manufactured in the United States of America

Contents

About the Author. . . .

Born in Alberta, Canada, Gordon R. Dickson moved to the U.S.A. at the age of thirteen and is now a U.S. citizen. He received his B.A. in English from the University of Minnesota, and still makes his home in that state. Mr. Dickson spent three years in the service during World War II—an experience which lends authenticity to his acclaimed "Dorsai" series, part of his lifework "Childe Cycle", about the adventures of interplanetary soldiers. His first published science fiction story, "Trespass", appeared in *Fantastic Story Quarterly* in 1950; since that time he has become one of the most popular authors in the field, and one of the most prolific. Twice president of *Science Fiction Writers of America,* Mr. Dickson is winner of both the Hugo and Nebula Awards and of the August Derleth Award of the British Fantasy Society.

IN IRON YEARS

Slightly after midday, the rain began. Jeebee wiped his glasses and turned the visor of his cap down to keep as much of the falling moisture off them as possible. Wet, they gave him a blurred, untrustworthy image of his surroundings; and although this rolling plains country with its sparse patches of timber and only an occasional devastated farmstead seemed deserted enough, nothing could be certain. In the beginning, in spite of it being March, the rain was not cold; and although it soon soaked through the blanket material of his jacket at the inside of his elbows and upper back, above the packsack, and with each step made damper and more heavy the front of his trousers above the knees, he was not uncomfortable.

But, as the afternoon wore on, the darkness of the heavy cloud cover increased, the temperature dropped, and the rain turned to sleet, whipped against the naked skin of his face as the wind strengthened from the east. Like an animal, he thought of shelter and began to cast around for it, so that when a little later he came to the pile of lumber that had once been a farmhouse, before being dynamited or bulldozed into a scrap heap, he gave up travel for the day and began searching for a gap in the rubble. He found one at last, a hole that seemed to lead far enough in under the loose material to indicate a fairly waterproof overhead. He crawled inside, pushing his pack before him, braced against having stumbled on the den of some wild dog—or worse.

But no human or beast appeared to dispute his entrance, and the opening went back in further than he had guessed. He was pleased to hear the patter of the rain only distantly through what was above him, while feeling everything completely dry and dusty around him. He kept on crawling, as far in as he could until suddenly his right hand, reaching out before him, slid over an edge into emptiness.

He stopped to check, found some space above his head, and risked lighting a stub of candle. Its light shone ahead of him, down into an untouched basement garage, with walls of cinder blocks and a solid roof of collapsed house overhead.

He memorized this scene below as best he could, put the candle out to save as much of it as possible, and let himself down into the thick, dust-smelling darkness, until he felt level floor under his bootsoles. Once down, he relit the candle stub and looked around.

The place was a treasure trove. Plainly no one had set foot here since the moment in which the house had been destroyed, and nothing had been looted from the cellar's original contents.

That night he slept warm and dry with even the luxury of a kerosene lantern to light him; and when he left the place three days later through a separate, carefully tunneled hole much larger than the one by which he had entered, he was rich. He left still more riches behind him. There was more than he could carry, but it was not just a lack of charity to his fellow human beings that made him carefully cover and disguise both openings to the place he had found. It was the hard-learned lesson to cover his trail, so that no one would suspect someone else had been here and would try to track him for what he carried. Otherwise, he would not have cared about the goods he left behind, for his path led still westward to Montana, to his brother Martin's Twin Peaks ranch—eight hundred miles yet distant.

His riches, however, could not help going to his head a little. For one thing, though he realized he was taking a calculated risk, he had ridden off on the motorcycle he had found among other items in the cellar. It was true that it was a light little trail bike and worth a fortune if he could only come across some community civilized enough to trade, rather than simply kill him for it. It was also true that on it, in open country like this, he could probably outrun anyone else, including riders on horseback. But it could be heard coming from a mile away, and gas was scarce. Also, possession of the bike was as open an invitation to attack and robbery as a fat wallet flourished in a den of thieves.

Outside of the motorcycle, however, Jeebee had selected well. He was now wearing some other man's old but still solidly seamed leather jacket; his belt was tight with screwdrivers, pruning knives, and other simple hand tools, and his pockets were newly heavy with boxes of .22-long rifle shells, ammunition for the .22 bolt-action rifle he had been carrying. In addition, he had canned goods, some of which might still be eatable—you could never tell until you opened a can and smelled its contents —and wrapped around his waist above the belt was a good twenty feet of heavy, solid-linked metal chain taken from under the ruins of what had evidently been a doghouse, in the back yard behind the debris of the main building.

He had sense enough by this time not to follow any roads. So he cut off between the hills, on the same compass course westward that he had been holding to for the past two weeks, ever since he had run for his life to get away from Abbotsville. Even to think of Abbotsville now set a cold sickness crawling about in the pit of his stomach. It had taken a miracle to save him. His buck fever had held true to the last; and, at the last, when Bule Mannerly had risen up out of the weeds with the shotgun pointed at his head, he had been unable to shoot, though Bule was only seconds away from shooting him. Only the dumb luck of someone else from the village firing at Jeebee just then and scaring Bule into hitting the dirt, had cleared the way to the hills.

It was not just lack of guts on his part that had kept him from firing, Jeebee reminded himself now, strongly, steering the bike along a hillside in the sunlight and the light March breeze. He, more than anyone else, should be able to remember that, like everyone else, he was the product of his own psychobiological pattern; and it was that, more than anything else, which had stopped him from shooting Bule.

Once, in a civilized world, reactions like his had signaled a survival type of pb pattern. Now, they signaled the opposite. He glanced at his reflection in the rearview mirror on the rod projecting from the left handlebar of the bike. The image of his lower face looked back at him, brutal with untrimmed beard and crafty with wrinkles dried into skin tanned by the sun and wind. But above these signs, as he tilted his head to look, the visor of his cap had shaded the skin and his forehead was still pale, the eyes behind the round glasses still blue and innocent. The upper half of his features gave him away. He had no instinctive courage—only a sense of duty—a duty to the fledgling science which had barely managed to be born before the world had fallen apart.

It was that duty that pushed him now. On his own, his spirit would have failed at the thought of the hundreds of unprotected miles between him and the safety of the Twin Peaks ranch, where he could shelter behind a brother more adapted to these times. But what he had learned and worked at, drove him—the importance of this knowledge that must be saved for the future. All around the world now there would be forty, perhaps as many as sixty, men and women—psychobiological mathematicians like himself—who would have come independently to the same conclusion as he had. For a second the symbols of his math danced in order in his mind's eye, spelling out the inarguable truth about the human race in this spring of dissolution and disaster.

Like him, the others would have come to the conclusion that the knowledge of pb patterns must be protected, taken someplace safe and hidden against the time—five hundred years, two thousand years from now—when the majority of the race would begin to change back again toward civilized patterns. Only if all those understanding pb math tried their best, would there be even a chance of one of them succeeding in saving this great new tool for the next upswing of mankind. It was a knowledge that could read both the present and the future. Because of it, they who had worked with it knew how vital it was that it must not be lost. Only—the very civilized intellectual nature of their own individual patterns made them nonsurvival types in the world that had now created itself around them. It was bitter to know that they were the weakest, not the strongest, vessels to preserve what they alone knew must be preserved.

But they could try. He could try. Perhaps he could come to some terms with this time of savagery. It was ironic, after all the promises of worldwide nuclear destruction and such, that the world had actually died with a whimper, after all.

No—he corrected himself—not with a whimper. A snarl. It had begun with a universal economic breakdown, complemented by overpopulation, overcrowding, overpollution—of noise and idea as well as of waste and heat. A time of frustration, mounting to frenzy, with unemployment soaring, worldwide. Inflation soaring, worldwide. Strikes, crime, disease . . .

—All the prosaic, predictable things, but reinforcing each other, had come to a head at once. And for a reason which had never been suspected, until the math of psychobiological patterns had been created—independently, but almost simultaneously, by people like Piotr Arazavin, Noshiobi Hideki . . . and Jeeris Belany Walthar, yours truly . . .

First there had come the large breakdowns—of the international economy, then of the national economy, then of local economies. Then, following economic systems into chaos, had gone the systems of world trade, of food production and other necessary supplies. Law and order had struggled for a while and gone down in the maelstrom. Cities became battlefields of the dead left by riot and revolution. Isolated communities developed into small, primitive, self-fortified territories. And the Four Horsemen of the Apocalypse were abroad once more.

It was a time of bloodletting, of a paring down of the population to those with the pb patterns for survival under fang-and-claw conditions. A new medievalism was upon the globe. The iron years had come again; and those who were best fitted to exist were those to whom ethics, conscience, and anything else beyond the pure pragmatism of physical power, were excess baggage.

And so it would continue, the pb mathematics calculated, until a new, young order could emerge once more, binding the little village-fortresses into alliances, the alliances into kingdoms, and the kingdoms into sovereign nations which could begin once more to treat with one another in systems. Five hundred years, two thousand years—however long that would take.

. . . And, meanwhile, a small anachronism of the time now dead, a weak individual of the soft centuries, struggled to cross the newly lawless country, carrying a precious child of the mind to where it might sleep in safety for as many centuries as necessary until reason and civilization should be born again—

Jeebee caught himself up at the brink of a bath in self-pity. Not that he was particularly ashamed of self-pity—or, at least, he did not think he was particularly ashamed of it. But emotional navel-contemplating of any kind withdrew his attention from his surroundings; and that could be dangerous. And, in fact, no sooner had he jerked himself out of his mood than his nostrils caught a faint but oily scent on the breeze.

In a moment he had killed the motor of the bike, was off it, and had dragged it with him into the cover of some nearby willow saplings. He lay there, making as little noise as possible and trying to identify what he had just smelled.

The fact that he could not identify it immediately did not make it less alarming. Any unusual phenomena—

noise, odor, or other—were potential warnings of the presence of other humans. And if there were other humans around, Jeebee wanted to look them over at leisure before he gave them a chance to look at him.

In this case the scent was unidentifiable, but, he could swear, not totally unfamiliar. Somewhere he had encountered it before. After lying some minutes hidden in the willows with ears and eyes straining for additional information, Jeebee cautiously got to his feet and, pushing the bike without starting the motor, began to try to track down the wind-born odor to its source.

It was some little distance over two rises of land before the smell got noticeably stronger. But the moment came when, with the bike ten feet back, and lying on his stomach, he looked down a long slope at a milling mass of grey and black bodies. It was a large flock of Targhee sheep— the elusive memory of the smell of a sheep barn at a state fair twelve years before snapped back into his mind. With the flock below were three boys, riding bareback on small hairy ponies. No dogs were in view.

The thought of dogs sent a twinge of alarm along the nerves of Jeebee. He was about to crawl back to his bike and start moving away when a ram burst suddenly from the flock, with a sheep dog close behind it, a small brown-and-white collie breed that had been hidden by the milling dark backs and white faces about it. The sheep was headed directly up the slope where Jeebee lay hidden.

He lay holding his breath until the dog, nipping at the heels of the ram, turned it back into the mass of the flock. He breathed out in relief; but at that moment the dog, having seen the ram safely back among the other sheep, spun about and faced up in Jeebee's direction, nose testing the wind.

The wind was from dog to Jeebee. There was no way the animal could smell him, he told himself; and yet the canine nose continued to test the air. After a second the dog began to bark, looking straight in the direction of where Jeebee lay hidden.

"What's it, Snappy?" cried one of the boys on horseback. He wheeled his mount around and cantered toward the dog, up the pitch of the slope.

Jeebee panicked. On hands and knees he scrambled backward, hearing a sudden high-pitched whoop from below as he became visible on the skyline, followed by the abrupt pounding of horses' hooves in a gallop.

"Get him—*get'm!*" sang a voice. A rifle cracked. Knowing he was now fully in view, Jeebee leaped frantically on the trail bike and kicked down on its starter. Mercifully, it started immediately, and he roared off without looking backward, paying no attention to the direction of his going except that it was away from those behind him and along a route as free of bumps and obstacles as he could find.

The rifle cracked again. He heard several voices now, yelping with excitement and the pleasure of the chase. There was a whistling near his head as a bullet passed close. The little trail bike was slow to build up speed, and the sound of its motor washed out the galloping beat of the horses' hooves behind him. But he was headed downslope, and slowly the bounding, oscillating needle of the speedometer was picking up space above the zero miles-per-hour pin.

The rifle sounded again, somewhat further behind him; and this time he heard no whistle of a passing slug. The shots had been infrequent enough to indicate that only one of the boys was armed; and the rifle used was probably a single shot, needing to be reloaded after firing—not an easy thing to do on the back of a galloping horse with no saddle leather or stirrups to cling to. He risked a glance over his shoulder.

The three had already given up the chase. He saw them on the crest of a rise behind him, sitting their horses, watching. They had given up almost too easily, he thought—and then he remembered the sheep. They would not want to go too far from the flock for which they were responsible.

He continued on, throttling back only a little on his speed. Now that they had seen him, he was anxious to get as far out of their area as possible, before they should pass the word to more adult riders on better horses and armed with better weapons. But he did begin, instinctively, to pay a little more attention to the dangers of rocks and holes in his way.

There was a new, gnawing uneasiness inside him. Dogs meant trouble for him—as one had just demonstrated. Other humans he could watch for and slip by unseen, but dogs had noses and ears to sense him in darkness or behind cover. And sheepherders meant dogs—lots of them. He had never expected to run into sheep this far east. According to his calculations—he had lost his only map some days ago—he should be no further west than barely into Nebraska or the Dakotas, by now.

A sudden, desperate loneliness swept over him. He was an outcast, and there was no one and no hope of anyone, to stand by him. If he had even one companion to make this long hazardous journey with him, there might be a real chance of his reaching the Twin Peaks. As it was, what he feared most deeply was that in one of these moments of despair he would simply give up, would stop and turn, to wait to be shot down by the armed riders following him; or he would walk nakedly into some camp or town to be killed and robbed—just to get it all over with.

Now he fought the feeling of loneliness, the despair, forcing himself to think constructively. What was the best thing for him to do under the circumstances? He would be safer apart from the trail bike, but without it he would not cover ground anywhere near so swiftly. With luck, using the bike, he could be out of this sheep area in a day or so. He had two five-gallon containers of gas strapped behind his saddle on the bike; that much fuel gave him a range of nearly four hundred miles, even allowing for the roughest going.—Four hundred miles—it was like the thought of gold to a miser. The bike was too valuable to abandon. Yes, it would be better to push through and simply hope to outrun trouble, as he just had, if he encountered any more of it.

He could, of course, hide out somewhere during the days and travel nights only; but travel at night was more dangerous. Even with a good moon he would have trouble spotting all the rocks and potholes in the path of the bike. No, the best plan was to make as much time as he could while the day lasted. When night came, he would decide then whether to ride on . . .

Thinking this, he topped the small rise he had been climbing and looked down at a river, a good two hundred yards across, flowing swiftly from south to north across his direct path west.

Jeebee stared at the river in dismay. Then, carefully, he rode down the slope before him until he halted the bike at the very edge of the swiftly flowing water.

It was a stream clearly swollen by the spring runoff. It was dangerously full of floating debris and swift of cur-

rent. He got off the bike and squatted to dip a hand in its
waters. They numbed his fingers with a temperature like
that of freshly melted snow. He got to his feet and remounted the bike, shaking his head. Calm water, warm
water, he could have risked swimming, pushing the bike
and his other possessions ahead of him on a makeshift
raft. But not a river like this.

He would have to go up or downstream until he could
find some bridge on which to cross it. Which way? He
looked to right and to left. To right was downstream; and
downstream, traditionally, led to civilization—which in
this case meant habitation and possible enemies. He
turned the bike upstream and rode off.

Luckily, the land alongside the river here was flat and
open. He made good time, cutting across sections where
the river looped back on itself and saving as much time as
possible. Almost without warning he came around a bend
and upon a bridge, straight and high above the grey,
swift waters.

It was a railroad bridge.

For a second time he felt dismay; a purely conditioned
reflex out of a civilized time when it was dangerous to try
to cross a railway bridge for fear of being caught halfway
over by traffic on the rails. Then that outworn feeling
passed, and his heart and hopes leaped up together. For
his purposes a railway bridge was the best thing he could
have encountered.

There would be no traffic on these rails. And for something like the light trail bike he rode, the right-of-way beside the track should be almost as good as a superhigh-
way. He rode the bike up the embankment, stopped to lift
it onto the ties between the rails, and remounted. A brief

bumpy ride took him safely over the river that moments before had been an uncrossable barrier.

On the far side of the river, as he had expected, there was plenty of room beyond the ends of the ties, on either side, for him to ride the bike. He lifted the machine off the ties to the gravel and took up his journey. The embankment top was pitted at intervals where rain had washed some of the top surfacing down the slope and away, but for the most part it was like traveling a well-kept dirt road, and he made steady time with the throttle nearly wide open.

There was another advantage to traveling along the railroad right-of-way that he had not thought of until he found himself doing it. This was that the embankment lifted him above the surrounding country and he could keep a good watch ahead for possible dangers. He was now past the rolling landscape he had been passing through earlier. Now, on either side of the track, the land was flat to the horizon, except in the far distance ahead, where the track curved out of sight among some low hills. And nowhere in view were there any sheep, or in fact any sign of man or beast.

For a rare moment he relaxed and let himself hope. Anywhere west of the Mississippi, across the prairie country, a railroad line could run for miles without intersecting any human habitation. With luck, he could be out of this sheep country before he knew it. Farther west, Martin had written in the last letters Jeebee had gotten from his brother, the isolated ranchers of the cattle country had been less affected than most by the breakdown of the machinery of civilization, and law and order, after a fashion, still existed. He could trade off the loot he had picked up from the cellar in comparative safety for the things he needed.

First of these was a more effective rifle than the .22. The .22 was a good little gun, but it lacked punch. Its slug was too light to have the sort of impact that would stop a charging man, or large beast. And there were still wolf, bear, and even an occasional mountain lion in the territory to which he was headed—to say nothing of wild range cattle, which could be dangerous enough.

Moreover, with a heavier gun he could bring down such cattle, or even deer or mountain sheep—if he was lucky enough to stumble across them—to supplement whatever other food supplies he was carrying. Which brought him to his second greatest need, the proper type of food supplies. Canned goods were very convenient, but they were heavy and impractical to carry by packsack. What he really needed was some freeze-dried meat. Or, failing that, some powdered soups, plain flour, dried beans, or such, and possibly bacon.

He had a packsack full of the best of that sort of supplies when he had finally tried to make his escape alive from Abbotsville. In fact, when he had packed it he had not really believed that the locals would not just let him go, that they really intended to kill him. In spite of the previous three months of near-isolation in the community, he had still felt that after five years of living there, he was one of them.

But of course, he had never been one of them. What had led him to think he knew them was their casual politeness in the supermarket or the post office, plus the real friendship he had had with his housekeeper, Ardyce Prine. Mrs. Prine had lived there all her life; and, in her sixties, was in a position of belonging to the local authoritative generation. But when the riots became too dangerous for him to risk traveling into Detroit to the think-tank at the university, the local Abbotsville folks must have begun to consider that they were stuck with him. And there was no real place for him in their lives, particularly as those lives began to shift toward an inward-looking economy, with local produce and meat being traded for locally made shoes and clothing. Jeebee produced nothing they needed. While Ardyce was still his housekeeper, they tolerated him; but the day came when she did not—only a short stiff note was delivered by her grandson, saying that she could no longer work for him.

After that, he had felt the invisible enmity of his neighbors beginning to hem him in. When he did try to leave and head west to Twin Peaks, he found they had been lying in wait with guns for him, for some time. At the moment of his leaving he had not been able to understand why. But he knew now. If he had tried to leave naked, they might have let him go. But even the clothes he wore they regarded as Abbotsville property with which he was running off, like a thief in the night. Bule Mannerly, the druggist, had risen like a demon out of the darkness of the hillside, shotgun in hand, to bar his going—and only that lucky misshot from somewhere in the surrounding darkness had let Jeebee get away.

But then, once away, he had foolishly gone through the supplies he carried like a spendthrift, never dreaming that it would be as difficult as it turned out to be to replace them with anything eatable at all, let alone more of their special and expensive kind.

But he had learned his lesson, now, three months later. At least half of him had become bearded and wise and animal-wary—ears pricked, eyes moving all the time, nose

sensitive to sound, sight, or smell that might mean
danger . . .

He fell to dreaming of the things he would want to
trade for as soon as he found someplace where it was safe
to do so. In addition to a heavier rifle, he badly needed a
spare pair of boots. The ones he wore would not last him
all the way to Montana, if the bike broke down or he had
to abandon or trade it off for any reason. Also, a revolver
and ammunition for it would be invaluable—but of course
to dream of a handgun like that was like dreaming of a
slice of heaven. Weapons were the last thing anyone was
likely to trade off, these days.

He became so involved in his own thoughts that he
found himself entering the low line of further hills before
he was really aware of it. The railroad track curved off
between two heavy, grassy shoulders of land and disappeared in the shadow of a clump of cottonwood trees that
lay at the far end of their curve. He followed the tracks
around, chugged into the shadow of the cottonwoods and
out the other side—to find himself in a small valley, looking down at a railroad station, some sheep-loading pens
and a cluster of buildings, all less than half a mile away.

As it had when he had smelled the sheep, reflex led him
to kill the motor of the bike and seek the ground beside
the track with it and himself alike, all in one unthinking
motion. He lay where he was on the rough stones of the
track ballast, staring through a screen of tall, dry grass at
the buildings.

Even as he lay there, he knew his hitting the ground
like this had almost certainly been a futile effort. If there
was anyone in the little community ahead, they must
have heard the motor of his trail bike even before it came
into view from under the trees. He continued to lie there;

but there was no sign of movement in or around the small village, or whatever he was observing, although the tin chimneys on several of the buildings were sending up thin banners of grey smoke against the blue sky.

Overall, what he was observing, ahead and below, looked like a sheep-loading station that had grown into a semicommunity. There were two buildings down there that might be stores, but the majority of the structures he saw—frame buildings sided with grey unpainted boards, could be anything from home to warehouse.

He rolled half over on his side and twisted his body about to get at his packsack and take out a pair of binoculars. They were actually toy binoculars, a pair he had brought for Martin's youngest son, a five-year-old. They were all he had been able to get his hands on before leaving Abbotsville, and they were something that in ordinary times he would not have bothered to put in his pack. But they did magnify several times, although the material of their lenses was hardly of a higher grade than window glass.

He put the binoculars to his eyes and squinted at the buildings through the eyepieces. This time, after a long and painful survey, he did discover one dog, apparently asleep beside the three wooden steps leading up to the one long, windowed building he had guessed might be a store. He stared at the dog for a long time, but it did not move.

Jeebee held the glasses to his eyes until they began to water. Then he lowered the glasses, took his weight off his elbows, which had been badly punished, even through the leather jacket, by the gravel and stones beneath him, and tried to conjecture what he had stumbled upon.

It was, of course, possible—the wild wishful supposition

came sliding into his head unbidden—that he had stumbled across some community where disease or some other reason had destroyed the population—including the dogs. In which case, all he had to do was step down there and help himself to whatever property might be lying around.

The ridiculousness of such an impossible streak of good fortune coming his way was a proper antidote to the fanciful notion itself. But certainly, the buildings seemed, if not deserted, almost too quiet to be true. Of course, it was the middle of the day; and if this was stockmen's country, most of the people in it could be out tending or guarding sheep . . .

Even that was a far-fetched notion. No matter how many might go out, no one in these days would leave this many buildings, with whatever they might contain, unprotected from possible looters. No, there must be people below—they were simply inside the buildings and out of sight.

At once the answer burst on Jeebee's mind, and he glanced at his watch. Of course. It was noon. Anyone around below and ahead of him would be eating a midday meal.

He lay and waited. Within about twenty minutes the door outside which the dog lay opened, and the first of several figures came out. With the first one the dog was on his feet, in what—as far as Jeebee could tell from this distance—was a friendly greeting. The dog stayed alert, and one by one, half a dozen people emerged, to scatter out and disappear within other buildings. All seemed to be male and adult. Shortly after the last one had disappeared, the door opened again and a figure in skirts emerged, threw something to the dog, and went back inside. The dog lay down to chew on whatever it had been given.

Jeebee lay where he was, thinking. He could hold his position until night and then push the bike around the station and continue on down the track beyond at some safe distance. While he was still thinking this, the whanging of a one-cylinder engine burst distantly to life, and a moment later a motorized railcar rolled into sight on the track beyond the buildings. It continued up the track, away from him and the station until it was lost to sound and sight.

Jeebee chilled where he lay, looking after it. A car like that could get its speed up to sixty miles an hour along good railway track. It could run down his motorcycle with no trouble at all. He had just been fortunate that it had not headed toward him, instead of in the other direction. Of course, he could have gotten off the embankment and into the ditch, among the tall weeds before he could have been spotted. But all the same . . .

Suddenly, he had made up his mind. There had to be an end to guessing, sometime. Somewhere he would have to take a chance on trying to trade, and this place looked as good as any. He got back on the trail bike and kicked its motor to life.

Openly and noisily he rode down the track and in among the buildings.

There was a clamor of barking as he entered. A near dozen dogs of diverse breeds, but all of sheep dog type, gathered around him as he rode the bike directly to the steps where he had seen the original dog and where all the people had emerged. The original dog was one of those now following him clamorously. Like the others, it crowded close but made no serious attempt to bite, which was—he thought—a good sign as far as the attitudes toward strangers of those owning the dogs were concerned.

He stopped the bike, got off, and with the .22 in hand, packsack on back, he climbed the three steps to the door. He knocked. There was no answer.

After a second he knocked again; and when there was still no answer, put his hand on the knob. It turned easily and the door opened. He went in, leaving the yelping of the station dog pack behind him. Their noise did not stop once he had disappeared from their view, but it was muted by the walls and windows of the building.

Jeebee looked around himself at the room into which he had stepped. It was fair-sized, with six round tables and four chairs apiece that all dated back to before the breakdown. Along one wall was a short, high bar, but with nothing but some glasses upside down on the shelves behind it. Beyond the bar was a further door, closed, which Jeebee assumed to lead deeper into the building. Stacked on one end of the bar were some dishes, cups, and silverware looking as if they had just been left behind by diners, the figures Jeebee had seen coming out of this building a small while since as he lay and watched from the embankment.

The clamor of the dogs outside suddenly increased in volume, then unaccountably faded away into whimpers and silence. Jeebee moved swiftly to the window and looked out.

Coming toward the steps leading to the building's entrance was a strange female figure. A woman who must have been as large as Jeebee himself, but dressed in a muffling nineteenth-century dress of rusty black cloth that fell to the tops of her heavy boots below and ended in a literal poke bonnet at the top. She walked with long and heavy strides, one hand holding a short chain leash. But the leash seemed unnecessary. It dropped slackly from its connection with the leather collar of the large dog pacing beside her, as if it was trained to heel.

It was this dog which had caused the rest of the pack to fall silent. It was no sheep dog, but a German shepherd half again as large as any of the other canines around it, its coat rough with the thick hair of a dog which had spent most of its winter out in the weather. Its collar was heavy and studded with bright metallic points, which, as it came closer, Jeebee made out to be sharp-pointed spikes.

It paid no attention to the other dogs at all. It ignored them as if they did not exist, walking by the side of the big woman with no signal of body or tail to show anything other than that it was on some purposeful errand. The other dogs had drawn back from it, had sat down or lain down, and were now silent, licking their jaws with wet uneasy tongues. Woman and dog came up the steps, opened the door and stepped into the room where Jeebee waited. As the woman closed the door behind her, the barking outside made a halfhearted attempt to start again, then dwindled into silence.

"Heard you on your way in here," said the woman to Jeebee in a hoarse deep voice like the voice of a very old person. "I just stepped out to get my watchdog, here."

Jeebee felt the metal of the trigger guard of the .22 slippery in his right hand. The woman, he saw now that she was close, was wearing a black leather belt tight around her waist, with a small holster and the butt of what looked like a short-barreled revolver sticking out of the holster. He did not doubt that she could use it. He did not doubt that the dog would attack if she gave it the order. And, flooding all through him, was the old doubt that he could lift the .22 and fire, even to defend his own life.

"Sit," said the woman to the huge dog. "Guard."

The German shepherd sat down before the outer door. His black nose pointed and twitched in Jeebee's direction for a second, but that was all the reaction he showed. The woman lifted her head, looking directly at Jeebee. Her face was tanned, masculine-looking, with heavy bones and thin lips. Deep parentheses of lines cut their curves from nose to chin on each side of her mouth. She must be, Jeebee thought, at least fifty.

"All right," said the woman. "What brings you to town?"

"I came in to trade some things," said Jeebee.

His own voice sounded strange in his ears, like the creaky tones of an old-fashioned phonograph record where most of the low range had been lost in recording.

"What you got?"

"Different things," said Jeebee. "How about you? Have you or somebody else here got shoes, food, and maybe some other things you can trade me?"

His voice was sounding more normal now. He had pulled his cap low over his eyes before he had come into town; and hopefully, in this interior dimness, lit only by the windows to his right, she could not see the pale innocence of his eyes and forehead.

"I can trade you what you want—prob'ly," the woman said. "Come on.—You, too."

The last words were addressed to the dog. It rose silently to four feet and padded after them. She led Jeebee to the further door and through it into another room that looked as if it might once have been a poor excuse for a hotel lobby. A corridor led off from a far wall, and doors could be glimpsed on either side along it.

The lobby room was equipped with what had probably been a clerk's counter. This, plus half a dozen more of the round tables, were piled with what at first glimpse appeared to be every kind of junk imaginable, from old tire casings to metal coffeepots that showed the dints and marks of long use. A second look showed Jeebee a rough order to things in the room. Clothing filled two of the tables, and all of the cooking utensils were heaped with the coffeepots on another.

"Guard," said the woman to the dog again, and once more it took a seated position before the closed door by which they had all just entered.

"Let's see what you got," said the woman. She motioned to an end of the clerk's counter that was clear. Jeebee unbuckled his recently acquired leather jacket— the dog's nose tested the air again—and began unloading his belt of the screwdrivers, chisels, files, and other small hand tools he had brought. When he was done, he unwrapped the metal chain from his waist and laid it on the wooden surface of the counter where it chinked heavily.

"Maybe you can use this," said Jeebee, nodding at the dog as casually as possible.

"Maybe," said the woman, with a perfect flatness of voice. "But he don't need much holding. He works to orders."

"Sheep dog?" asked Jeebee, as she began to examine the tools.

She looked up squarely into his face.

"You know better than that," she said. "He's no stock

dog. He's a killer." She stared at him for a second. "Or, do you know? What are you—cattleman?"

"Not me," said Jeebee. "My brother is. I'm on my way to his place, now."

"Where?" she asked, bluntly.

"West," he said. "You probably wouldn't know him." He met her eyes. It was a time to claim as much as he could. "But he's got a good-sized ranch, he's out there— and he's waiting for me to show up."

The last, lying part came out with what Jeebee felt sounded like conviction. Perhaps a little of the truth preceeding it had carried over. The woman, however, looked at him without any change of expression whatsoever, then bent to her examination of the hand tools again.

"What made you think I was a cattleman?" Jeebee asked. Her silence was unnerving. Something in him wanted to keep her talking, as if, so long as she continued to speak, nothing much could go wrong.

"Cattleman's jacket," she said, not looking up.

"Ja—" he stopped himself. Of course, she was talking about the leather jacket he was wearing. He had not realized that there would be any perceptible difference in clothing between sheep and cattlemen. Didn't sheepmen wear leather jackets, too? Evidently not—or at least, not in the same style.

"This is sheep country," the woman said, still not looking up. Jeebee felt the statement like a gun hanging in the air, aimed at him and ready to go off any minute.

"That so?" he said.

"Yes, that's so," she answered. "No cattlemen left here, now. *That* was a cattle dog." She jerked her thumb at the guard dog, swept the tools and the chain together into a pile before her as if she already owned them. "All right, what you want?"

"A pair of good boots," he said. "Some bacon, beans, or flour. A handgun—a revolver."

She looked up at him on the last words.

"Revolver," she said with contempt. She shoved the pile of tools and chain toward him. "You better move on."

"All right," he said. "Didn't hurt to ask, did it?"

"Revolver!" she said again, deep in her throat, as if she was getting ready to spit. "I'll give you ten pounds of parched corn and five pounds of mutton fat. And you can look for a pair of boots on the table over there. That's it."

"Now, wait . . ." he said. The miles he had come since Abbotsville had not left him completely uneducated to the times he now lived in. "Don't talk like that. You know —I know—those tools there are worth a lot more than that. You can't get metal stuff like that any more. You want to cheat me some, that's all right. But let's talk a little more sense."

"No talk," she said. She came around the counter and faced him. Jeebee could feel her gaze searching in under the shadow of his cap's visor to see his weakness and his vulnerability. "Who else you going to trade with?"

She stared at him. Suddenly the great wave of loneliness, of weariness, washed through Jeebee again. The thinking front of his mind recognized that her words were only the first step in a bargaining. Now it was time for him to counteroffer, to sneer at what she had, to rave and protest—but he could not. Emotionally he was too isolated, too empty inside. Silently he began to sweep the chain and the hand tools into a pile and return them to his belt.

"What you doing?" yelled the woman, suddenly.

He stopped and looked at her.

"It's all right," he said. "I'll take them someplace else."

Even as he said the words, he wondered if she would call the dog and whether he would, indeed, make it out of this station alive.

"Someplace else?" she snarled. "Didn't I just say there isn't anyplace else anywhere near? What's wrong with you?—You never traded before?"

He stopped putting the tools back in his belt and looked at her.

"Look!" she said, reaching under the counter. "You wanted to trade for a revolver. Look at it!"

He reached out and picked up the nickel-plated short-muzzled weapon she had dumped before him. It was speckled with rust, and when he pulled the hammer back, there was a thick accumulation of dirt to be seen on its lower part. Even at its best, it had been somebody's cheap Saturday night special, worth fifteen or twenty dollars. Jeebee did not really know guns, but it was plain what he was being offered.

His head cleared, suddenly. If she really wanted to trade, there was hope after all.

"No," he said, shoving the cheap and dirty revolver back at her. "Let's skip the nonsense. I'll give you all of this for a rifle. A deer rifle—something about .30 caliber, and ammunition. Skip the food, the boots and the rest."

"Throw in that motorcycle," she said.

He laughed. And he was as shocked to hear himself as if he had heard a corpse laugh.

"You know better than that," he said. He waved his hand at the pile on the counter. "All right, you can make new hand tools out of a leaf from old auto springs—if you want to sweat like hell. But there's one thing you can't make, and that's chain like that. That chain's worth a lot. Particularly to somebody like you with stuff to protect. And if this is sheep country, you're not short of guns. Show me a .30-06 and half a dozen boxes of shells for it."

"Two boxes!" she spat.

"Two boxes and five sticks of dynamite." Jeebee's head was whirling with the success of his bargaining.

"I got no dynamite. Only damn fools keep that stuff around."

"Six boxes, then."

"Three."

"Five," he said.

"Three." She straightened up behind the counter. "That's it. Shall I get the rifle?"

"Get it," he said.

She turned and went down the corridor to the second door on the left. There was the grating sound of a key in a lock, and she went inside. A moment later she re-emerged, relocked the door, and brought him a rifle with two boxes of shells, all of which she laid on the counter.

Jeebee picked up the gun eagerly and went through the motions of examining it. The truth of the matter was that he was not even sure if what he was holding was a .30-06. But he had lived with the .22 long enough to know where to look for signs of wear and dirt in a rifle. What he had seemed clean, recently oiled and in good shape.

"You look that over, mister," said the woman. "I got another one you might like better, but it's not here. I'll go get it."

She turned and went toward the door.

"Guard!" she said to the dog, and it came to all four feet, its eyes fixed on Jeebee. She passed through the door, closing it behind her.

Jeebee stood motionless, listening until he heard the distant sound of the outside door slamming re-echo through the building. Then, moving slowly so as not to trigger off any reflex in the dog, he slid his hand to one of the boxes of cartridges the woman had brought, opened it with the fingers of one hand and extracted two of the shells. He laid one on the counter and slowly fed the other into the clip slot of the rifle. He hesitated, but the dog had not moved. With one swift move, he jacked the round into firing position . . .

—Or tried to. The firing chamber would not close. Manually, he pulled back its cover and swore silently. The woman had outthought him, even in this. The shells she had brought him were of the wrong caliber for this particular rifle. The shell he had just put in was too big to more than barely nose itself into firing position.

Slowly, he took the shell out and laid the gun down on the counter. The proper size ammunition, of course, would be in that room down the corridor, but his chances of getting there . . .

On the other hand, he might as well try. He took a step away from the counter toward the corridor.

Immediately the dog moved. It took one step forward toward him. He stared at it. It stood like a statue, its tail unmoving, no sound or sign of anger showing in it, but neither any sign of a relaxation of its watchfulness. It was the picture of a professional on duty. Of course, he thought, of course it would never let him reach the door of the room with the guns, let alone smash the door lock and break in. He stared at the dog. It must weigh close to a hundred and fifty pounds, and it was a flesh-and-blood engine of destruction. Some years back he had seen video film of such dogs being trained—

The distant sound of voices, barely above the range of audibility, attracted his attention. They were coming from outside the building.

He took a step toward the windows. This moved him also toward the dog, and at this first step the animal did not move. But when he stepped again, the dog moved toward him. It did not growl or threaten, but in its furry skull its eyes shone like bits of china, opaque and without feeling.

But his movement had brought him far enough out in the room so that he could look at an angle through the windows and glimpse the area in front of the building where the three steps stood to the entrance door. The woman stood there, now surrounded by five men, all with rifles or shotguns. As he stood, straining his ears in the hot, silent room, the sense of their words came faintly to him through the intervening glass and distance.

". . . Where y'been?" The woman was raging. "He was ready to walk out on me. I want two of you to go around back—"

"Now, you wait," one of the men interrupted her. "He's got that little rifle. No one's getting no .22 through him just because you want his bike."

"Did I say I wanted it for myself?" demanded the woman. "The whole station can use it. Isn't it worth that?"

"Not getting shot for, it ain't," said the man who had spoken. "Sic your dog on him."

"And get the dog shot!" shouted the woman, hoarsely, deeply.

"Why not?" said one of the other men. "It's no damn good, that dog. Killed four good sheep dogs already, and nobody dare go close to it. For that matter, it don't do

what you want, so easy. You should have shot it yourself,
back when we pulled down Callahan's place."

"That's a valuable dog! Like this's a valuable machine!"
The woman waved at the motorcycle. "You got to take
some risks to make a profit."

"You go in and send him out here!" said one of the
men, stubbornly. "You send him out not suspecting anything and give us a chance to shoot him with some safe."

"If'n he comes out," said the woman. "He's going to
want to come out traded, with a loaded carbine instead of
that .22. You want to face that, damn you? You going to
argy with me? I done my share of facing him. Now it's up
to you all—"

The argument went on. The loneliness and emptiness
crested inside Jeebee. He sank down into a sitting position on the boards of the floor, dropping the .22 across his
knees and covering his face with his hands. Let them
come. Let it be over . . .

But he sat there as the seconds ticked away, and he
found that he was not quite ready to die yet. He lifted his
head and saw the muzzle of the dog staring eye-to-eye
with him—not six inches between their faces.

For a moment the dog stood there, then it extended its
neck, and sniffed at him. Its black nose began to move
over his upper body, sniff by sniff exploring the jacket;
and a sudden wild hope stirred in Jeebee. Casually, he
closed his hands on the rifle still in his lap and with his
left hand tilted its muzzle toward the head of the dog
above it as his left hand felt for the trigger. At this close
range, even a small slug like this right through the brain
of the dog . . .

His finger found the trigger and trembled there. The
dog paid no attention. His nose was pushed in the unbut-

toned opening at the top of the jacket, sniffing. Abruptly he withdrew his head and looked squarely into Jeebee's eyes.

In that moment Jeebee knew that he could not do it. Not like this. He could not even kill this dog. His buck fever was back on him . . . and what did it matter? Even if he killed the animal, the men outside would kill him eventually. And what kind of a fool guard dog was it, that would let him put a gun directly to its head and pull the trigger?

"Get away!" he snarled at it, slamming it with his fist on the side of the head.

The head rocked away from him with the blow. But it turned back; the china eyes looked undecipherably into his; and the head dropped, dropped . . . until a rough red tongue rasped on the back of the hand with which he had struck.

He stared at the door. Then, almost before he had time to think, habit and instinct—his whole out-of-date pattern moved him unthinkingly. He reached out and gently soothed the thick fur of the bowed neck.

"Sorry, boy. Sorry . . ." he whispered.

The big dog leaned its weight against him, almost tumbling him over backward. But even now it did not wag its tail in ordinary canine fashion. The tail moved horizontally, tentatively and slightly, and then went back to being still. The great jaws caught Jeebee's stroking hand by the wrist and chewed gently and lovingly upon it. The eyes looked directly into Jeebee's again; and now they were no longer opaque china, but glass windows opening on long twin tunnels down to where a savage single-purpose fire burned.

Like the waters from a bursting dam, the offering of

affection from the animal exploded into Jeebee's arid soul. Like water to a parched throat, it was almost painful in its first touch—and then Jeebee found himself with both arms around the neck of the big dog, hugging the beast to him.

But, even as he blossomed interiorly, Jeebee's mind began its working. It was the jacket, of course, his mind told him. The jacket, and the dog alike, must have come from the ruined house where he had found the chain and taken shelter that night. The jacket must still smell of the cattleman who had owned the dog originally, and several days of wearing the leather garment had mingled its original owner's scent with Jeebee's until they were one scent only. Also, above all, the jacket and Jeebee both would not smell of sheep and sheep handling, of which all this station, its people and buildings, must reek to the dog's sensitive nose.

Nonetheless, what had happened was a miracle. He could not get over that. He almost cried and laughed at once, sitting on the floor with his arms around the dog, dodging the wet tongue searching for his face. He should have remembered, he told himself, that back when the years had been of iron there had been miracles, as well. And both had come to life again.

That thought reminded him of the danger in which he still stood. He scrambled to his feet and ran to the locked door of the room the woman had entered, the dog close at his heels. A blow of the rifle butt of the .22 broke the cheap lock of the door handle, and the door itself swung open to show him a rack of rifles and shotguns—a hanging row of handguns.

He grabbed a revolver and the one rifle he recognized, a Weatherby Magnum 300, and found boxes of ammunition for both weapons among the many other such boxes filling a shelf along the far side of the small room. He loaded the Weatherby and the revolver and shoved the revolver into his belt, boxes of the two kinds of shells into his pockets. Then, with the big dog following, he ran out again into the corridor, toward its far end.

A little farther on, the corridor turned left at a ninety-degree angle and cut across the width of the building to a dead end, pierced by a window shielded by a glass curtain. Jeebee looked out the window and saw two men, with three of the station dogs, standing and waiting, watching.

Hidden behind the curtain, Jeebee smashed the glass of the window with the muzzle of the .22 and fired it steadily out of the broken window into the air until it was empty. Then he threw up the window and jumped out.

The two men outside, unhurt, were running away. They disappeared from sight around the far end of the building, the three dogs at their heels. Jeebee looked about, saw the loom of the hills over the roofs to his right, and ran that way between two buildings.

He loped between the buildings, suddenly remembering that half of his possessions were back on the bike and the bike was lost forever. A tingle of fear tried to be born in him, but was drowned in the adrenalin of the moment. This was no time to think of anything but getting away. He dodged from one alley between a pair of buildings to another and broke out at last beyond a final pair of the structures to see his way clear to the hills, with only a long slope of waist-high stunted-looking corn before him. Just emerging from the cornfield and headed toward the station, only fifty feet from him, was a man with a shotgun and a pair of dogs trotting ahead of him.

The man halted at the sight of Jeebee and lifted his shotgun uncertainly. The guard dog went past Jeebee in a silent rush toward the two smaller dogs. One of the two spun and bolted. The second stood its ground a second too long and went down with a howl that turned into a choked-off death yelp as the guard dog's jaws closed on its neck.

The man's shotgun, which had been lifting to aim at Jeebee, swung instead to point at the guard dog.

Jeebee dropped the .22 and jerked up the Weatherby. This time, without thinking, he fired to kill.

A few minutes later, hidden among the corn, he turned to look down through the stalks at the station. A number of figures milled around down there between the buildings and the edge of the planted field, but none of them were trying to follow.

He turned and headed away between two of the hills, keeping the corn as cover between himself and the station. He had lost the .22 in that last moment when he had shot the man coming out of the cornfield; half of his goods and bike were abandoned behind him. But the big dog pressed close against his leg as they both moved on, and Montana was a certain destination now. He was no longer alone. The world as it was, and he as he had become, had moved toward each other finally.

A strengthened vessel carried knowledge westward.

HOMECOMING

As they came to the top of the ramp, Jeb Halvorsen felt the little hand of the krillian thrust into his own. He looked down and saw that the small Danibor marsupialoid was shrinking against him the way a child might.

"It's all right, Tommy," he said soothingly. "I'm not going to go off and leave you."

"I'm good," said Tommy, turning the large eyes in his narrow, kangaroolike face up to Jeb.

"I know you are." Jeb reached over with his free hand and patted the round furry head that came to a little below his belt. "Don't worry now. These are only human people like you knew back on Danibor. It's just that there's a lot more of them here on Earth. They won't hurt you; and anyway, I'll take care of you. Come on. We go this way."

They turned to their left, down the long, echoing, pillared distance of Customs Row with its alphabetical divisions. The ramp they had taken up from the landing area of the ship that had just brought them in from Danibor and Alpha Centauri had brought them out in the K section. It was a short stroll to the H section where Jeb's luggage would be delivered.

In fact when they got there the luggage had already arrived. It stood piled in a rough pyramid of boxes and cases all but identical with the similar stacks of luggage on the ruled squares about it. They went to it, passing a pleasant-faced young blonde girl who occupied the square to their right.

"Now you wait here," Jeb told Tommy. "I've got to go get a ticket. I'll be right back. Stay with the luggage."

He turned and went off, threading his way between the piled-up squares of luggage back to the rear wall of the section. A stack of large plastic numbers was hanging on a hook there. He took the top one—it was number eighteen—and carried it back to the square where Tommy waited beside his luggage.

Tommy was sitting down with his back against a suitcase, his eyes enormous on the blonde girl on the next square, who was trying to talk to him. Her face, animated now in conversation, had glowed into unexpected prettiness. She was a small girl and very white-skinned, as if she had spent months out of any sunlight whatsoever.

"He's cute," she said, looking up as Jeb approached. "He's not Earth-native, is he?"

"No, he's a mutant variform of Danibor in the Vegan system. His parent strain was *Onychogale*—nail-tailed wallabies, a sort of kangaroo," said Jeb. "They were mutated to provide a balanced ecology on Danibor—but this one's a personal pet of mine."

"I never had a pet when I was little—" she said, a little sadly, looking down at the krillian. Then she smiled at Tommy. "Would you like to come back to Mercury and be my pet someday?"

"No," said Tommy, and the transient glow of her smile was suddenly wiped away by shock. She looked up, hurt, at Jeb.

"It's all right," said Jeb. "He didn't really understand you. This variform can talk a little, but they're still not much brighter than a young chimp, say, though they've got a dog's desire to please. They're awfully affectionate." He put a hand gently on Tommy's head. "You get attached to them."

She smiled again, from him to Tommy. She leaned over and held out her hand. After a moment the krillian reached out and grasped it trustfully with his own small fingers.

"I'm good," said Tommy.

"I'm sure you are," she said. "Good as gold." She looked up at Jeb. "Are you Daniborian? Or are you from Earth?"

Jeb smiled a little twistedly.

"I'm buying my way back," he said.

"Oh." She colored a little.

"It's nothing I'm ashamed of," said Jeb. "I was shipped out on a surplus-population draft like lots of people you've known yourself. And I'm coming back on a talent-and-funds immigration visa. You're Earth yourself?"

"Yes," she answered. "I've lived most of my life on Mercury—but we never lost our citizenship here. My father was a transfer engineer on loan from a Baltimore company to its New Mercury branch." She hesitated. "Can I ask what your talent is?"

"Sound engineering," Jeb said. "I came up with a few new wrinkles in the field. The funds part of it came from a little device I patented to control noise levels on city streets. You know how this re-entry business works, don't you?"

"No. How?" She was watching him interestedly.

"To satisfy the funds requirement, you have to put up

a bond in International Earth Credits. To get that type of currency, you have to have something that you can sell or hock on Earth itself. I hocked my rights to the noise-level-control patent."

She opened her mouth to say something further, but at that moment a Customs inspector came threading his way among the squares, calling out, "Number fifteen!"

"That's me," she said, turning away quickly. She held up her hand. "Over here, officer!"

The Customs man came toward her. Tommy had escaped from her grasp while she was talking to Jeb and was now over on the other side of their pile of luggage, sniffing and staring about interestedly. Two more numbers were called in quick succession, and then came, *"Eighteen!"*

Jeb held up his hand. "Over here!"

The Customs officer who approached was a stocky, thin-haired man with a darkly tanned face and a pleasant smile. He shifted his record board into the crook of his arm as he came up and punched for a new entry.

"Name?" he said. "Place of departure? Planetality? Open your luggage, please—we aren't allowed to touch them until you do so."

His fingers punched rapidly, taking down Jeb's answers, as Jeb went about the pile of luggage, spreading it out and snapping the cases open. The officer followed him, peering at the contents of each, punching out his record and keeping up a small string of conversation.

"—nothing to declare? Right. What have you got here?"

"It's some of my Daniborian clothes," said Jeb. "I was told I could bring in my own personal apparel."

"That's all right," said the Customs officer. "Native

woolens, though. You'll have to declare that you have no intention of reselling them. Wool's got quite a snob value Earthside these days. Do you so declare?"

"Sure," said Jeb. "I wanted them mainly as souvenirs. These pipes too—"

"That's all right. All these things, you understand, have a certain value because they are off-planet in origin. What's in the metal case?"

Jeb opened it, revealing the neatly racked rows of spools.

"Scientific library and records of some work I've been doing," he answered.

"I'll put them down as so declared. You assure me that in this library there are no items of seditious or immoral literature, or anything otherwise forbidden to importation under the Earth United law?"

"I do," said Jeb. "And that about winds it up, except for this case here." He opened it. "Odds and ends I've got kind of attached to."

The officer looked over a collection of articles ranging from a paper knife to a pipe reamer.

"That's all right," he grinned. "As long as you haven't a diamond or two tucked away amongst it."

"Give you my word," said Jeb, smiling back. "The whole lot isn't worth ten Universal Units."

"I believe you," said the officer. "You should see some of the junk people have paid a couple of hundred light-years' worth of freight on that comes through here. All right." He punched the last few of his buttons. "You haven't any Daniborian fruit, vegetables, seeds, spores, or other vegetation about your person or your luggage?"

"Not a one," said Jeb.

"Then sign here." He presented the record board to

Jeb. "Thumbprint to the right of your signature. That's fine. I'll go file this now, and as soon as it's taken up, your luggage will be delivered to the central city depot. You can pick it up there."

"Thanks," said Jeb. "Thank you very much. You've been a lot less rough about some of this stuff than I expected."

"Oh, we're human, too," said the officer. "Though to listen to some of the stories you hear about us—" Stepping back, he almost stumbled over Tommy, who had just then come around the stack of luggage after visiting a neighboring pile during the inspection. "Oops!"

"That's all right," said Jeb. "You didn't hurt him. Say hello to the officer, Tommy."

But Tommy merely sat and stared up at the Customs man with wide-eyed curiosity. And the Customs man looked back down at him with no less interest.

"What is he?" the officer asked. "Some sort of kangaroo? He's yours, isn't he?"

"Yes," said Jeb. "No, he's not a real kangaroo. He's a krillian. He'd speak to you when I tell him, but he's having too much fun right now looking at your uniform ornaments. Tommy, say hello to the man."

"What's a krillian? I never heard of one," said the inspector. "Some species native to Danibor?"

"No, he's a variform—a mutant, you know—of the nailtailed wallaby here on Earth. They bred them to—" Jeb broke off suddenly. "Is something wrong?"

The officer was frowning.

"I don't know," he said. "Wait here just a minute, will you, please?" He turned and disappeared among the luggage piles, back in the direction of the Customs office for their alphabetical sector.

"Hi," said a voice. Jeb turned. It was the blonde girl on the next square. "How are you and Tommy coming? I'm all finished."

"We are too, I guess," answered Jeb slowly. "The officer just told us to wait a minute until he came back." He looked at the girl. Her face was flushed with pleasure and quite appealing.

"They're nice, aren't they?" said the girl. "I expected all kinds of trouble over some gifts I was bringing in. Oh, not *real* trouble, I mean, but red tape and signing papers and bonds and stuff. But he just waved it off. How was your man?"

"Nice guy," said Jeb.

"Now my vacation starts," said the girl. "Three months of it and then I'll be going to college on the West Coast. Now that it's really here, and I'm really in, I'm ready to burst with excitement."

"Play with me, please?" said Tommy, from beneath them, putting up a hand to clutch at her skirt.

She smiled radiantly down at him. "Of course I'll play with you, Tommy! What would you like to play?"

"Play tag?" said Tommy, bounding suddenly up into the air as if propelled by a spring like a jack-in-the-box, and coming down on top of one of the luggage cases.

"Not now, Tommy," said Jeb. "There isn't room to play tag here."

Tommy's slender ears drooped slightly. "Tag?" he said wistfully.

"No!" snapped Jeb.

Tommy's reaction was instantaneous. He almost

cringed, and Jeb, immediately remorseful, put out a hand to stroke the soft head.

"It's all right, boy," he said. "I'm not mad at you. It's just that we can't play tag right now."

"I love you," said Tommy, putting out a sudden pink tongue to kiss Jeb's caressing hand.

"I know. I love you, too," said Jeb automatically. He was aware suddenly that the girl's eyes were on him, and that they were shining with tears.

"I'm sorry," she said, dabbing at them with a small handkerchief. "It's just that today is—so much and everything—and then the two of you . . ."

"Well," said Jeb awkwardly.

Over the heads of the surrounding crowd and the tops of the luggage piles, he saw relief coming.

"Here's our officer now," he said.

The girl turned to look.

"There's somebody with him," she said.

And indeed there was another man just behind the one who had checked Jeb's luggage, a slightly heavier, older man with graying hair and the silver bar of a senior lieutenant in the Customs service on the shoulders of his uniform. They both came up to where Jeb, the girl and Tommy were standing. The lieutenant was carrying some papers in one hand and he seemed harassed.

"Mr. Halvorsen?" he said.

"Yes," said Jeb.

"This is your entry permit for a Daniborian marsupialoid?" He showed a sheet.

"Yes." Jeb frowned at him.

"Well—uh—perhaps we better step back into my office for a minute. You can go, Harry." The Customs officer turned and left. "This way, Mr. Halvorsen. Bring the marsupialoid with you, will you, please?"

"Here, Tommy," said Jeb.

He took Tommy's hand and began to follow the lieutenant back toward the Customs offices. He felt a tug at his elbow and turned, still walking, to see the girl hurrying along behind them.

"What is it?" asked the girl. "Is something wrong?"

"I don't think so," said Jeb.

"Can I come along?"

"I don't see why not."

The lieutenant led them into a large room where a number of the Customs officers were busy at work, recording and checking; and through this room into a smaller office with a desk and several easy chairs facing it.

"If you'll sit down for a minute, Mr. Halvorsen—" The lieutenant saw the girl and the eyebrows on his round, not unpleasant face went up. "Miss—?"

"She's with us," said Jeb.

"Not in your party?" said the lieutenant.

"No. Just a friend. You don't mind?" spoke up the girl, quickly and a little breathlessly.

"I—suppose not. Well, sit down, please," said the lieutenant, seating himself behind the desk and spreading out the papers upon it. "Mr. Halvorsen, this entry permit of yours for the marsupialoid—name Tommy—" he glanced at Tommy, who was sitting high beside Jeb's chair and peering over the desk surface at him—"it was made out on Danibor."

"All my papers were, of course," said Jeb. "Why? Something the matter with them?"

"No. Not with them. Not even with *this*." The lieutenant twitched the entry permit for Tommy. "The form's proper and made out correctly. It's just—well, I feel rather bad about this, Mr. Halvorsen. You've been the victim of a mistake on the part of whoever issued this permit back on Danibor."

"What mistake?" Jeb's voice came out with a harshness that surprised him.

"I can understand *you* not knowing, but there's no excuse for whoever's in charge of the office on Danibor. This form has been removed from the lists."

"Is that all?" Jeb could not help smiling a bit.

"You don't understand," said the lieutenant, hitching his chair forward. "The form has been dropped because there's now a law against reintroducing any of the mutated variforms to Earth."

Jeb stared at him. "Earth is where they come from in the first place."

"I know." The lieutenant waved a wide, slightly embarrassed hand. "But it's a genetic matter—not merely the variforms themselves, but what sort of disease mutations they may have developed on other worlds. Especially over several generations." He coughed, gazing at Tommy. "He is a cute little fellow, isn't he?" He smiled at Tommy, suddenly became serious and turned again to Jeb. "The law was passed half a dozen years ago. A mutated virus that attacked Earth life could be a problem to an overcrowded world like this."

"But wouldn't a virus that attacked Earth life attack early imports of Earth life on the world where it first appeared?" Jeb put his hands on the edge of the desk. "There's fresh, unmutated life—people, stock, vegetation —being shipped out to all the colony worlds all the time. They'd be the first to catch it."

"Well, possibly—I don't know all the ins and outs of it," said the lieutenant. "Maybe there were other reasons, too. I don't know. It's not my job to justify the law, only to enforce it." He looked at Tommy again. "I'm sorry. I know he must be quite a pet. I've a dog myself at home." He returned his attention to the desk and shifted the papers, stacking them together neatly.

"This is crazy!" burst out Jeb. "Look, the permit was issued. There must be some way around this. Tommy's not like a dog—he's more intelligent, for one thing. And he's lived with me for eight years. We were alone together out at a survey station on Danibor. He couldn't live without me—"

"I'm sorry," said the lieutenant. His face softened, became sympathetic and concerned. "Look, you don't understand. According to a strict interpretation of the order, I should order him destroyed—"

"Oh, *no!*" It was the girl's voice crying out suddenly.

Tommy jerked up his ears and hopped hastily over to her. He licked at her face.

"Don't cry," Tommy said in distress.

She put her arms out and hugged him protectively.

"Please," said the lieutenant. "It's not me. It's the law. The law forbids the importation of variforms and orders them destroyed where they're found on Earth. It's not *that* bad for you. I'll give you a couple of hours to decide what you want to do about it." He nodded at Tommy. "If you can find some means of getting it off Earth in that time, I'll let it go."

"You were calling him *he* a few seconds ago," said Jeb between his teeth.

"Was I?" said the lieutenant. "It doesn't matter. My duty stays the same. And if you're thinking of asking me, or bribing me, to forget the law and let him slip by the basis of the entry permit—please don't make it embarrassing for both of us." He got up from his desk and crossed to the door. "I'll give you a couple of hours. Until then, no pass to leave the Customs area will be issued to you."

"I think I hate you," said the girl.

"You don't understand—either of you," he said gently. "There's no room for exceptions to the rules nowadays. There's too many of us crowded together on Earth for that." He went out, pausing a second in the doorway, with his hand on the door button. "You'll save yourself a great deal if you give up and turn it over to be destroyed now," he said to Jeb.

"The hell I will!" cried Jeb savagely at the closing door.

It clicked shut. He turned to the girl and then to Tommy with fury on his face.

"The hell with it," he repeated. "We'll get out of this place, both of us."

She looked at him, as if across some sort of abyss.

"You know you can't leave," she said.

He opened his lips furiously to speak. But the words died somewhere inside him and after a second he closed his mouth again without saying anything.

"I know," she said, "how hard it is to get back to Earth after you've lost your citizenship. I've heard them talk. My father says it's like climbing a mountain that gets higher every day."

"Yes," he said emptily.

He got to his feet and walked across the office to a window on the far side that looked beyond the Customs building to the first, light, soaring buildings of the city beyond.

"I'll ship him back to Danibor," he said.

She played with Tommy's ears tenderly.

"Don't you have friends back there who'd take him—"

"I guess so," he said. "Brad Alokua—he'd take Tommy. Tommy likes him." He turned back to the doorway. "I'll go over to Shipping and arrange it." He held out his hand, and Tommy, leaving the girl, hopped to him and took it.

"Come on, boy," he said, and went out. The girl followed after.

They crossed the wide area that belonged to Customs and took a walkway to the Outbound area. Here, as at Customs, the destinations were arranged alphabetically. They went to the desk that handled Aldebaran through Evenside.

"Where to?" asked a clerk, coming up on his side of the desk as they approached. He was a lean, young man with dark hair and more of a local accent than the Customs officer or the lieutenant had shown.

"Danibor—" began Jeb.

"Papers?" The clerk held out his hand.

"No, it's not for me," said Jeb. "I just came in from Danibor. But I've found out that I can't bring my krillian in with me. I want to ship him back."

The clerk dropped his hand and, turning slowly, stared down at Tommy.

"This here?" he said. "Is that a krillian?"

"Yes," said Jeb, a little shortly.

"No offense," said the clerk. "I've just never seen one. So you want to ship him back. You're a Daniborian yourself?" He opened a drawer before him and took papers out of it, laying them on the top of the desk.

"With an Earth immigration visa," said Jeb.

"Your Daniborian citizenship's still in effect then, until

your final papers are issued." The clerk stamped several blanks on the papers. "Weight of krillian?"

"Twenty-three point four kilos."

"Fine," said the clerk, finishing off his papers. "Shipping fee will be—let's see—fourteen hundred and thirty-nine International Earth Credits."

Jeb sat still for a moment.

The clerk looked up.

"So much?" asked Jeb.

"That's right."

"When we came out—"

"I know," said the clerk. "Everything was a lot lower in price. It's a matter of shipping space. The heavy traffic is outbound from Earth, so the freight and passenger fees are high. Coming in from Danibor, there was plenty of space, so—"

He shrugged.

Jeb felt a touch on his elbow. He turned around and saw the girl leaning toward him.

"I could help out," she said.

He swallowed hard. "Thank you."

She passed him a small wad of notes. He dug out his own money case and counted the contents. He was four hundred and thirty short. He took them from her fold of money and returned what was left to her.

"Thanks," he said, with difficulty. "I'll pay you back."

"It doesn't matter," she said. "Really it doesn't."

He passed the money over to the clerk, who counted it and put it into an envelope, which he sealed.

"All right," said Jeb. "Where do we take him now?"

"Take him? Oh—" said the clerk. He consulted a paper on the side of his desk. "You're in luck. Bring him back in three weeks to this desk here. I'll give you a pass and directions to the Shipping area—"

"*Three weeks!*"

Startled, the clerk looked up at him.

"Why, yes—"

"But we've got to ship him off inside of two hours!" cried Jeb.

The clerk blinked at him.

"Oh, that's impossible," he said at last. He even smiled, a little uncertainly. "You're not serious. Even if a ship was leaving today, it'd take five hours to have him taken aboard—"

"But we've got to get him off!" Jeb's voice rang harshly out over the area, and at a neighboring desk another clerk and his customer looked over to see what the matter was. "Three weeks—that's crazy. I just came in on a ship that must be going back sooner than that."

"Oh, the *Dancia*," said the clerk. "She's going out this afternoon. But she's all emigrant this trip. No room for freight."

"Tommy didn't come as freight. He came in my cabin."

"Well, there you are." The clerk spread his hands on the desk like a reasonable man. "If you were taking him back personally—but you couldn't on this ship unless you were emigrating."

Jeb sat glowering at the clerk. A sudden touch on his elbow made him turn. The girl's face was urgently close to his.

"My family—" she said. "On Mercury. We could send Tommy to them."

"Mercury? Great!" Jeb leaped gladly to his feet. "Which way—"

"Down at the end of the row here," said the clerk, pointing away to Jeb's left.

Jeb saw, diminutive in the distance, a hanging sign proclaiming PLANETS OF THE SOLAR SYSTEM. He turned and went swiftly toward it, hearing the quick clicking of the girl's heels catching up behind him. Tommy bounced happily alongside.

"Race?" he said, looking up at Jeb. "Race me?"

"Not now, Tommy."

The Inner Planets section was a good four long city blocks away. When at last they arrived at it, warm and breathing hard, both of the humans, they found under the enormous floating overhead sign a multitude of desks.

"This way!" The girl pulled him forward to a desk.

"Sit down, please," said the clerk—a woman this time, about middle age. She smiled at all of them, and particularly Tommy, who warmed to her interest.

"I'm good," he informed her.

The clerk's sudden startlement was interrupted by the girl. Words tumbling urgently from her lips, she explained the situation. The older woman's face gentled.

"Of course, honey," she said, patting the girl's hand and reaching into her desk. She came up with a sheaf of papers. "The next ship for Mercury doesn't leave for six hours. But once you get him aboard, no one'll touch him. Now you give me your parents' name and their home address."

The girl produced her papers. The clerk nodded to the sound of the girl's voice, taking down the necessary information, while Jeb stood back, feeling at once relief, and a sensation of lostness, as if he had been betrayed into a wilderness, caught up in something beyond his own and proper control.

"Here—" he started to say. And then he stopped. He had nothing to tell them. And anyway, occupied as they were, they had not heard him.

Tommy's small, tight grip closed on the fingers of Jeb's right hand. He patted the krillian on the head absently. There was something unreal about this whole business. They would ship Tommy off to Mercury—to a good home. And after that? Jeb would make the hop from time to time . . .

No, he could not make it seem real.

"All right," the woman behind the desk was saying. She handed Jeb a paper. He took it numbly. He had planned and worked to come back to Earth from the day he had seen that he must go out in an emigrant draft . . .

"What?" he said.

"—off to your right there," the woman was repeating. "Back to the Delivery area, Freight, Section C, Livestock. You'll find it all right."

"Thanks." Slowly Jeb stood up.

"Come on," said the girl. She led the way off.

A short distance off, among the many faces and bodies of the crowd, they found the area they were looking for. There was a counter with an entryway in it and behind it a wall pierced by a door labeled TO LOADING SECTION. The man behind the desk took the papers from Jeb in silence and read them, stamping this section and detaching that.

"All right," he said. He was a lean man in his forties. "This the one?" He reached over the counter for Tommy, and Tommy drew back. "Shy, eh?" He turned and came around through the entryway. "Is he vicious?"

"No!" said Jeb sharply.

The man shrugged at him. "Maybe you better tell him he's to go with me. It helps sometimes."

Jeb looked down. Tommy was pressed close against his leg.

"Tommy," he said. Tommy looked up. "Tommy, you go with the man here."

Tommy stared up at Jeb, his eyes enormous. He did not move.

"Tommy—"

"Probably," said the man, "I better just—" His hands moved swiftly and abruptly to snatch up Tommy—and in that same second Tommy turned and clung with all of his strength to Jeb's leg.

"Tommy—" said Jeb. "Tommy— Let go, will you!" he exploded at the man.

The man let go and straightened up, his lean face a little darkened and hotly flushed.

"Tommy," said Jeb, closing his hands gently but firmly around the slim forearms of the krillian. "Tommy, listen now. It's all right. You've just got to go with him, that's all." He felt the small, warm arms, downy-soft with their fine fur, clinging piteously to him. "Tommy, please!"

A double shock wave, of cold, then hot, washed through Jeb. In one twin flash of vision he saw the new, raw cities of Danibor and the long dream of Earth.

"Let go!" he snarled, and wrenched at Tommy. The furry arms pulled away a little, but clung.

"I'll get him for you," said the man. "There's a simpler way." He bent down and clamped his hand over Tommy's muzzle, closing the mouth and nostrils. "When he starts to strangle, he'll let go."

Tommy made no effort to fight the hand. He only pressed as close to Jeb's leg as possible and hung on.

"*Stop it!*" screamed the girl.

Both men started suddenly and the man from Shipping let go, and they looked at her.

"Can't you see he isn't going to? Can't you see he'll die first?" she cried.

"He won't die," muttered the man. "Just pass out and relax, that's all."

"You!" She turned on Jeb. "How can you do that? It just won't—it just won't work."

Jeb was petting Tommy's head automatically. His hand trembled a little.

"Look, I can't fool around all afternoon," said the man. "Bring him in yourself if you want to."

"No." Jeb found his voice. "Go on." The man frowned at him. "I said go on. It's all right. I mean we're not sending him right now, after all." He swallowed.

The man looked at Jeb, turned to take a long look at the girl, turned again without a word, and went. They watched him pass again behind the counter.

"It's all right, Tommy, it's all right now," Jeb was saying.

Tommy slowly let go. Jeb picked him up and looked past one quivering furry shoulder at the girl.

"You could go with him!" she flung out.

"To Mercury?" said Jeb harshly. "What's on Mercury for me? I might as well go back to Danibor."

"Just to leave him there—"

"We'd still have to split up sometime!" he said, taking his own anger out on her. "What's the use of delaying?" He turned about and started to stride off.

"Where are you going?" She was running after him, alongside him, almost crying.

"Back to that Customs lieutenant," he said, staring straight ahead. "It's up to him."

They threaded their way back through the indifferent crowds to the Customs section and the office of the lieutenant.

The lieutenant glanced up from his desk as they entered, his gray, calm eyes swiftly understanding.

"Too bad," he said.

"There must be some solution!" the girl burst out. "There *must!*"

The lieutenant got up from behind his desk. He went over and opened another door to an inner office.

"Tommy," he said, "you wait in here."

Tommy stayed still, close to Jeb.

"It's all right, Tommy," said Jeb, with a dry mouth. "It's all right this time. I'll be in."

Slowly Tommy moved away from them and into the room. The lieutenant shut the door on him and returned to his desk.

"Sit down," he said.

"But there must be *some* way!" cried the girl.

The lieutenant turned to face her.

"You ought to know better," he said. "You're from the Inner Planets." He considered her. "No, you're too young. You don't realize."

"I realize there must be some kind of solution that doesn't mean killing him because nobody can wait more than an hour to find one!" she flared at him.

"That's where you're wrong," said the lieutenant. "That's where you're completely wrong."

"How?" she challenged him.

"The situation is urgent," the lieutenant said, "exactly because it's a situation. No, you don't understand. You're from Mercury—well, that's out a little way from the business of Earth. And your parents must have kept you wrapped up safe from the hard facts of life. Halvorsen here I don't blame. Being from a frontier planet where there's no urgency, he would not know. But you should."

"There's no danger." She glared at him. "You don't even know yourself of a good reason for the ruling."

"It doesn't matter whether the ruling's good or not. Now listen." He spoke almost kindly. "This is the hub of our universe here, Earth. This is where all the big work, the big business goes on. Everybody wants to come here; nobody wants to leave. Ask Halvorsen." He pointed his chin at Jeb. "So no single individual's important here. It's the room that's important, the bit of ground you occupy. If you don't want to play by the rules, somebody else'll gladly take your place. There's no room on Earth for the kangaroo, but there is for Halvorsen. He takes it or he doesn't, and he takes it right now or his chance is over. All of us—me too—only hold our room as long as we stick by the rules. There are too many people and too little room for anything else."

"It's not like that!" She was really starting to cry now. The tears made twin tracks down her young cheeks.

Jeb looked away, but the lieutenant continued to stare gravely at her.

"But it is," he said. "Halvorsen's got a brilliant future here—otherwise they would not have let him back. It's worth the sacrifice of whatever Earth asks of him. Right, Halvorsen?"

There was a moment of silence in the office. Even the girl, looking intently at Jeb, held her breath.

"Right," said Jeb in a low voice, looking at neither of them.

"That's correct," said the lieutenant. "Believe me, I'm sorry for both you *and* Tommy." He opened the drawer of his desk. "I'm not the ogre you'd like to think me, miss. I just don't have any choice—like the rest of you. Perhaps, Halvorsen, you'd rather take care of it yourself?"

Jeb, looking up, saw the other extending a handgun to him across the desk. He hesitated a second, then took it, thrusting it inside the loose bulge of his tunic, where it was hidden.

The girl sobbed. He went into the other office, closing the door behind him.

The other office was decorated as a library, with one large window giving on the city. Tommy had been sniffing about the shelves of tapes, but he stopped and sat up with bright, intelligent interest as Jeb came in.

"Go now?" asked Tommy.

"Pretty soon," said Jeb. He was surprised that his voice came out steady, though to his own ears it had a dead, strange ring, like the voice of someone he did not know. "Just a minute. Come over here, Tommy—to the window."

He walked to the window and stood facing out. Tommy hopped over to stand beside him.

"See?" Tommy asked.

"Yes," said Jeb. "Look down there, Tommy."

Together they gazed out at the far carpet of buildings rolling away to the horizon. The sight of them at last made Jeb catch his breath a little, in spite of himself. It was all there. Earth.

"Trees?" Tommy was saying, breathing against the window. "Trees?"

"There aren't any trees, Tommy," answered Jeb.

"No trees?"

"And no grass," said Jeb. Tommy's ears went back in disappointment. "No place down there for you to play." With a little effort, Jeb conjured up the picture of Tommy, cramped and prisoned in an apartment. "It's not much fun for a krillian here on Earth, Tommy. Not much fun at all."

"Sheep—?" faltered Tommy, in the faint tone of one who pleads for the realization of some smallest crumb of his hopes.

"No, no—" With a sudden start, Jeb came back to his purpose in this room. His voice hardened, the words extruding like steel between his teeth. "Yes, I think there are some sheep down there. See? Down there."

"Sheep?" Tommy's ears flicked up and he pressed his nose to the pane of the window eagerly. "Sheep?"

"Don't you see them?" said Jeb tightly. He reached into his tunic and drew out the gun. "Keep looking. Down there. See them?" He pointed the gun's muzzle at the back of the small, furry head.

"See? Sheep?" Tommy's ears flicked in this direction and then that, like semaphores. Jeb's jaws were clenched so tightly together they felt welded shut. The butt of the handgun slid a little in his slippery grip, and the muzzle end of the barrel wavered.

"Keep looking, Tommy!" he said in a stifled voice. "Keep looking."

His finger tightened on the firing button. He could feel its half-marble roundness cold against the tip of his forefinger.

The wavers of the barrel increased, built up until the whole arm was trembling violently.

He laid arm and gun down on his other hand for a second to steady it, then lifted them again. He squinted like a man facing into a merciless sunglare. His whole arm and shoulder were quivering.

Suddenly, he threw the gun across the room. Startled, Tommy jerked around.

Jeb let out a long breath in a sigh of exhaustion.

"Nothing, Tommy," he said. "Never mind." He went across the room and picked up the gun. "I think the sheep are gone now. Let's go back into the other room."

With Tommy hopping ahead of him, they returned. As they came through the door, the lieutenant's eyebrows went up. Jeb tossed the gun down on his desk.

"We're going back to Danibor," he said in a tight voice. "Both of us. On that emigrant ship."

A small female cyclone blew across the room into Jeb's arms and began crying wildly against his shoulder. Tommy was pogo-sticking with excitement all around him. Over the top of the blonde head pressed into his tunic, Jeb scowled furiously at the lieutenant.

The lieutenant shook his head, putting the handgun back into the drawer of his desk.

"It's your funeral," he said, "if you want to give up your chance at Earth and everything it could do for you. I'll bet you can't give me one good, logical reason for what you're doing."

"Maybe not," said Jeb. "But it looks like we have two different sets of standards about what's worth having, me, you, you home-planet people; and whether mine's better or not, I seem to be stuck with it."

"I love you!" cried Tommy, leaping up to lick Jeb's face, without the slightest idea of why this should be an emotional occasion, but convinced it was nonetheless.

"Me too!" wept the girl.

They both clung to Jeb.

"Well," said the lieutenant, "it takes all kinds to make a universe."

A TASTE OF TENURE

1

In 2212, when Walt Onegh died, Arm Brewer, Director of Staff, recommended Tom Calloway to fill the empty position as Director of Crews at Midwest Construction. The board, of course, confirmed.

One of Tom's first acts was to drop by Arm's office and thank him.

"I'd hoped—" he said. "But not so soon."

Arm clapped his big hand on Tom's shoulder. His cropped white hair aureoled his healthy pink face.

"Not a moment too soon," he said. "You're management material, Tom. A man of principles is rare in this cutthroat world of ours."

"You overestimate me," said Tom. But he glowed inside. It was true he had hoped; but not quite as modestly as he implied to Arm. Fifty was not old these days. But neither was it young. And he would be fifty-one in three weeks. And with people knifing each other in the back for every little job or advantage . . .

"Run along and take over your offices," said Arm genially. "You inherit from Walt, lock, stock and barrel. Suite 312."

"Suite 312," echoed Tom, savoring it. For the three hundreds were third level. Executive.

The meaning of lock, stock and barrel became more apparent when he actually stood in the outer room of his two-office suite, however. It obviously included Christine Nyall and the plant.

It was the plant which, of the two, struck him more strongly at first glance. Among the silver and opalescences, the businesslike glitter of the office, it stood out like a drab of nature, its thick, shiny green leaves spread out flatly above the crystal pot.

"Why, what is it?" Tom asked, forcing a smile.

"A sort of rubber plant," Christine Nyall replied. She ducked her head above her stenomachine, then added, with almost a touch of defiance, "Mr. Onegh liked a touch of green about the place."

She did not meet his eye when speaking. It was this more than anything else that disturbed Tom, who had taken pride all his life in meeting everyone with a level gaze and a clear conscience. It was painfully obvious to him at this moment that Christine was being turtle-cautious. That was what came from being formerly Walt's secretary, and thus now a holdover.

The plain fact of the matter was that there was now no job for her, with Walt dead. In the glutted labor market of overpopulated Earth, there was not any other position available for her within the company—unless Tom made one. And Tom did not. His own secretary, Bera Karlson, had been with him twenty years. He had no intention of replacing her with this old woman. On the other hand, by virtue of her age and length of service, Christine was Class A Secretarial. She had tenure. She could not be discharged short of the legal retirement age.

It was an uncomfortable situation, with its only possible solution lying in Christine's voluntary retirement. And it was clear she had no present intention of that.

"Um," said Tom, stepping over to the plant. He looked down at it. It was not a pretty thing, he thought; and on one broad and fleshy leaf a small spot showed whitely.

"It seems to have a touch of blight," he said.

"Oh no," said Christine, swiftly. "That's just a little bald spot."

"I see," said Tom. He turned away and went on into the private office to examine that which would be his.

Afterwards, he took the problem of Christine home with him. It was still obsessing him after dinner, when he woke to the realization that his wife had been speaking to him and he had not been listening at all.

"What?" he asked. And looked at her contritely. "Sorry, Josi. I had my mind on the office."

She smiled at him forgivingly, this slim, amazingly youthful woman to whom he had been married for the last nineteen years. He had married late and, as he firmly believed, for love. And all that had come out of his marriage, including his two young sons—one fifteen and one eleven—had made him idyllically happy.

"What's bothering you?" she asked.

"No," he said. "Tell me what you were talking about, instead." She shook her head.

"I'll save it," she said. "You first."

He stretched and straightened up on his couch, looking across to where she sat half-curled upon an overstuffed hassock, brown against the white of it, her long limbs and the slight angularity of her body softened by the lounging pajamas tightbelted around her slim waist.

"It's Christine Nyall," he said. "She's not retiring."

"Oh?" said Josi. "But that doesn't affect you, does it?"

"I'm afraid so." He grimaced slightly. "She's a hold-over. And with no place to go she'll be staying in my outer office. You see—" He explained the holdover system, and tenure.

"But can't you make her do her sitting around some-place else?" asked Josi.

"Not without risking a writ of prejudice and a work fine, if a court convicts me," he said unhappily. "The tenure law reads she must be kept 'on the job'. And the job is that of being secretary to the Director of Crews."

"Oh," said Josi. There was silence. Finally he broke it by asking what had been on her mind.

"I shouldn't bother you with it now," she said.

"Nonsense. I shouldn't bring the office home with me, anyway. Go ahead."

"—Can't you talk her into retiring?"

Tom sighed.

"The only thing I can do is make life in the office a liv-ing hell for her," he said. "I've known it done before by other men with the same problem. Only I'm just not built to do something like that."

"No," she answered, looking at him.

"No." He looked down at his hand, which had closed itself into a fist. He opened it, wiggled the fingers, then looked again at Josi.

"We'll forget it," he said.

"Now, what was it you wanted to talk about?"

She got up from the hassock and came over to sit down beside him. He looked curiously at her.

"Something important?" he asked.

"Yes. Tom—"

"What?"

"You're Class A Management now," she said. "You've got tenure. You don't have to work any more. We don't need to go on living close to the Company Offices."

"No—" He still looked at her, slightly puzzled. "But what about it? Where would you want to live?"

"Away from the city."

He looked at her in astonishment, convinced that she must be joking. But her face was unsmiling.

"But there is no *away* from the city," he said. "Not nowadays. You know that, Josi. There's no unimproved land left anywhere in the world."

"There's the Preserves," she said.

"The Preserves!" He blinked. "But you can't live in them. They're parks. Deliberately restricted—you know that—by the government, so we'll have a few scraps of open country to look at and remember the past."

"Oh yes," she said. "But they have tourist lodges."

He smiled with sudden understanding. He reached out for her hands. Josi let him take them, but they lay limp and quiet in his grasp.

"Honey," he said. "I hate to disappoint you, but these cabins and things might as well be on Pluto as far as you and I are concerned. I know it looks like you can live around the Preserves. But you can't. Those tourist quarters have all been bought up years in advance by the big travel agencies. To get them you'd have to sign up for what they call perpetual tours—all-expense luxury set-ups. And the prices are fantastic. Why, for you and me and the boys, just the four of us, it'd be twenty or thirty thousand a year." He smiled at her consolingly.

She still refused to smile back. Her face was calm and still.

"Forty," she said.

"Forty?" He frowned.

"Forty thousand a year, Tom, for the four of us."

He shook his head. Her words seemed to buzz in his ears.

"Forty thousand?" he echoed. "How do you know?"

"I've been checking up."

"But Josi—" He ran out of words, trying not to think what he could not help thinking. "You didn't suppose, seriously—"

"I've never supposed anything else," she replied. And he wondered then how she could look him in the eye and say it. "I've been waiting for this for a long time, Tom— longer than you'd believe. Since my first baby was born."

He shook his head again, unbelievingly.

"We can do it now," she said. "With your increase in salary and if we use the savings and borrow against your pension. We'll have enough for five years; and by that time you'll have got another income boost."

"Josi!"

"Oh, stop staring like that!" she snapped, suddenly. "Did you think I'd let my boys miss out on a chance at what the real world once was, if there was any way at all to give them even a taste of it?"

He sat back on the couch, dazed. "It isn't like you."

"Because I've been a good wife all these years and done what *you* wanted, and lived where *you* wanted? You thought I never had a selfish desire of my own? Oh, Tom, *Tom!*" She clutched his hands with a strength that shocked him. "How long are you going to go on pretending that people are still like they were in the old days? There's no civilization left now. You ought to know that!

It's claw, tooth and nail! And I'm looking after my children!"

"Josi," he said.

She shook her head at him. "Tom," she said, "do you know how many people there are on Earth now?"

"Yes," he said. "And I know they're considering laws to control the population expansion."

"Control it!" She laughed like someone he had never seen before. "If they'd talked of controlling it fifty years ago, it might have helped us. What's going to help us now? It's my babies that have to grow up in a world where there's ten people for every job and no future for even the ones who get it. The only way they can *live* is if they make the right friends. And the only way they can meet the right friends is to go where they are. And that's the Preserves!"

"Josi!" said Tom. "Nothing like that's necessary. I hope I've made a moderate success of myself in the world. And I can truthfully say I've done it by decent, honorable methods!"

"You!" she cried. "Oh, *you!* The great anachronism!"

"Josi—" But she was beyond all reasoning.

2

As Tom came in through his outer office on his way to his desk the following morning, the rubber plant took his eye again. It grated on his overwrought nerves like a shabby challenge. He was on the verge of bursting out at Christine to get rid of it, when he became suddenly aware of its extraordinarily protected position on a new little ledge, hugging the wall by her desk—now pushed to the farthest possible distance from the desk of Bera Karlson, who had moved her own equipment in on the opposite side of the room. Abruptly he realized that he had been on the verge of taking out his own unhappiness on an underling—a thing he had never before allowed himself to do. He nodded to both women; and made himself smile.

"Good morning," he said.

They answered together—Bera with a tinge of tension in her voice, Christine almost in a whisper. He went on into his own private office, the door sucking gently closed behind him.

He dropped in the chair at his own desk; and for a minute he sat limply, his eyes closed. The long, unfinished, unclear, unrewarding argument with Josi the evening before had left him drained of energy and clogged with bitterness. He had gained nothing but her promise to let him think this matter of the Preserves over for a few days before talking of it again.

He straightened with an effort and glanced at his appointment screen. The name of Orval Lasron glowed at him from its gray, opaque surface. He stared at the two words, troubled by some slightly ominous echo at the back of his mind, which they evoked. Surely, he did not know the man? After a moment, he gave up. Buzzing Bera to admit Lasron, he got up and crossed over to the one wall-wide window that looked down to the Executive Waiting Lounge, three floors below.

He heard Bera's voice speak out over the annunciator down there and a stocky, short man in middle age, with lumpy features, rose from a table. He crossed over to where the angle of the wall below cut him off from Tom's sight.

After a second, the man rose into sight on a floating

magnetic disk, which came to a stop outside the window. Tom touched the dissolve button and extended his hand. Lasron stepped through the now non-existent window. His handshake was brisk and impersonal.

"I interrupted your drink down there," said Tom. "May I—"

"No, thanks," said the other.

Tom led the way back to his desk and both men seated themselves. Face to face, Lasron was somewhat more impressive than he had been at a distance. There was a hardness to his bunchy features and his eyes seemed to show the light of a constant, buried anger.

"And what can I do for you, Mr. Lasron?"

"You don't know me," stated Lasron. He crossed one thick leg over the knee of the other.

"No."

"I'm the local agent for the Secretarial Code," said Lasron. "I didn't know you, either. You were in Sales before, were you?"

"That's right. Our labor relations were all handled higher up."

"Yes." Lasron shifted in his chair with an abrupt, impatient movement. "Well, you've got a holdover. Christine Nyall."

"I know," said Tom, sobering. "A shame that—"

"I don't think so," interrupted Lasron. "Christine doesn't think so. She intends to remain on the job. Quite happy in it. It's standard procedure in these cases to drop around on the one in Management responsible. Just as a reminder." He paused. "You understand."

"No," answered Tom, sitting straighter. "I don't think I do."

Lasron sighed.

"All right," he said. "Any evidence of prejudice and we'll slap a writ on you for a fine. Deal with an illegal outfit and we'll spend half the money in the treasury, if necessary, to get a felony rap to stick to you."

"Now, wait! Now, look here," said Tom. "Just a minute, Lasron. Just what do you think you're insinuating? My record is perfectly clean and fair. I know some people on Management Level have the popular reputation of pulling dirty tricks in cases like this. But for your private information—"

Lasron waved one hand, wearily.

"I have a code of ethics!" snapped Tom. "No, I don't pretend I wouldn't like to see Christine happily retired. But—" He became suddenly aware that he was talking to a man who was staring out the window, humming a small tune nervously to himself, his fingers beating small, jerky time on the arm of his chair.

"Good," said Lasron, when Tom stopped. He got to his feet. His eyes of buried anger burnt briefly and impersonally on Tom, as if the man across the desk was something mechanical, troublesome and potentially dangerous. "I won't take up any more of your time."

Tom rose also, and punched the dissolve button.

"Drop by any time," he said, defiantly. "You don't have to make an appointment. Just walk in."

Lasron looked at him briefly. He appeared to be about to say something, then turned away. He nodded his head and stepped through the dissolve window onto the disk which wafted him down and out of sight.

Tom was left standing with a feeling of ugly inadequacy. He half-turned to his interoffice with the intention of calling Arm Brewer, to report the agent's threats. But it would be a bad beginning in the new position to go running for help right off the bat. He turned away again.

Then he thought of calling in Christine and challenging her about the agent's behavior. But that was not strictly fair, either. Time, he thought, sitting down at his desk again—time would iron matters out automatically.

Two days later Josi reminded him of his promise to consider the move to the Preserves. He put her off, saying he had not had the chance to think, pleading the situation at the office.

"Just don't take too long, Tom," she said.

She said it in such an odd, unusual tone that he looked at her startled, and then looked away again before she could catch him staring. He wanted to ask her what she meant; but discovered suddenly he was afraid to.

That night he slept badly, and when he did get to sleep he slept late.

It was later than usual when he stepped through the entrance to his outer office. He could feel immediately that there was something wrong. As she answered his good morning, Christine kept her eyes fixed on the surface of her desk; while Bera, glancing deliberately at him, gave him a look of peculiar outrage, features set and a little pale. Tom shouldered past them both into the security of his own office, hoping to avoid the matter, whatever it was.

He was given no choice. On his appointment screen, Bera's name stood out brilliantly, in the space where his first appointment should have been. Tom hesitated for a moment, to put a small barrier of time between his entrance and Bera's admission; and then pressed her button and summoned her in.

She came and sat down opposite him. It was abundantly clear that a crisis point had been reached, for as she sat on the edge of her chair her body was rigid with the glass-brittle tension of a woman on the verge of explosion.

They began calmly enough, but Bera's low voice quickly climbed the scale toward hysteria. She did not want to complain. He knew that she never complained; but—she reminded Tom of all the years she had worked for him. She asked him if he had ever had any reason to complain. She thought that over the years—and so on. Inevitably came the tears.

She sat in the big visitor's chair and cried, a large-boned, not unlovely woman at the end of her thirties; but past the point where tears could look good on her. Tom gave her a drink and waited until the emotion was controlled.

He was shocked to discover the whimpering fear that underlay her outburst.

"Why, Bera," he said, as soon as she was in fit shape to listen, "what makes you think I'd ever get rid of *you?* Why, I could no longer get along without you than—" he hunted for an enormous metaphor and could think of nothing but—"my right arm."

Bera gulped, "But *She* has tenure and I haven't, and you only need one of us."

"Then I'll just have to put up with both of you," he said, in a poor attempt to be jocular. "Anything else is ridiculous." He frowned. "Besides, I think after a while she'll get tired of not having a real job to do around here, and retire."

"No, she won't—the old biddy!" said Bera with sudden viciousness. "She wants to hang on forever."

"Now, you know that's not true," said Tom. "She just liked her job. All of us do."

"Well, I don't care. She doesn't belong in our office. Why doesn't she just go?"

"Where do you want her to go?" asked Tom, reasonably.

"I don't care. It isn't as if she'd starve to death. You make as much money retired nowadays as you do working."

"Well, she's not going to get your job," said Tom. "Now straighten up, Bera, and forget this nonsense. As far as I'm concerned, Christine has already retired."

"Then she shouldn't be allowed to clutter up the office with things like that plant of hers."

"Why, it's not a bad looking plant," said Tom. "I think it's rather a nice idea, having it there. Hardly anyone keeps flowers or plants around nowadays."

"It gets in my way," said Bera, sullenly. Tom felt it was time to put his foot down.

"I'm sure you can work around it," he said. "Try it for a few weeks, anyway. If Christine is still here after then, and the plant still interferes around the office, we'll see about getting rid of it. All right?"

Tom got to his feet, which forced her to rise as well. "Try and get along with Christine, then, Bera. I'm leaving now. I just dropped by today to take a look at things. You can tell anyone who calls that I won't be back before tomorrow. Handle them as you like."

"Yes." She wiped her eyes.

"So long, then." He went out, closing the door on her answering good-by. In the outer office, Christine was sitting at her desk, her face expressionless and a sheet of paper filled with aimless doodlings before her.

"Well, I'm off for the rest of the day, Christine," he said.

"Good morning, Mr. Calloway," she replied, without looking up.

He went out the door.

When the tension in the outer office did not improve, he took a trip to the other side of the building to talk to Arm.

"Tom!" Arm jumped to his feet as Tom entered, and came forward bouncily, his heavy face smiling under its white hair. "How's our newest member upstairs here? Have a drink?"

"No thanks," said Tom. "How've you been, Arm?"

"How could I be? Eighty-seven and sound as the Company's credit rating!" Arm slapped his wide chest. "Why don't you and Josi step out with me one of these nights and find out for yourselves? See if the old bachelor can't outdo you yet?"

"I wouldn't doubt it. I'll talk to Josi about it," said Tom, smiling. "Arm, I hate to come running to you with troubles right away, but I've got stuck in a situation."

"That the straight sheet?" Arm punched for a drink and set it on the edge of his desk. "What is it?"

"Christine Nyall. Old Walt's secretary."

"Christine—? Oh, the holdover!" Arm looked at Tom, pulled a long face and rocked abruptly with hearty laughter. "Now, that is rough. If only she'd been some young bounce, huh, Tom?"

Tom smiled agreeably, if perfunctorily.

"Well, well." Arm sobered. "So you've got old Walt's girl on your hands. You knew about her and Walt? Yes, I see you did. Well, now, what's the problem?"

"Well, since I brought Bera up with me, I've really no need for Christine. But she's trying to stick it out."

"They all do."

"For myself, I don't mind too much—after all, she's bound to retire eventually. But it crowds the office, you know how we are for space. And, worst of all, she's upsetting Bera."

"Well, now, that is serious," said Arm. "A good secretary, broken in over the years. I can see why you wouldn't want her disturbed. Why don't you do something about it?"

"But that's the point. What can I do?" said Tom. "She's got tenure. The representative of the Secretarial Code was around just a week or so ago to remind me of that. What *can* I do?"

Arm looked across the desk at him with a curious expression on his big face.

"You haven't been approached yet, then?" he said, slowly.

"Approached? By who?"

Arm's drink had been sitting unnoticed all this time. He picked it up now and sipped at it.

"There's people," he said, "who make a point of being useful in just such situations."

"There are?" Tom searched his expression for a clue. "In the face of the tenure law? What can they do? Who are they, anyway?"

"They contact you."

"But I mean—oh," said Tom. "Oh, oh I see!"

"I don't know anything about them myself," Arm said, sipping on his drink. "Nothing whatsoever. I've just heard about them."

"Of course," said Tom. There was a fumbling moment of silence.

"Sure you won't have a drink, after all?"

"Thanks," said Tom automatically. Arm had already punched for a full glass without waiting for an answer. Now he handed the drink over. Tom took it, his eyes staring unseeingly through the wall of Arm's office.

"Hi!" said Josi, meeting him at the front door, when he arrived at home.

"Hello, honey." He kissed her. They went inside.

"You've been drinking," she said.

"I had a few at the office with Arm," he answered, as they sat down. "He wants us to go out with him one of these nights."

"That's nice," said Josi.

"You don't sound very enthusiastic," he said.

"No, I suppose not."

"Josi!" he burst out. "Josi, will you snap out of it? Can't you understand I've got a crisis brewing in that office of mine? If I don't handle this right, what do you think my chances of promotion will be?"

"I'm just waiting," she said.

"Here I am up to my ears in business troubles—"

"And spending the morning getting drunk with Arm."

It developed into a first class fight.

3

The outer office had become an armed camp. There was no disguising the atmosphere of antagonism that existed there. Tom dodged through it as quickly as he could, and remained buried in the inner office during the hours of his working day.

But this was no solution. Bera became more and more

unreliable until it became obvious, even to Tom, that her work had become clearly secondary to her feud with Christine. On Tuesday, at the beginning of the third week, Tom was disturbed at his desk by what could only be the sounds of a scuffle.

He went swiftly to the door of the outer office and jerked it open. The two women were standing facing each other, breathing hard, and the jar which held the plant was clutched with fierce protectiveness in the arms of Christine. As the door opened, she turned to look at Tom for a single moment, then turned back and put down the plant once more in its accustomed place. She reseated herself, silently. Bera turned and walked jerkily back to her own desk and also sat down. Neither one said a word.

He waited until they were ostensibly busy again, then walked through the office and out of the front door. He did not say a word to Bera; and the back of his neck was aware that she stared after him with bitter, fearful eyes, while the woman across from her sat silent and depressed, her head down and her eyes hopelessly fixed on her desk.

Feeling as if he was choking, Tom made his way out of the building. He avoided the lobby lounge below and took an aircab to a rooftop bar nearby—the Parisien, it was called. Its small round tables and wire chairs were imitative of an old-fashioned sidewalk cafe. He ordered a tall scotch and tried to relax.

Things, he thought, could not go on like this. Twenty-four hours had been the limit on family quarrels between Josi and himself for years now. But the present one about the move to the Preserves seemed to renew itself daily. Softly, he pounded on the white, slick surface of the table with his fist. Trouble at the office. Trouble at home. And the two things feeding on each other to keep themselves alive. The tension between Josi and himself was blurring his usual decisiveness so that he was fumbling the office problem. And the office problem wore his nerves thin so that one word from Josi was enough to set him off. Why couldn't Josi be a help instead of a hindrance at a time like this? And why couldn't Christine be sensible and retire?

The scotch came. He accepted it automatically, indifferent to the anachronism of a live waiter instead of the usual delivery panel set in the table. The truth was, he had started out with a sneaking sympathy for Christine. It was not impossible for him to put himself in her shoes, to feel an empathy with her. He had, therefore, been half-inclined to let things drift, to let her sit out her remaining days in his office—perhaps even in time to give her small bits and pieces of work to make her feel necessary. He had never imagined such a violent reaction, however, from Bera. Who would have supposed . . .

A shadow fell abruptly across his table.

He looked up and saw gazing down at him a distinguished looking man of his own age. A handsome fellow, slim, with a touch of easy amusement at the corners of his thin mouth.

"Well, Mr. Calloway," said the man, "you're a hard person to get in touch with."

He sat down. Tom stared at him in astonishment.

"Hard?" He looked more closely at the man. "Do I know you?"

"May I introduce myself?"

He put the question with such unnatural stilted formality that for a second Tom did not realize that it was an actual question, and not a rhetorical one.

"Is there any reason why you shouldn't?" asked Tom.

"Joe Smith," said the other, taking this as permission and offering his hand. "Utility Services."

Tom shook hands automatically.

"Utility Services?"

"Of course you don't know us. We aren't listed. In fact," Joe Smith turned to signal the anachronistic waiter, "legally we don't exist."

A bell rang in Tom's mind. He sat up straight behind his scotch and looked penetratingly at his visitor.

"And illegally?" he asked.

The man laughed.

"We understand you have a problem, Mr. Calloway— thanks—" he accepted his glass from the waiter. "A hold-over."

"Who told you?"

"Why," said Smith, "it's a matter of public record, isn't it?" He looked at Tom. "We're prepared to help you out."

"How?"

Smith waved a hand.

"Depends on the difficulty. Once it was merely a matter of offering a job with some dummy firm. But the Secretarial Code is well up on simple tricks like that, lately. In the case of your Christine—let's see. She was supposed to have been having a long-term affair with her former employer, wasn't she? Perhaps someone who resembled him a great deal could bring about her resignation."

"Now, look here," said Tom.

"Yes, Mr. Calloway?"

"I certainly wouldn't stand for anything like that."

Smith raised his eyebrows.

"What did you expect?" He leaned forward over the

table, lowering his voice. "I'll tell you what you expected —a miracle. We don't deal in miracles. Just results."

Tom flushed.

"All right, Smith," he said. "I don't think we've got any business to do together."

"I think we have," said Smith. "Or rather, you have business to do with us. If not now, later. We're a business fact of life in this modern world, Mr. Calloway. Ugly, if you insist on looking at us that way, but just as unavoidable as any other fact of life."

"I don't think so," said Tom grimly.

"Don't you?" queried Smith. "Open your eyes, Mr. Calloway. This isn't the last century. It's the present. There's no way to hide from the facts of life now."

"I'm not sure I know what you're talking about," said Tom. "But I'll tell you this. I've lived by my own code of ethics all my life. And got along all right. So go peddle your dirty papers someplace else."

"No, no," said Smith, shaking his head. "It's all very fine to have ethics, Mr. Calloway, but they simply don't work in business. They've gotten to be a luxury nobody can afford any more. Save your ethics for home. Tell them to the kids for bedtime stories when you tuck them in for the night. But don't go messing up your career with them. You'll regret it. Indeed you will, Calloway. People like this Christine *expect* to get kicked out. They just hang around creating a fuss until they are."

"If you think you can say that—" Tom checked himself suddenly, remembering the office as it had been lately. Remembering Josi. "My wife—" he began, without thinking. Then he stopped.

"What about your wife?"

"None of your business!"

"Oh? But I take it," said Smith, looking at him closely, "you weren't about to listen to her, either?"

Tom shuddered suddenly and quite unexpectedly.

"It's all nonsense," he said.

"Someone walk over your grave?" said Smith, not entirely unmaliciously. "You ought to know the truth as well as your wife. As well as me, for that matter." He waved his arm out over the parapet of the rooftops, at the endless buildings surrounding them. "Look at that. Full up. Ripe. Starting to rot, wouldn't you say?" He grinned at Tom.

"What're you talking about?" said Tom. "There's unlimited frontiers. New worlds . . ."

"You want to go? Do I want to go?" Smith sat back, shaking his head and took a drink from his glass. "Easier to stay here and face facts, Calloway. And the fact you've got to face—" he tapped with his fingernail on the shiny white tabletop, his nail making a hard clicking sound against it— "is that you must do for this Christine or, indirectly, she's going to do for you. If you don't get her out of that office, the mess'll grow. It'll grow until you find yourself into it too deep to pull yourself out. I've seen this sort of thing before." He got up. "Think about that, Calloway. You or her. And the longer you hesitate, the more likely it's going to be both of you."

It was evening before Tom found Christine Nyall.

After Smith left, Tom had tried to call her at the office. Bera told him the older woman had gone for the day. Bera did not have Christine's address, either, so Tom had been forced to go to a public tracing center. It took the center three hours to come up with a list of places where she might be found.

He located her at last, sitting at one of the small tables around the wide expanse of dance floor in one of the midage groups recreation centers. She sat alone, a barely touched drink in front of her, the glowingly white translucent dance floor throwing a pale illumination on her overpowdered face. He strode over and sat down opposite her.

"Christine," he said.

She turned from her blank contemplation of the dancing couples on the floor and looked at him. As his identity registered, her features slid into the carefully controlled expression he was used to seeing at the office.

"Mr. Calloway," she murmured.

"Hello." He stumbled, suddenly at a loss for words. "Er —another drink?"

She touched the glass before her.

"Thanks, no," she said.

"I see," he said. "Well, I think I'll have one." He pressed buttons and waited for a few short seconds until a filled glass rose from the slot in the center of the table. He took it, swallowed largely and put it back on the table. "I've had a hard time finding you."

The words reminded him immediately of the man named Smith. He put his drink down with a gesture of revulsion. He looked at Christine, almost pleadingly.

"Look, Christine," he said, "do you really think you'd feel happier belonging to my office staff than you would, retired?"

She reached for her glass and turned it.

"Yes," she said, "yes, I do."

"You know," he said, trying to joke, "sooner or later we all have to quit."

She looked up sharply. He saw her eyes were terrified.

"Not until retirement age!" she said. "I've got tenure!"

"Of course, of course. I know you've got tenure," said Tom. "But you do see—you're just putting off the inevitable, don't you?"

"I only want my rights. That's all!"

Tom took a heavy gulp from his glass. He pushed it away from him.

"Look," he said, "I want us to be friends. I know how I'd feel if I was—well—put in an awkward position with some years yet to go to retirement. I'd like to do what's best for you. And I know Bera. She can be difficult to get along with."

"I don't mind," said Christine carefully.

"Oh come now," said Tom. "Informally—just between the two of us—I know she's been raising cain ever since we moved into the new office."

"Bera's all right," she answered. "I like Bera."

Tom gaped at her. The statement was too monstrous to refute.

"Christine!" he burst out, finally. "Let's be honest, anyway!" She looked stubbornly down at her drink. "Look, if you really want to stay, you can. I'll talk to Bera. Or the three of us will all get together and thrash this thing out. That is, if you really want to stay."

She glanced up obliquely, almost slyly, at him.

"I can stay anyway," she said. "My tenure guarantees it."

"Of course! Of course you can stay!" cried Tom.

"That's not what I'm talking about. I'm talking about fitting you in, making a useful place for you."

"That's all right." She raised her head to look him squarely in the eye. "You don't have to bother about me."

"Good Lord!" shouted Tom. "Do you like things the way they are?"

"You might as well give up, Mr. Calloway," she said. "I know what my rights are, and I'm not going to give them up. If you've got any questions you can call up the Secretarial Code and talk to Mr. Lasron. Of course, I'll have to report to him you tried to talk to me here, today."

For a moment Tom stared at her in amazement.

"You stupid woman!" he burst out finally. "Can't you see I'm trying to help?"

Christine's face went white and frightened. She jerked as if she had been struck. For a moment she sat as if paralyzed; then she made a small noise in her throat and scrambled up. She was hurrying off, before Tom could stop her, between the tables.

"Christine! Wait!" he called after her. But she was already gone.

It was late when he at last got home. Josi was waiting for him in the lounge room.

"Had your supper?" she asked a little sharply, as he came in.

"I'm not hungry." He dropped into a chair.

"Would you like a drink? Or—" she stood over him—"have you had too many already?"

"Josi," he said wearily, putting his head in his hands, "don't start in on me now."

She sat down opposite him.

"I'm sorry, Tom," she said. "But we've got something

to talk over. I've been waiting for you since this afternoon."

"Can't it wait?"

"No, Tom."

A note he had never before heard in her voice made him look up.

"I'm leaving things up to you, Tom," she said. "I went down to the tourist agency and told them to go ahead with our reservations."

"Josi!"

"You listen to me now. The plans are at a premium. I can't afford to wait. The Preserves may be filled up, or the price increased any day now, to where we can't afford it."

"Josi, listen!"

"No. Now I'm doing the talking, Tom," she said. "I told you I was going through with this. And I meant it. The reservation is in my name. If you won't come along, then I'm getting a divorce. My settlement will pay for the first few years of the plan; and after that we'll work things out any way we can. But whether you like it or not, whether you come or not, the boys and I are leaving for the Preserves. It's up to you, Tom."

She rose to her feet and left him, sitting in the lounge, numb and old and alone.

4

The next morning found him having breakfast at a poolside restaurant not far from the office. He had slipped out of the house to avoid Josi, for reasons that were at the moment unclear to him. He sat at his small table under a striped awning, staring out at the early morning swimmers in the pool. The coffee seemed tasteless.

He had spent the whole of a wakeful night trying to believe what Josi had told him. Accepting it was something else again. First he had to believe she would do such a thing. It was all the more wildly improbable for the reason that he believed Josi still loved him. Only there seemed to be some startling and hitherto unsuspected limits to that love.

How, he wondered, staring at the pool, had Josi reached such a point? He tried to think back over their discussions—well, be honest and call them arguments. Had there been some point at which he had driven her to desperation? Thinking back, he could remember no such point. In fact, he had never given a definite "no" to the idea. He had merely been doubting and wanting to put off his decision until he could settle the problem of Christine.

That could only mean—he came back to the point not for the first nor even for the hundredth time since the previous evening—that Josi had simply long ago decided to eliminate him from the family. She had thought not *my husband, our family;* but simply *my children and I.* She had cut him out.

Or had he ever belonged?

After a while, he got up and went to the office.

When he came in this morning, Bera was absorbed in her work; but Christine looked up at him with a momentary strange, unreadable expression. He brushed past both of them and went on into his own office.

He sat down at his desk. He had never been an early morning drinker; but now he punched for scotch. After a moment, the tall glass rose to the surface of his desk and he took it. It tasted alien and bitter, like the coffee he had drunk earlier. But he forced himself to swallow it.

After a little while, the hard edges of his world softened somewhat. He straightened up and looked at his appointment screen.

There, waiting for him, was the name of Lasron. He got up from his desk and looked out the window, down into the lounge.

There was Lasron waiting. Tom made out the man's thick body seated alone at a table before a glass from which he was not drinking. His fingers seemed to be drumming on the table top. Impatient. Well, he would just have to wait. Tom came back to his desk and pushed the button that summoned Christine.

She came in hesitantly, closing the door behind her instead of letting it suck shut automatically, and approached his desk.

"Sit down," said Tom.

She seated herself carefully on the edge of the big visitor's chair.

"Christine," he said, "I wanted to talk to you."

"I know," she answered. She was watching her own fingers, which she had laced together and was turning, backwards and forwards, in her lap.

"You know?" he said.

"I'm so terribly sorry, Mr. Calloway," she said. "I want to apologize—"

He stared at her in startlement. But she was hurrying on, tripping over her own words in her haste.

"I just couldn't help it after working here so long. I couldn't help thinking it was our office—mine and Mr. Onegh's. And then, when you're older and you've got no one—to be cut loose, to just eat and sleep and die and be forgotten—you go a little crazy, I guess."

"Well, now," said Tom, "Christine—"

"And they make matters worse for us down at the Secretarial Code. They warn us Management will try all sorts of dirty tricks to make us resign, when we've got tenure. They get us so worked up, Mr. Calloway, that we can't trust anyone. And I didn't trust you. I called Mr. Lasron last night, after you talked to me. It wasn't until after I punched off the phone, that I thought to remember you hadn't been anything but kind. You didn't even complain about the plant."

Tom found his voice a little hoarse, and cleared it. "No point in being unfair."

"I know. I just couldn't believe it." She twisted her hands. "I want to tell you about that plant, Mr. Calloway. It—" She hesitated, and her powdered face twisted into a slight grotesqueness. "It meant a good deal to me. You must know about me and Mr. Onegh."

"Yes," said Tom.

"A lot of people knew." She was stroking one blue-veined hand with the fingers of the other, as if in fascination with the process. "They knew I loved him and they guessed—that was before his wife died—that we were getting away for a weekend, now and then. But nobody here knew we once had nearly a whole year together."

Tom jerked his head back from the window.

"Yes." She nodded a little. "It was before you came to the Company. There was an underground city supply unit to be set up in the Midlands, on Venus. The Company took the bid. Mr. Onegh was sent out as Management Representative when we got the job. I took a leave of absence; and he pulled some strings to get me an appointment on the Government Inspection Crew. So we both went out, and no one here knew about it."

She stopped. Tom was staring at her. She went on.

"It was a year," she said. "We could have stayed on Venus. I wanted to. But Walter—" Her voice trailed off.

"He thought," said Tom, and was jarred at the sound of his own voice, so strange it sounded, "of his wife and his job here."

"Yes," she whispered.

Her index finger made little circles on the arm of the chair. She spoke again.

"He was a coward," she said. Tom started and looked at her with a sort of horror.

"I thought you loved him?"

"I did." She raised her head. "He wasn't a coward when I first met him. It was the years made him that. All the years and the sneaking around corners with me. And the business getting tighter and tighter every year, so that even someone who'd been with the Company as long as he had didn't feel safe."

"Class A Management. With tenure." Tom's throat was dry, suddenly.

She smiled sadly at him.

"Oh, they've got dirty tricks for Management level, too," she said. "When I was working with Walter—" Her voice trailed off, embarrassedly.

Tom sat still in his chair. He opened his mouth, closed it again and suddenly, almost with violence, shoved himself to his feet. Turning, he stepped to the office window and looked out. Across from him, over the airy depths of the lounge below, he could make out Arm Brewer, his white thatch vigorously in movement beyond the pane of his window on the opposite side of the lounge.

"What about the plant?" Tom said without turning. "You were going to tell me about the rubber plant."

"Well, you know how Venus is," her voice rang in his ears. "The carbon dioxide blanket, the dust storms, nothing green anywhere. It was against the shipping rules, but he took the plant along when he went to Venus—for me. To make me happy. For that one year it grew in our home."

Out and below Tom, the lounge eddied in its steady movement of continual coming and going. Salesmen, jobhunters, caterers, favorseekers, representatives like Lasron—the flotsam of the commercial sea. All waiting. All hungry.

Yes, thought Tom.

Just then, through the wide-swinging entrance of the lounge came the tall, thin figure of Mr. Smith. For a moment, Tom hung, not even breathing, staring down at the tall man.

Behind him, Christine talked on. But he heard her only as background noise. Smith had just nodded to Lasron, sitting at his table; and Lasron had lifted a hand in acknowledgement.

Mr. Smith paused to speak to the receptionist, his elegant head a little on one side. He turned and went over the opposite wall soaring up from the lounge. A disk came immediately to life on the floor, and he stepped aboard. It bore him upward to the window of Arm's office, opposite. The window dissolved before him as Arm reached out a hand in greeting. They went inside together and—did their heads turn to look for a moment in the direction of Tom's office as they went?

Tom had a sudden dizzying sensation of falling. It was as if the lounge below reached up with clutching fingers to drag him down. He clung to the window drape beside him for a minute, finding the heavy metallic cloth slippery in his damp hands. He took a deep breath, straightened and turned.

"Yes, yes," he said, interrupting Christine. "I appreciate your telling me about the plant. But I think that in spite of the sentimental attachment you have for it, we'll have to get rid of it."

Her mouth open, she stared at him. In her astonishment she looked almost imbecilic.

"You understand," he went on, the words coming automatically, "I'm a liberal-minded man myself. But I can hardly be expected to put up with a souvenir of this type. After all, this is a business office, not a bedroom. I was a young man once myself—fairly recently, too. And I had my—er—fun. And I recognize that a single woman and a man with a perpetually ailing wife might have their problems on a physical plane. But to flaunt mementos of—well, it seems to me to be a little too much."

She looked up at him with a rabbit-like fascination, as if he had suddenly revealed scales and a moveless eye. He met her look squarely. It was odd, but he felt no need to avoid her. His eyes were heavy as pebbles in his face, and as insensitive to what he gazed at.

"So I'll just ask you to put it away somewhere right now," he said. He paused. "Naturally, I'm going to have to submit a memo on this to the Company psychiatrist. I believe you need help, Christine. Women often do at your age. I'll do what I can by attaching a complete account of what you told me about you and Walter—"

With one quick, gasping intake of breath, she was on her feet. She turned and ran from his office. The impersonal machinery of the door closed it politely behind her.

Tom sat down at his desk. He felt as if he should be shaking, but he was not. He laid his hands on the desktop but felt nothing.

After a while he became aware of the sound of Bera's buzzer, calling for his attention. But he ignored it. It was not until some little time after that, that the door to his office opened and she came in. Her eyes were wide, showing too much white; and her lips trembled.

"What is it?" he asked.

"Mr. Calloway—Mr. Calloway, it's Christine!"

He looked carefully at her. "What about Christine?"

"I'm worried. Perhaps I've been— I didn't think."

"Will you tell me," he said, "what it is? If you don't mind, Bera!"

"She locked herself in the supply closet in our outer office. She won't come out, and she doesn't—doesn't answer."

"Oh?" said Tom. "I see." He took a slow breath and leaned back in his chair.

"I'm scared. She took the plant. Oh, Mr. Calloway, I didn't mean to be so nasty to her! If she's—"

"Control yourself, Bera." Tom got up from his chair. "I'm sure it's quite all right. Perhaps the door locked accidentally. Perhaps she had a little fainting fit in there. After all, she's not as young as she once was. Why don't you run down and get the janitor up here to unlock the door? Don't make a fuss about it. Just say the door's locked and we can't find the key."

"Oh, yes! I'll run!" said Bera. "I'll run right away!" She dashed out of the room.

After she had gone, Tom sat still for a second. Then he reached out and punched for a private connection to Arm Brewer on the interoffice phone.

Arm's face sprang into view on its screen.

"Who? Oh, Tom. What can I do for you?"

"Just give me a few pointers about something when you've got time, Arm," said Tom. "Josi and I are thinking of taking one of those perpetual tours around the Preserves—"

"Preserves? Sure!" boomed Arm. "I've been on them. Tell you all about it, if you want. How's things down at your end there?"

"I'm afraid I'm going to have to let Bera go after all," said Tom, steadily. "And keep Christine. Bera's gone all to pieces lately. Lets her work go, and spends all her time picking on Christine. Of course, there's no tenure problem with Bera."

"Ah? I hadn't realized that," said Arm, raising white eyebrows. "Well, that settles your little problem."

"Yes. I'm afraid so." Tom sighed. "Too bad. I'd never have considered this if she'd—but, well, this is easier all around. She's been making life hell for Christine."

"Yeah. I heard something about that. Look, talk to you later, okay, Tom? I've got a little deal on right now."

"Fine. Thanks, Arm."

"Not at all. Any time."

Tom broke the connection and sat back, waiting for Bera to return. For a while he heard nothing but silence. But then, at last, there was the muffled sound of voices reentering his outer office. For a moment they murmured busily together; then there was the sound of a lock turning. Then silence.

—When the scream came, he was expecting it.

High and clear in Bera's voice, he had been expecting it all along. Sitting still at his desk, he did not move. Only the muscles of his body froze all together as if the blood in them had congealed at the sound; and the sweat stood suddenly out on his forehead like living water from the rock.

THE HOURS ARE GOOD

The mists of preconditioning rolled away. Harold Smith-Jones came back to himself on the hospital-like metal table of the Technical Center. They were just cranking the hood up off him.

"There you go," said one of the white-coated technicians, giving him a hand up. Off the table and once more on his feet, Harold frowned at the youngster.

"—*sir!*" he corrected.

"There you go, sir," the technician made haste to amend.

Harold's frown relaxed. He did not approve of this modern laxity—but they were good boys. He did not approve of riding subordinates, either.

He allowed himself to be helped on with his regency coat. A tall, blond young boy was standing back from the group a bit, waiting. His new decoy, no doubt. A good type, in jumper and slacks, athletic, his only adornment the thin, sharp-edged strip of polished steel that held the watch on his wrist. The boy was somewhat tight-faced and looked nervous.

"Cheer up, there!" said Harold, giving him a friendly whack on the back. "All in the day's work."

The decoy managed a grin. A trifle sick—but a grin. Good lad, thought Harold, and, leaving the room, headed out for the job.

As he stepped, a moment later, out of the gray building's austere entrance, the brilliant September sunlight struck him a sudden, dazzling blow, and for a moment the street before him wavered and blurred.

"Steady on, now—" he thought, catching hold of the left arch of the entrance. He felt the gray stone rough under his palms, took a deep breath, and the street steadied and came back in focus.

The preconditioning again, of course, he told himself. It must be he had developed a sensitivity to the hypnotic drug they used to put him in a receptive state for instructions. Slight allergic reaction on his part, possibly. He made a mental note to mention the fact in his report later.

There was no point in his being uncomfortable. On the other hand, it would hardly do to take on a job without the protection of full preconditioning. Under the latest laws dealing with this sort of thing, the opposition had the right to question him if they happened to get their hands on him before he reached the street afterward. Only if he showed obvious evidence of preconditioning, so that he could tell them nothing of how he had planned the job, would there be no point in their doing so. And such questioning could be—well, there was no point in dwelling on unpleasant details.

Not that anything would go wrong. Not with a job he himself had researched and planned. Not with a possible new world's record staring him in the face.

Thirty-four consecutives. *Thirty-four!* Without a hitch, or a scratch upon him. He would take a little vacation after this one, thought Harold. Rest on his laurels.

He took another deep breath and stepped hard on his left foot. The outline of the small plastic gun could be felt through the inner sole, and at the feel of it the old magic flooded through him once again, like a spate of warm wine. Ah, he thought, never mind fame and riches, never mind palaces and beautiful women. Give me a gun.

With confidence and even good humor returned, he got down onto the nearest strip of the moving sidewalk before him and let it carry him off.

The sidewalk slid him off down the block and swept around a corner. As he came around the curve, he caught sight of his own dark image, obscurely reflected in a passing store display window. Perfect, perfect!

A heavy-bodied, somewhat small man in regency coat, breeches and jackboots—with lilies of the valley in the little vases at each ankle. Thank God nowadays everybody dressed the way they wished. When he had been a boy, back in the nineteen-sixties, everybody he remembered had dressed alike. But now, with the overpopulation pressures, nobody cared much whether the individual lived or died, let alone how he dressed. A damned, dull time, the past, no matter what the historical entertainments liked to pretend. He preferred the present.

Of course, for business reasons, mainly. With any costume permissible, it was that much easier to create the image of a harmless, pompous, little fat man.

On the other hand, thought Harold, his feet changing slideways without consulting his brain, maybe his liking for the present was based on the fact he was in a special situation. Few people had his opportunities for what you might call excitement and adventure. After all, he reminded himself, he had originally intended to be a wine-taster, having that wonderful discrimination of taste that is born in one person in a million. If it hadn't been for that little psychotic upset (but everyone had them these days) he might not have lost it, and never gone into this business at all. And never discovered what an aptitude he had for it. Ah, yes— "*Some are born great. Some have greatness thrust upon them . . .*"

On the other hand . . . Harold found himself glancing at a street sign, and changed to another moving sidewalk with the automated reaction of good preconditioning. On the other hand, aptitude itself was really only the corner-stone of his success. Study, study—plan, plan—practice, practice—*that* was the real secret; that and his attention to details like seldom using the same decoy more than twice, and little touches like the lilies of the valley on his boots. And the man in the street thought all it took was a good target eye and a touch of sadism.

Harold stepped off the sidewalk into an entrance bla-zoned above with the legend MOTHER TURNER'S TEA ROOMS. Marvelous, thought Harold, the way the precondi-tioning had brought him right to the place when every jot of knowledge about the job had been hidden from his mind by the hypnotic block. He'd had no idea where he was heading until the moment of recognition right now. The boys in the technical department deserved a com-mendation in his report. And would get it.

Entering, he nodded to himself. One of the decently ex-clusive gathering places. Wisely, these places kept their prices up and excluded the salaried mob, who never ceased to be baffled by the fact that the Tea Rooms offered no better drinks or accommodations than their own cocktail lounges. They missed the point entirely.

Harold passed on into a dim-lit foyer. Two men con-verged on him immediately.

"Mind stepping on this metal plate, sir?" —hum of de-tectors.

"Excuse me, sir." —hands patting him swiftly all over.

"Not at all, boys. I know you've got a job to do." Harold's voice rang heartily; a generous man, a jolly, fat man with an untroubled conscience. With a cheerful wave of his hand, he turned to the right. There, before an arched interior entrance, was a placard.

WILLIAM X. KLANNERT
Editorial Auction

That's right—the little nodule of pre-planted information said in Harold's head, releasing its interior surprise of information. Klannert was the author of that best-selling new philosophical novel, *Existence's Worth;* and this was one of those publicity affairs promoted by his publishers under the guise of auctioning off a subsidiary right or two. Really, just a good public relations excuse to introduce Klannert to magazine editors, TV and film people, etc. He himself, Harold pre-remembered suddenly, was supposed to edit one of the intellectual weeklies under the name of Spence.

"Oh, Mr. Spence! *Here* you are! Martini?"

Harold became suddenly aware of a seductive blonde in flame-purple, standing just inside the entrance to the placarded room and tempting him in with a full cocktail glass. A hostess, of course—preconditioned to recognize all those to whom invitations had been distributed. Harold himself (or the technical boys) had been thorough with this detail, too. Harold went graciously toward her.

"Why, thanks, no," he said. "I never drink." True enough. Did the gunmen of the old West—the good ones, that is—drink while awaiting their moment of truth? And how much more foolish for Harold. "Iced tea, perhaps."

"Of course, Mr. Spence. Of *course!*"

She swept off to get him one. He glanced about the room. There, that was Klannert over there—the peaceful-faced, silver-haired man seated on the little dais at the end of the oval room, a crowd clustered around him.

"Your iced tea, Mr. Spence."

"Thank you, ma'mselle. Cheers!"

"Oh, *cheerio*, Mr. Spence!"

He continued on into the room, glass in hand, caught up immediately in the good-sized crowd.

"Oops, terribly sorry—" He had collided with a small brunette.

"My fault, really. Say, I don't know you, do I? I'm Hepzibah Collins. *Wasteland.*"

"Aneas Spence. *The Fabliau Weekly.*"

"You must give me your biog and I'll have it preconditioned into me the next time at the office. I do feel it's everybody's duty to know everyone they meet, don't you?"

"Absolutely." Harold fumbled artistically in a huge pocket of his regency coat. "I don't seem to have a biog slip with me—"

"Oh, dear. Well, tape it to me. There's Samantha! Sam!"

She disappeared into the crowd. Moving off himself, Harold came on to a small empty balcony and stepped up on it for a look at the crowd.

The number of people he saw rang a sudden icy tocsin of warning in his mind. There were at least twenty or thirty more here than his formal estimate of attendance had calculated. In a small room with a single exit, such a mob could hamper escape; and he would not legally be free from capture or reprisal until he was actually out of the building.

Harold carefully set down his glass of iced tea and took another deep breath, putting his weight once more on his left foot to feel the solid shape of the gun. The situation at once became clearer. He congratulated himself on his early study of Yoga. Like every other bit of knowledge he had painstakingly acquired, it paid off a thousandfold at times.

Now that he thought of it more objectively, the crowd might not hamper him. It might even help him by interfering with pursuit. Harold smiled. Once again his wisdom in leaving the final situation fluid and adaptable was proving itself.

He turned his attention to the business of spotting Klannert's bodyguards. Klannert would be expecting someone to try to do a job on him sooner or later. Everyone in the public eye knew such things were inevitable. Harold let his gaze search the crowd. That girl—Hepzibah Collins, the *Wasteland* editor—was one, of course. An expert frisker, undoubtedly; her collision with him would have been for the purpose of double-checking the detectives' search. Odd existence, thought Harold, momentarily struck by that strange, sad, philosophical turn of mind that had been growing on him these last few years. Imagine making a living going through life bumping up against people! Still, some sorts of persons might actually enjoy it.

The hostess was undoubtedly another.

And then that tall, heavy senatorial type. An excellent actor, but Harold had not studied over fifty thousand job reports in the past fifteen years for nothing. This man had been a bodyguard in the Claire Dumont job in April '89.

Then there was—good lord, whom did they expect to fool with that? That beetle-browed plug-ugly who was supposed, no doubt, to look so much like a bodyguard that nobody could suspect he would be one. And that was the lot—no, wait. That small old lady over there. She looked perfectly innocent; but the minute Harold's eyes noted the way she held her silver mesh purse, he knew. Those hands had had judo and karate training.

Harold paused, out of thoroughness, to take one last survey of the crowd. But there were no more opposition people to be uncovered. If there had been, he would have known who they were, even if his conscious gaze could find no flaw in them. Sixth sense, in his case, so many people in the Organization said. Nothing of the sort! It was the result of long years of study so intense that few minds could have stood up under it.

But it was time for that decoy of his to be here. Harold turned toward the entrance and spotted the slacks-and-jumper outfit. Then he stiffened slightly. The young fool!

His decoy had brought a good-looking redheaded girl along as part of his camouflage. What was the matter with the boy? Had he been asleep during Harold's lectures to the apprentice classes? A decoy's job was to draw the attention of the bodyguards *gradually* upon himself. Any woman could either attract too much attention or else sidetrack it unduly. With this woman—well, it was damned lucky that Harold's timetable had not called for elaborate pre-action proceedings.

For the boy's own good, Harold should censure him in his report. But on the other hand, he thought, softening, why make an official matter of it? Teach the lad a lesson instead—Harold smiled slightly to himself—by taking that good-looking redhead away from him afterward. Harold seldom went out of his way now for female companionship, but it was an accepted fact that no woman could resist a successful professional in his line of work. And it would drive home to the boy that lessons were to be learned. Possibly save his life as well, someday.

It was time to begin work.

Harold left the little balcony and went down into the crowd. The cocktails, he noticed, had been flowing freely and the people were already beginning to clump in little gossipy or argumentative groups. He wandered around awhile and then joined one about halfway between the balcony and the dais where Klannert still sat.

"—Nobel Prize," a short, belligerent, broad-shouldered, middle-aged man was saying. He had a bushy, black, ill-trimmed spade beard which he was thrusting at all his hearers. "Deserved every cent of it! What? Man *is* more than merely a sustaining mechanism! No one like Klannert!"

"Come now," said Harold, smoothly intruding. "Mechanism, after all, is an accepted sociological theory. All of us like to see it questioned, for form's sake, if nothing else. But to throw it out completely—"

"Who're you?" said the bearded man.

"Spence. *Fabliau Weekly.*"

"I know your rag!" said the bearded man. "Didn't think you'd have the nerve to stick your nose in here!"

Smiling—for the *Fabliau* was wholly imaginary—Harold bent his head politely.

"I think my lead article in the issue before last answers your arguments," he said.

"Lies, lies, lies—" sputtered the bearded man. But

Harold was already on his way to another group one step nearer to Klannert.

He paused with this group—they were also singing Klannert's praises, but Harold refused to let himself be drawn into conversation this time. He had already made the point—for anyone who happened to be taking an unduly suspicious interest in him—that he was not trying to make himself unobtrusive by hiding his own point of view. In fact, he had avoided drawing unusual attention to himself by drawing a small amount of the usual sort of attention to himself. At the second group he listened awhile, smiled noncommittally and moved on.

That feeling, almost of sadness, slipped over him again as he continued to circle about the room.

It was all so simple, if you knew what you were doing. Experience taught you what the opposition would expect. You gave them something else. It was as easy as that. So simple it was almost a little pitiful.

Look at Klannert up there. A good man, by the standards of those who considered themselves good men. But he had offended somebody or other. Who, of course, would never be known; the Organization was strict about protecting clients. But somewhere, somebody had signed the necessary credit chit—and here was Harold, about to put a period to the life that had been considered good.

And for what? Not really for the money. A little for the excitement of the business. Possibly a little more because this would make a new world's record. But really because that was the way the world wagged these days—for himself, for Klannert, for everybody.

We are all bound by the wheel of life, thought Harold, with a touch of soft melancholy. All to the same wheel.

After this, he *would* take a vacation, get away for a long rest to some place where he could be a common man once more among men. It was time, and overtime, for a change.

He stopped. He had worked his way clear across the room on a slant. He stood now by some egg-yellow wall draperies, not fifteen feet from where Klannert sat. Elsewhere about the room, the people were all huddled in small, busily talking groups. There was space to run between the groups. Now. Once excitement had struck, they would mill around, getting in each other's way and in the way of pursuit. But by that time, he should be in the foyer, if not out into the safety of the public street.

He looked for his decoy. There the boy was, still with the girl, standing out among the less attractive mortals grouped around Klannert, very satisfactorily. The hostess, Harold noted with satisfaction, was standing with apparent casualness quite close to them.

Harold smiled entirely to himself, internally, with that same touch of melancholy. He glanced around without seeming to. His glass of iced tea was almost finished. He drained the last few drops from it; and as he did, it slipped from his fingers.

It dropped with a soft thump to the thick carpet, rolling half out of sight under the draperies. Exclaiming in annoyance, he bent over as if to pick it up.

Instead, without any undue attempt at concealment, his hand went to the toe of his left boot. Toe and hand lifted together, the top part of the boot and bootsole peeled away from the bottom half, and the plastic gun slipped out into his fingers. He straightened up—

—and something tremendously heavy crashed down on him from behind. He was aware of himself suddenly, on his knees and going down further, with the full weight of another adult on his back. His head was foggy. He could still see and hear, but everything had a dreamlike quality about it. He felt the thick, deep carpet pressing up against the palms of his hands as he flung them out to break his fall. He had a sudden kaleidoscopic glimpse of nearby faces turning to stare in his direction. And then, thin and clear, above the sound of voices still talking, he heard a woman scream.

The weight on his back rolled suddenly off. Turning his head, Harold saw that his assailant had been the belligerent, spade-bearded man who had been holding forth to the first group of talkers. The man was now scrambling to his feet and launching himself in the direction of the room's entrance. For a second the crowd opened out a little, and Harold had a sudden glimpse of his decoy, barewristed, running for the entrance, while the girl with him stopped and half turned, lifting a gun with cool expertness and sending several shots into the spade-bearded man.

Scrambling to his own feet as the spade-bearded man went down, Harold caught sight of Klannert stumbling down from the dais. His hands were up at his chest; and sticking out from between two fingers was a thin strip of metal, a strip of steel about the width of a wristwatch band. As Harold watched, Klannert's knees gave way and he sank down below the bodies of the people who were rushing toward him.

Harold grabbed at his fallen gun—but in that second, hard hands seized him and hustled him through the crowd. Twisting his head back over his shoulder, he saw he was in the grasp of one of the detective-bodyguards and an unidentified stranger. They impelled him swiftly into the lobby.

"They'll shoot me now—" thought Harold, his heart yammering at his throat. Then, like the thudding of some huge, sickening velvet hammer, despair came to shatter his panic. What did it matter? Caught on the job—a failure—execution left to a decoy. Or had he been double-crossed?

He became aware that those holding him had stopped, and the detective had stepped across the room, leaving Harold pinned by the stranger in an efficient judo hold. Harold could not turn his head to see, or make out the words of the conversation. Suddenly they were interrupted by an ugly laugh from the detective. Heavy footsteps returned behind him.

He was grabbed and rushed forward to the open entrance—hurled roughly out into the street.

Harold staggered, windmilling for balance on the slideway outside. Laughter echoed behind him. He whirled, wild with rage. The gun was still clutched in his hand. They had forgotten it. He jerked it up before him—

—and, abruptly, the mists of preconditioning vanished from his brain. They left him with the suddenness of support jerked away. He stared at the entrance to Mother Turner's Tea Rooms, and then at the gun down in his hand. He began to weep.

Quite a crowd had accumulated about him. A city policeman came pushing through it, to stand before Harold, red-faced and sweating.

"All right, all right! Move on!" he shouted. The crowd started to drift away. He turned on Harold. "What're you doing with that in your hand? Don't you know it's illegal? Where's your license?"

Harold shook his head, unable to speak. The policeman snatched the gun from him and turned it over in two freckled hands. His expression faded from anger to exasperation. He shoved the gun back into Harold's hands and turned away.

"Get off the street," he said to Harold, and then, to those of the crowd that still lingered, "All right, all right—move along! The gun's a fake. He's only a decoy, just snapped out of conditioning. Nothing more to see. Move along now!" He shoved Harold impersonally. "You too."

Harold moved off, weeping, clutching the imitation gun in his hand, the salt tears streaming down his face.

GIFTS

The paper boy, cutting across soft spring grass of the front lawn in the bright sunshine of a late May afternoon, was so full of bubbling expectations that he did not see Jim and almost threw the newspaper into Jim's face.

"Oh, here, Mr. Brewer," he said, checking and handing it up the height of the three concrete steps. He squinted against the sun up at the chunky, adult body in blue wash slacks and T-shirt and the square-boned face under short red hair. "We're having a P.T.A. carnival at school, tonight. You coming?"

"I guess not tonight, Tommy," said Jim.

"They're going to have a shooting gallery," said Tommy, and hurried on to the neighbors.

Jim, turning, went back through the screen door into the living room.

"Something?" called Nancy, from the kitchen. He went on in to her, still carrying the paper. She was standing by the sink, peeling potatoes for the casserole of a Friday dinner, the transparent, tight-tied apron making her look slimmer and blonder and younger—like a new bride just beginning to play housewife.

"What?" Jim asked.

"I heard you talking." She looked aside and up at him.

"Just the paper boy," he said. "Wanted to know if we're going to a P.T.A. party at the school, tonight."

She laughed cheerfully.

"Tell him to wait until Joey's old enough for school. Then we'll go to all the P.T.A. parties."

"If we can afford it." Jim batted the paper idly against the refrigerator. "It's a fund-raising deal, of course. You have to spend—nickles and dimes, but it adds up."

She watched him.

"Worrying, hon?" she asked. He shook his head; then grinned at her.

"Just thinking. A week of filling prescriptions and selling home permanent-wave kits doesn't add up to much. A two-year-old house like this—a three-year-old car—and what's left over? A lot of running just to stand still."

"You'll have your own drug store, some day."

"Some day is right."

She finished off the potato in her hands without taking her eyes off him.

"You're hungry," she said. "Go sit down. Dinner'll be ready soon."

"All right." He went back into the living room, opening the paper as he went. He was just sitting down in the green armchair across from the television when the doorbell chimed.

"I'll get it," he called to the kitchen. Nancy did not answer. Just as he had called, Jim had heard the back door slam, and the noise of their son, Joey, and Pancho, the family cocker, was filling the kitchen air.

Jim approached the front door and saw through the screen the dark faces of two slim, middle-aged men, tall in business suits. The Community Fund, thought Jim, remembering suddenly that this was the week of their drive for a new hospital.

"May we come in?" asked the taller of the two.

"Sure, come on in." Jim opened the screen for them and led the way to the living room. He was turning over in his head the possible amounts one would have to subscribe. "Sit down." The two men sat side by side on the sofa. "What can I do for you?"

"My name is Long," said the taller one. "And this is White."

"Pleased to meet you." Jim half-rose from his own chair to shake hands with both of them. They looked enough alike, he thought, to be brothers.

"Mr. Brewer," said Long, "you have a dog in the house."

"Why, yes," answered Jim. He looked at them, suddenly frowning, and then a slight scraping noise, as of claws on a polished floor caught his eye and he turned his head to see Pancho standing in the entrance to the kitchen, head and tail up, staring at the strangers. The cocker spaniel was perfectly still and rigid, leaning forward, nose extended, almost in point. Then, slowly, with the delicate care with which he approached birds in cover, the dog began to advance. Step by slow step he came up before the two men, who had not moved, but sat watching with patient eyes. Before them he halted. Then, equally slowly, he began to back away from them, step by step, until he came up hard against Jim's legs, pressing sideways against them with hip and flank, his head still turned to the two on the couch. Through the thin material of his slacks, Jim felt Pancho's whole body trembling.

"Easy, boy," said Jim, automatically, putting his hand on the furry head. "Easy." He stared at the two; and then suddenly a coldness ran down the narrow line of his spine and he felt the fine hairs on his own neck begin to rise as his body tensed in the chair. He was watching the two faces, so much alike, and he saw them now as motionless and impersonal as masks.

"Yes," said the one called Long. "You see that we aren't human."

Jim said nothing. But he could hear the sound of Nancy's and Joey's voices in the kitchen and he was slowly, as slowly as Pancho had moved, shifting the weight of his body forward in the chair, so that it would be over the bone and muscle springs of his knees.

"Please," said the one introduced as White. "There's nothing for you to be afraid of. We won't harm you. And you can't harm us. We only want to talk to you."

Jim was poised now. He was thinking that he could leap forward and yell at the same time. But there was the danger that Nancy and Joey would only be bewildered by his shout and come instead into the living room to see what was the matter.

"What about?" said Jim.

"You've been chosen," said Long, "at random. Not entirely at random, but mainly so, to answer a question for us. That's all there is to it." He looked into Jim's eyes; and Jim had the impression that he smiled suddenly and warmly, although Long's lips did not move, or any part of his face. "It's a question that concerns your interests, only, not ours. Only you ought to get over being afraid of us. Here—"

He extended his hand toward Pancho. He did not snap his fingers or beckon in any way, but merely held out his fingers, waiting. And after a slow, still moment, the dog began to move, step by step away from the comfort of Jim's legs and toward the stranger. He approached the hand as he might approach a new dog in the neighborhood, stiffly and with caution. For a long second, with neck outstretched, he sniffed at the fingers—and then, with a change as dramatically sudden as the snapping of a violin string, his tail wagged and he shoved his head forward onto the hand of Long.

Long brought forward his other hand and scratched Pancho between the ears. He looked up at Jim.

"You see?" he said.

"That's a dog," said Jim; but he had relaxed, none the less. Not completely, but relaxed. "Well, what is it?"

"Did you ever think much about ethics, Mr. Brewer?" said Long, still petting Pancho.

"Ethics?" Jim looked from one to the other of them.

"Perhaps you might call it morality," said White. "The duty of morality. The duty to your neighbor."

"We get a lot of that here," said Jim, thinking of the P.T.A. and the Community Fund and all the many other drives and collections.

"You have a lot," said White. "But did you ever think much about it?"

"You don't think about things like that," said Jim, still watching them. "You just do them."

"But," said White, "there are two sides to that coin. The coin called charity."

"What do you mean?" said Jim. He looked from White to Long, who was still holding Pancho's head in one slim palm, and stroking between Pancho's ears now, with the other. The dog's eyes were closed in an ecstasy of pleasure.

"We're talking," said Long, suddenly, "about the ethics of Charity. If your dog here were lost far from your home, and trying to find his way back—if he were obviously hungry, you'd think someone else was a good person, if he or she fed him?"

"Certainly," said Jim.

"And what if the dog were interested only in getting back to you. Would it still be a kindness to tie him up until he did eat? And perhaps force him to stay, in an effort to feed him up again?"

"That's what we'd call a mistaken kindness," said Jim. "Look, what's the point of all this?"

"The point is the ethics of Charity," said Long, "and that we feel the same way about them you do. Charity isn't a kindness when the one receiving it doesn't really want it. It's an instinct among civilized people to give help—but the instinct can be mistaken."

"I still don't get what you're driving at," said Jim.

Long let go of Pancho, who shoved a furry head forward onto his knee. He reached into his right-hand suitcoat pocket and took out something small enough to be hidden in his hand.

"Mr. Brewer," he said, "when you were very young, did you ever dream of having something—something magical that could grant all your wishes?"

Jim frowned at him.

"Doesn't everybody?"

"Everybody does," said Long. He turned his hand over and opened it out. Lying in his palm was what looked like a child's marble, a glassy small globe of swirled color, green, and rust, and white. He half-stood and passed it into Jim's automatically receiving hand. "There you are."

"There I am, what?" demanded Jim, staring at it.

"There you have your wish-granter," said Long.

Jim looked back up into the dark face of the slim man and smiled a little.

"No," said Long. "It's quite true. Close your hand on it and wish."

Jim looked back at the marble. The others waited. Long had gone back to petting Pancho.

"No, I don't think so," said Jim, handing the marble back. Long accepted it, put it back in his pocket. They both stood up, and went toward the door.

"Wait," said Jim, getting up himself. "You're going?"

"We took it you had answered us," said White.

"No, wait—" said Jim. "Come on back. Let me see that again."

The two of them returned to the couch and sat down. Long passed over the marble. Jim took it, sitting back down himself, and turned it over curiously in his fingers.

"Anything?" he said.

Once more Jim had the impression of a smile from the unmoving countenance of Long.

"Almost anything," he said. "The almost doesn't have to concern you."

Slowly, Jim closed his hand over the marble. He squeezed his eyes shut and thought. He opened them again.

He was standing in the drugstore where he worked. A middle-aged woman customer was just walking out past him, filling his nostrils with an invisible cloud of her cologne. Behind the drugs and toiletries counter Dave Hogart, the owner, was looking up at him, his face wrinkled in surprise.

"Jim. I didn't see you come in. What're you doing back down here?" he said.

"Uh . . . aspirin," said Jim. "Fifty of the kid aspirin, Dave. Joey's got a slight cold."

Dave turned and reached to an upper shelf, turned back and handed Jim the bottle. He rang it up on the charge key of the cash register, the fingers of his left hand resting swollen and hunched on the bare counter beside the register.

"How's the arthritis?" Jim found himself asking, suddenly.

Dave jerked his head up with a grin.

"Not bad enough to make me want to retire yet," he said. "Want to buy the store?"

"Wish I could," said Jim.

"I guess we're going to be ready to make that deal about the same time," said Dave. "Hope Joey's all right in the morning—" Another customer was coming into the store. "See you, Jim." He moved off.

Both their backs were turned. Jim closed his hand on the marble and wished again.

He was back in his own living room. He sat down again in his chair and noticed the small transparent bottle of orange-colored tablets was still in his hand. He set it carefully down on the coffee table by his chairside and looked up. Long and White were still sitting, watching him.

"I don't understand," said Jim. "I just don't understand."

Long pointed to the hand of Jim's that still held the marble.

"That," he said, "isn't important. We only wanted something to show you, something to convince you with. The whole story's much bigger."

Jim glanced suddenly toward the kitchen entrance and the voices of Joey and Nancy coming through it.

"Don't worry," said White. "They won't think to come in until we're through here."

"You see," said Long, "we don't come from anywhere near the family of worlds that go around your sun. But we couldn't help discovering you people, when you started doing things. We've been watching you for some years now. You people are like we were—a long time back on our own world. You have the same troubles, the same sorrows, much the same hopes. You remind us very much of us, in the beginning."

"You're that much like us?" said Jim, dazedly.

"Well, not so much as you might think just by looking at us—and again, much more so than you would realize in ways you've yet to learn about," said Long. "The point is, we look at you—with your conflicts, your diseases, your pains and famines—all your lacks. And many of them are things we can do something about. We could heal your sick, we can give you longer and more useful lives. We can help you to go out among the stars and find more living room. We could open up great new fields of opportunity for you."

"Well," said Jim, looking from one to the other, "why tell me about this? Why don't you?"

"Because we're not sure it would be right," said White. "We're not sure you want our help."

"For those things?" said Jim. "Are you crazy? Of course we do."

"Are you sure?" said Long.

They sat watching him; and Jim stared back at them. The moment stretched out long between them.

"Of course I'm sure," said Jim at last.

"I hope so," said White. "Because the decision is up to you."

Jim jerked his gaze suddenly over to look at White.

"Us?" he said.

"No," answered White, knitting his long fingers together in his lap. "Just you, you alone."

"Me?" cried Jim, and then checked his voice to hold it down below a level that would carry into the kitchen. He stared at them. "Just me? Why? Why *me?*"

"We picked you at random and on purpose," said White. "We think you are most likely to give us the truest answer."

"But you don't want me!" said Jim, turning to Long. "I'm nobody to make a decision for the whole world! Look, there's the President. Or the United Nations—"

"You see," said Long, patiently, "the question isn't a logical one. It isn't an intellectual one, to be investigated by charts and speeches and discussions. It's an emotional question, dealing with deep and basic instincts. It isn't *what* help we can give you, it's—do you *want* help? Any help? Help of any kind?"

He stopped speaking and waited. Jim did not say anything.

"Are you still so sure?" asked White, gently.

Jim sagged slowly back in his chair. He turned his head slowly and looked at the aspirin bottle. Beyond it, the window was just beginning to tint with the first translucency of twilight. Slowly, he shook his head.

"I don't know," he said, in a low voice. "I don't know."

"You can think it over," said White. "Take tonight and think about it. We can come back for your answer, tomorrow."

"I'm not the man," said Jim, weakly. "I'm not the man to ask—something like that."

"You are the man," said Long, as they got up, "because we picked you to be the man."

Jim rose also. The faces of all three of them were very close together. He felt their alienness now, more strongly than at any earlier moment since they had come in.

"Let me help you with a little advice," said Long. "Forget that you're deciding for a world. Don't try to think of how all the rest will feel. Decide only for yourself. I promise you, what you sincerely feel, the great and lasting part of your people, those who work and marry and have children and endure, will feel the same."

They turned away from him and went through the screen door into the strong glare of the sunset. Jim heard the screen door slam quietly behind them.

"Dinner's ready!" called Nancy, from the kitchen.

Incredibly, he actually forgot about it during the general chatter and excitement of dinner. It was only later, after Joey had been put to bed and he and Nancy were sitting in the living room watching television, that it all came back to him. He waited until the western they happened to be watching came to its noisy climax and then got up from his chair.

"I've got some letters to write," he told Nancy.

He went into the extra bedroom, that they called the office, and shut the door. He sat down in the chair before the card table that did service as a desk and turned on the lamp. Its light shone warmly at the bookcases and second-hand overstuffed chair that had been their first furniture purchase for the apartment he and Nancy had moved into after their honeymoon. He got out his fountain pen, the notepaper and envelopes—and then took the marble once more from his pocket and laid it on the white sheet of paper before him. It glowed back up at him, reflecting the lamplight.

"I've got to think this thing out," he told himself.

But no thoughts came. Once he closed his hand around the marble hesitantly, but then let go of it again without using it. He tried to imagine what the world would be like if he should tell Long and White that his answer was yes. No hospitals, different kinds of cars, he supposed—he was not very good at this kind of imagining. If everybody had everything they needed, what about money—and jobs.

He checked suddenly. Funny it had not occurred to him before. Of course, his own job would be one of the first to go. Well people wouldn't need medicine. And as for all the rest of the stuff a drugstore sold, beauty aids and the rest, there would probably be new versions that would last for a lifetime. Magazines would probably be left, candy, ice cream, toys . . . What would happen to Nancy and Joey if he had no job? What would eventually happen to him?

But he was forgetting. Under the new set-up they wouldn't want for things they needed. No need to worry there. But what would he do? He couldn't just sit around for the rest of his life. Or could he? There were things he'd always wanted to do, like deep-sea fishing, and places he'd always wanted to go. But would that be enough?

On second thought, there would probably be thousands of new jobs opening up. Long and White obviously belonged to a people who had work to do. Perhaps there would be something he would like better than pharmacy, something that would give him a feeling of really getting somewhere, making progress . . .

After some while, he glanced at his watch. It was almost eleven; he had been sitting here close to two hours. And nothing was decided. He stood up, feeling the weight and weariness of his own body. His eyes smarted from staring at the light reflected from the blank white paper before him. He put everything away, turned out the lamp and went to his and Nancy's bedroom.

Nancy was already in bed and reading the newspaper. She looked up as he came in.

"What time do you go in the morning?" she asked.

"Not until noon," he said. "Dave's opening up tomorrow." He took off his shirt and went about the business of getting ready for sleep. Nancy put the paper away on the shelf underneath the night table beside their double bed. She yawned and slid down under the covers.

"I've got to take Joey shopping tomorrow," she said. "He's just bursting out of his socks."

"Yes," he said. He turned out the light and got into bed. The peaceful darkness washed in around him. He lay there, slowly breathing. There was a movement under the covers and he felt Nancy's hand touch gently upon his arm.

"What's wrong?" she asked softly.

He sighed, deeply and gustily; and, turning toward her, he told her the whole story about White and Long, and all that they had said and done.

Nancy always had been a good listener. She listened now, without interrupting him with questions, her face a pale blur in the little light filtering in around the edges of the window shades. Toward the end of it they were both sitting up in bed; and Jim got up to turn on the light and retrieve the marble from his pants' pocket. He brought it back to her and got into bed again.

She took it from his hand and turned it over in her own fingers. The light from their bedstand lamp caught and glinted from its surface, making the three colors seem to flow as she turned it, as if they were being stirred about within a transparent shell. She looked at Jim.

"Could I?" she said. "Do you suppose—"

"Go ahead," said Jim.

She closed her fingers about the marble and closed her eyes. A fur stole appeared on the blanket before them. Nancy opened her eyes again.

"Oh!" she said, on a little intake of breath. She reached and touched the fur with a feather touch, stroking it almost imperceptibly with the ends of her fingers. She got up suddenly, climbing over Jim, who was on the outside of the bed, carrying the stole, and went to the mirror of her dressing table. She put the stole around her neck and held it there with both hands, gazing into the mirror. Watching her, standing there in her nightgown with the fur around her, Jim felt a sudden ridiculous tightening in his throat.

"Nancy," he said.

She turned about and came back to the bed, climbing in again and reaching for the marble. As her hand closed about it, the fur vanished.

"Nancy!" said Jim. "You didn't have to do that. You can keep it."

"If you decide, I'll get it back," she said. Without warning she kissed him on the cheek. "Thank you, darling."

"I didn't do anything," said Jim.

"Thank you for saying I could keep it."

He squeezed her hand in his; but he still frowned at the marble lying before them on the blanket.

"What'll I do? What'll I do?" he murmured.

He felt the light touch of her hand on his shoulder.

"Why don't you sleep on it," she said. "You'll think better in the morning."

"All right," he sighed. "I'll try. Only I don't think I can."

But he did sleep. He had not known how tired he was and unconsciousness had flooded in on him almost in the moment in which he closed his eyes. Only with sleep came the dreams, a multitude of them—vast confused fantasies of enormous ships that sailed above cities under hothouse domes. And houses unroofed to the ever-present air, beneath the domes. And people at work with shining machines whose purpose he could not comprehend.

Then, later on, the dreams changed back to the ordinary world; and there came the only one that he was ever to remember clearly afterward. In it he stood on the customer's side of a counter in the drugstore where he worked; and facing him on the counter's other side was Joey, in a white pharmacist's jacket. Joey, grown to a man now. A young man, but with the hair already receding on his forehead and tired lines of premature age on his face; and the drugstore about him was dingier and more shabby than Jim remembered. Joey handed him a bottle filled with small, pink, children's aspirin.

"Take this to my boy," Joey was saying. "It's not much, but it's the best we have."

Jim took it from him; and as Jim did so, he noticed that Joey's fingers had swollen, arthritic joints as Dave's hand had. Joey saw his eyes fall on them, and took the hand away, hiding it under the counter.

"I'm sorry, Joey!" cried Jim, suddenly.

"It's not your fault," said Joey. But he had turned his head away; and would not look at his father.

Jim woke, sweating.

He lay flat on his back on his side of the bed. Beside him, Nancy slept sweetly, breathing silently, with her face pressed against her pillow. Pale lines of beginning dawnlight were marking the windows around the edges of the pulled window shades.

Jim breathed deeply; and slowly, quietly, got up out of the bed. He dressed while Nancy continued to sleep, looking over at the alarm clock on the night table. Its white hands stood at the black numerals that told him it was five-thirty, an hour and a half before the alarm was due to go off. Dressed at last in slacks and shirt, he went out through the silent living room to the front door, opened it, and went down the steps onto the front walk.

He stopped, breathing in the fresh morning air and looking at the sky. It was as cloudless as clear water and the new rays of the morning sun made it scintillate as if it was possessed of a light of its own. The lawns up and down the block on either side of him and across the street glittered greener than ever with the night's dew. The other houses all seemed sleeping; but as he watched Chuck Elison came out of his kitchen door five doors down on the street's other side and climbed into his panel truck with "Elison Plumbing" painted on its side. Chuck's wife, Jean, came out the kitchen door to stand in her apron and wave at him as he backed down his driveway, turned the truck up the street, and drove off. She went back into their house.

Jim turned slowly from his gazing at the street, to look at his own house. The yellow trim around the screens and windows was beginning to flake a little. He should repaint before the heat of the summer months really got under way. And the grass would need cutting, soon—by Sunday, anyway.

Under the picture window of the living room the early tulips were in bloom, the yellow tips of their scarlet petals forming neat, scallop-edged cups. He reached out a forefinger, bemused, to touch one. He could not remember, just now, seeing any flowers in his dreams of the domes and ships. Undoubtedly they had been there, but— never had he felt before how beautiful these small plants were . . .

A slight sound of shoes on the sidewalk behind him made him straighten and turn. Long stood there alone, the morning sun lighting up his strange, dark face. For a moment they merely looked at each other saying nothing. Then Long spoke.

"Do you want more time?" he asked.

Jim sighed. Once more he looked around the street on both sides of him.

"No," he said. Slowly he put his hand into the right-hand pocket of his slacks. The marble was there. He took it out and handed it over to Long.

Long took it and put it back in his own pocket.

"You're sure?" he asked, looking closely at Jim.

"I think," said Jim, and sighed again, "we ought to get it for ourselves."

Long nodded, thoughtfully. He was turning to go when Jim stopped him.

"Was that the right answer?" Jim asked.

Long hesitated. For a second there seemed to be something strange and sad, but at the same time warm and friendly behind his eyes; but it was gone too quickly for Jim to pin it down.

"That's not for me to say," he said. And then, astonishingly, he did smile—for the first and only time; and the smile lit up his face like sunset after a storm has blown away. "But ask your grandson."

And, suddenly, as shadow, he was gone.

ZEEPSDAY

TRANSCRIPT:

TRIAL 47 Court Session 19238472635402847565635 of the Galactic Court of People's Manners, within the Federation of Planet-Originated Races.

RECORDER:

This trial record by Aki, brood-brother of Po, Domsker from Ju, graduate court reporter. Recorded in accordance with reportorial precept—"Let it be a full record; let no least spuggl twung unnoticed and unremarked."

RECORD BEGINS:

Two ulbls (four hours, twenty minutes, Human time; 38 Gisnk, Sloonian time) after sunrise on Beldor, Galactic Court World. A blithe day with the courtroom well filled with polite audience, of many varieties of goodly life forms. To the left of the Judge's bench, the compound of the defendant, one Garth Paulson, a Human from Earth, surrounded by friends and well-wishers. To the right, the compound of the plaintiff, Drang Usussis, a Nesbler from Sloon, similarly surrounded by friends and well-wishers. Approach of his honor, the presiding judge, Umka, a Bolver from Bol, is noted.

COURT BAILIFF: His honor, Judge Umka, now rolling upon his bench. All those fearing offense to personal and delicate sensibilities are warned to retire.

JUDGE: Thank you, Bailiff. You may scurry off now. Where is my scanner—ah, yes, I see here by the legal challenge submitted to me that the plaintiff charges the defendant with having committed a personal and verbal impoliteness upon the plaintiff, specifically the defendant's audible reference to the plaintiff upon one occasion as a being possessing four tentacles. Ah—um—do these three dozen old eyes deceive me? It seems to the bench from here that the plaintiff in question does indeed seem to be possessed of f—

MYSELF (*interrupting in accordance with legalized tradition and duty of court reporters on such occasions*): Psst, your honor—(*the rest of my words off the record*).

JUDGE: Oh—ah. Thank you, clerk. The bench extends its courtesies to the *three*-tentacled Mr. Usussis and the purchasing press agent—is that correct?—Mr. Paulson.

DEFENDANT: Press agent is correct, your honor. I am the city purchasing press agent for the city hall of the City of Los Angeles in the Metropolis of Los Angeles, Earth.

JUDGE: And Mr. Usussis. Your occupation?

MR. USUSSIS: Your honor, I am a registered dilettante, of the planet of Sloon, long may its purple oceans reek.

JUDGE (*pounding for order*): Order! Order! The court will not permit patriotic outbursts of this sort. The plaintiff is cautioned that the sensibilities of those here present may not be offended. Mr. Usussis, this is a challenge of a minor nature you have brought before this court, but it seems to the bench that your compound is well-peopled by legal talent of the highest order. And is not that the great criminal legalist, Spod Draxel of Nv, I see beside you?

MR. USUSSIS: It is indeed, your honor. However, he and these other gentlebeings are merely present as friends and well-wishers of the plaintiff in no official capacity. I shall attempt to prosecute my case with my own feeble talents.

JUDGE (*turning to defendant*): And you, Mr. Paulson, seem equally well supplied. Is not that Earth's foremost Corporation Sharpie I see in your compound?

DEFENDANT: It is indeed Sol Blitnik, your honor. However, as is the case with the honorable plaintiff, he and these others are merely chance acquaintances who have prevailed on me for a seat in my compound, the better to amuse themselves with witnessing this trial. I, also, will defend myself to the best of my poor ability.

JUDGE: Very well. The bench cautions both plaintiff and defendant against extraneous issues. We will proceed. Will the plaintiff take the stand and submit to questioning?

(*The plaintiff slithers across the floor and mounts the stand.*)

JUDGE: Will the defendant open the action of his response to the challenge of the plaintiff?

(*The defendant consults with the chance acquaintances in his compound.*)

DEFENDANT: We—that is, I think, your honor, that it would save time and trouble if the plaintiff were to commence by stating his cause of offense briefly in his own words, for the court's benefit.

JUDGE: It is so ordered. Go ahead, Mr. Usussis.

PLAINTIFF: The occasion was actually a simple one,

your honor. I was transacting a minor piece of business with the defendant at the time. We had just signed a contract for the purchase of certain Sloonian commodities recently become in high demand in the city of Los Angeles, when the defendant suddenly began to scratch himself vigorously. When I inquired politely what was the matter, he replied, "Now I get it. I should have known better than to trust a slippery customer like you, you—" and here, your honor, he made use of that obscene, disgusting, and unmentionable accusation against myself which is the reason for my present action against him in this court.

JUDGE: Allow me to interrupt for a moment. The bench would like to know whether the plaintiff is seeking punitive action in this case, or merely an injunction restraining the defendant from further verbal assault?

PLAINTIFF: Your honor, I want an injunction backed up by a threat of punitive action to the full rigor of the law—a two-year sentence, I believe.

JUDGE (*severely*): The plaintiff is warned against attempting to instruct the bench. A two-year sentence is, indeed, possible for a breach of politeness between races. However, the sentencing and conditions of sentence are up to the court.

PLAINTIFF (*humbly*): I apologize, your honor.

JUDGE: Your apology is accepted. (*turning to defendant*): It seems that the plaintiff has adequately stated the situation at the time of the alleged insult. What does the defendant wish—by the way, will the defendant explain to the bench why his chance acquaintance Sol Blitnik has adopted a position with his lips almost touching the defendant's ear?

DEFENDANT: I humbly beg the court to excuse my

infirmities. The ear in question has a slight itch which is eased by Mr. Blitnik's murmuring into it from time to time.

JUDGE: That's all right, Mr. Paulson. I was merely curious. Proceed.

DEFENDANT: Is the plaintiff aware that the city of Los Angeles is identical with the Metropolis of Los Angeles?

PLAINTIFF: I am, naturally.

DEFENDANT: And that the cities of Cairo, Hong Kong and Capetown are suburbs of the same Metropolis of Los Angeles?

PLAINTIFF: Well—I—uh—

WELL-WISHER (*from the plaintiff's compound*): Objection!

JUDGE: Order in the court! Spectators will not interrupt court proceedings.

PLAINTIFF: Your honor, I object.

JUDGE: On what grounds?

PLAINTIFF: Er—the question is immaterial and irrelevant.

JUDGE: How about that, Mr. Paulson?

DEFENDANT: Your honor, I am trying to show that the plaintiff was attempting to mislead the court when he referred to the business between us as minor and that that business has a direct bearing on the conversation which culminated in the offense alleged.

JUDGE: Objection overruled. Continue, Mr. Paulson—by the way how does your ear feel now? I notice Mr. Blitnik working on it again.

DEFENDANT: Much better, thanks, your honor. Will your honor direct the witness to answer that last question?

JUDGE: Answer the question.

PLAINTIFF: Well, yes, I do.

DEFENDANT: In short, what you have referred to as minor business was actually concerned with millions of units of manufactured items for the planet Earth as a whole. Right?

PLAINTIFF: Well, yes.

DEFENDANT: Your honor, I would now like to call my secretary, Marge Jolman, to the stand.

JUDGE: Very well—you are dismissed, Mr. Usussis. Subject to later recall, if necessary, of course.

(*The plaintiff slithers off the stand and back to his compound. From the compound of the defendant approaches a Human female—young, well-developed and red-haired. Slightly nervous, the witness performs a brief version of the Human hand-clasping ceremony with the defendant as he helps her up on the stand.*)

PLAINTIFF (*from his own compound*): Your honor, objection!

JUDGE: On what grounds, Mr. Usussis?

PLAINTIFF: This witness is known to be contemplating mating ceremonies with the defendant. I ask your honor to consider the possibility that this may cause her to be prejudiced.

JUDGE: For, or against him, you mean?

PLAINTIFF: For, your honor. Human matings are considered to be on grounds of affection.

JUDGE: Prejudice on grounds of affection or animosity are a practical impossibility for this court to take into account. Otherwise you yourself would have to be disqualified from pleading on the grounds of obvious prejudice, Mr. Usussis. Is there any direct connection between the contemplated mating ceremonies and your charge of impoliteness?

PLAINTIFF: No *direct* connection, your honor, but—

JUDGE: Overruled. Proceed, Mr. Paulson.

DEFENDANT: Marge, do you remember being at work in my outer office the day Mr. Usussis first came to see me?

WITNESS: Oh, yes.

DEFENDANT: Will you tell the court what he said to you on that occasion.

WITNESS: Well, I don't remember his exact words—

DEFENDANT: With your honor's permission, I will ask the witness to tell us the substance of what the plaintiff said to her at that time.

JUDGE: Go ahead. Plaintiff can always object after he hears how she puts it.

DEFENDANT: Go ahead, Marge.

WITNESS: Well, he had an appointment to see Garth— I mean Mr. Paulson, but he hadn't said what about. So I asked him. He said it was about Zeepsday.

JUDGE: Zeepsday? I don't—

MYSELF: Your honor, psst—(*the rest of my words off the record*).

JUDGE: Of course. Naturally. Hrmph! Continue.

WITNESS: I asked him what that was; and he said that was what he had come here to explain and could he see Mr. Paulson about it. I called Garth on the intercom and told him, and he said for both of us to come in.

JUDGE: Just a minute. Has plaintiff any objections so far?

PLAINTIFF: Not at this time, your honor.

DEFENDANT: And what took place in my office, Marge? Will you tell the court that?

WITNESS: Well, you wanted me to take notes, you said. So I stayed. Then you asked Mr. Usussis what it was all about. And he said it was a delicate matter and he didn't want to step on the toes of any human taboos he might not know about. But what was the reason no humans made use of Zeepsday?

(*The witness pauses and seems flustered.*)

JUDGE (*encouragingly*): Go ahead, Miss Jolman.

WITNESS: Well, Garth said, "What do you mean, Zeepsday?" and then Mr. Usussis explained that he didn't know the human word for it, but it was the day that came between the days we called Wednesday and Thursday.

JUDGE: Just a minute. I think that this is a point that ought to be clarified before we go any further. I think the witness can step down for a moment. Is there a temporal authority in the courtroom?—No, no, I don't want an expert from either the plaintiff's or the defendant's compound, disinterested as those gentlebeings may be. I want one from the courtroom audience. You sir—there in the back—would you consent?

(*A Vbuldo from O rises in the back of the courtroom and clanks forward to the stand.*)

JUDGE: Will you tell us your name and qualifications, sir?

WITNESS: Gladly. I am Porniarsk Prime Three and have advanced degrees in temporals general.

JUDGE: Will you explain in the simplest possible terms the temporal situation under consideration, here?

WITNESS: With pleasure. The plaintiff, being a Nesbler from Sloon, is native to a Stress Two area of the Galaxy. As a result, he is particular to a curvilinear time with a factor of .84736209, approximately. The temporal quantity being radial to space curvature, it results in a greater positive number of temporal divisions to the same temporal area for one from Nesbler than for one from Earth, where an alinear time with a factor of .76453839476, approximately, is in present effect.

JUDGE: And the practical result of this—?

WITNESS: That the plaintiff has a total of eight days in his week for seven of the defendant's. In short, the days Monday, Tuesday, Wednesday, Zeepsday, Thursday, Friday, Saturday and Sunday.

JUDGE: Thank you. You are dismissed.

(The witness bows, descends from the stand and clanks back to his seat in the audience section of the courtroom.)

JUDGE: Recall the previous witness.

(The Human female Marge Jolman reascends the stand.)

JUDGE: Miss Jolman, you have heard the last witness. Was this, in essence, what Mr. Usussis told you and the defendant?

WITNESS: Yes, your honor. He wanted to know what we humans did during the twenty-four hours between midnight Wednesday and the first minute of Thursday morning.

JUDGE: Do you mean to imply that the plaintiff intimated his belief that Humans also had eight days in their week?

WITNESS: That's what it sounded like, your honor.

JUDGE: Hmm—well, go on with your questioning, Mr. Paulson.

DEFENDANT: Thank you, your honor. Now, Marge, what did I say when Mr. Usussis said that?

WITNESS: You didn't believe it. And Mr. Usussis offered to show you.

DEFENDANT: Thank you. That's all.

JUDGE: Cross-examine, Mr. Usussis?

PLAINTIFF: Not at this time, your honor.

JUDGE: You may step down.

(*Witness returns to seat in defendant's compound.*)

JUDGE: And now, Mr. Paulson?

DEFENDANT: Your honor, I would like to call Gundar Jorgenson, also of Earth, to the stand.

JUDGE: Proceed.

DEFENDANT: Gundar—

(*A middle-aged male Human, large for the species, approaches and mounts the stand.*)

DEFENDANT: Will you tell the court your name and oc-cupation?

WITNESS: Gundar Jorgenson, from Earth. I am a tem-poral physicist.

DEFENDANT: Will you tell the court what your connec-tion is with this case?

WITNESS: I will. One sparkling spring morning last May, the defendant requested me to accompany him on a visit to Zeepsday—

(*Consternation in the court. Cries of* Objection! Objec-tion! *from the plaintiff's compound.*)

JUDGE (*pounding for order*): Order! Order in the court! Another outburst like that and I shall clear the courtroom. Will the defendant approach the bench?

DEFENDANT: Here I am, your honor.

JUDGE: Mr. Paulson, I must admit I had my suspicions earlier that in this trial the action was trending toward matters outside—the jurisdiction of this court. Surely the defendant is aware—and if he is not, I am sure any of his chance acquaintances sharing the compound with him at present can enlighten him—that any case concerning temporal illegalities must be considered by the High Crimes Commission. Both planets involved must be sequestered, their native products embargoed, and a hundred-year decontamination process of both parties put into effect. Does the defendant mean to charge the plaintiff with an actual derangement of the temporal structure around his home world?

DEFENDANT: No such thought entered my mind, your honor. As has already been stated, I am merely an inexperienced private citizen engaged in a small altercation with another citizen over a minor matter. As your honor knows, a conviction for the derangement of temporal structure is practically a legal impossibility; and in fact it is for that reason that the High Crimes Commission has seen fit to make the situation so uncomfortable to both the criminal and his victim that both parties, innocent and guilty, would shrink from becoming involved in such a case. Certainly I would not wish to be responsible for bringing such grief upon my world. Consequently, I would like to clear up any doubt in the court's mind about what actually happened, in a temporal sense. It is my theory that none of the temporal irregularities concerned in this trial actually happened; but that those of us who seemed to be concerned with them were actually only hypnotized into believing they had.

JUDGE: Hypnotized! And does the plaintiff agree to admit that he hypnotized the defendant?

PLAINTIFF (*smirking*):   I do, your honor, with the stipulation that the defendant in this case subconsciously wanted to be hypnotized, so that the action cannot be said to have been taken against the defendant's will.

JUDGE: Does the defendant agree to the stipulation?

DEFENDANT: I do, your honor, provisional to the theoretical nature of my contention.

JUDGE: Does the plaintiff agree to the theoretical nature of the defendant's contention?

PLAINTIFF: In theory I agree to the defendant's theory.

JUDGE (*looking somewhat glazed about the lower two dozen of his eyes, mutters something*).

MYSELF: What was that, your honor?

JUDGE: Nothing—nothing. Continue questioning your witness, Mr. Paulson.

DEFENDANT: Mr. Jorgenson, you were associated with me on our theoretical visit to Zeepsday. Will you tell the court what we did and what we discovered there?

WITNESS: I would be more than glad to. As I said, one balmy May night, we left the common, ordinary Earth behind—

JUDGE: Just a minute, Mr. Paulson. Why do you need a technical expert to testify to the facts of something that theoretically did not happen or exist?

DEFENDANT: I assure your honor, these non-existent facts have a vital bearing on the case.

JUDGE: Well . . . well—continue.

DEFENDANT: Go ahead, Mr. Jorgenson.

WITNESS: We left in a Sloonian spaceship. Earth fell away behind us. At a distance from the world, where the planet seemed to swim like some great clouded crystal ball in emptiness, we waited until 12:00 midnight, Wednesday. Then, at the witching hour, we activated the temporal distorter on the ship—

DEFENDANT: You mean the illusion of a temporal distorter.

WITNESS: Oh, yes. The temp—this illusion, that is—was the largest I had ever seen. My acquaintance with such heretofore had been confined to tiny laboratory models.

JUDGE: Of illusions, or of temporal distorters, Mr. Jorgenson?

WITNESS: Temporal distorters, your honor. Still, I knew the principle on which it worked. Briefly, it dilated an aperture in the normal temporal structure; and through this aperture one may discover any excess time that may be available in the area.

JUDGE: Just a minute. I would like to ask the former technical witness a question. You needn't come up to the stand, Mr. Porniarsk Prime Three; but is this description essentially correct?

VBULDONIAN VOICE (*from the back of the courtroom*): Quite correct, your honor.

JUDGE: Continue, Mr. Jorgenson.

WITNESS: Sure enough, when we landed again on Earth at 00:06 A.M. Zeepsday, we found a deserted planet.

JUDGE: Deserted planet?

WITNESS: Deserted indeed, your honor. The cities, highways and homes of Earth were there as they had always been; but they were untenanted by a living soul. We stared, amazed. Here was the broad expanse of lands—

JUDGE: Excuse me a minute. Is the witness by any chance an amateur poet or writer?

WITNESS (*with a mild rush of circulatory fluid to the face*): As a matter of fact, I am, in a slight way. How did your honor guess? I've actually published a few minor items in *Literary Frontiers*. Not for money, of course. I don't believe in commercializing my art, but—

JUDGE: The bench applauds the witness's altruism; but perhaps, in these sordid legal chambers, it would be better if the witness restrained himself to ordinary prose.

WITNESS: No place is too sordid for the soul of poetry to enter—

JUDGE (*somewhat grimly*): Perhaps not; but until it is admitted as a witness, it will have to preserve the order of this courtroom by remaining silent. Continue, Mr. Paulson.

DEFENDANT: Go ahead, Mr. Jorgenson.

WITNESS: Well—I mean—anyway, there weren't any people there. I made some tests.

JUDGE: Of this illusion.

WITNESS: Yes, your honor. I had wished to expose a few guinea pigs or hamsters as test subjects first. But it turned out to be unnecessary. As far as my tests could distinguish, this was good, perfectly experienceable time, comparable to Earth's own in every respect.

DEFENDANT: As a result of this experience, what was your conclusion on our return at the end of twenty-four hours to normal Earth Thursday?

WITNESS: It was my conclusion that Earth had an extra day available in every week, of which we humans had been failing to take advantage.

DEFENDANT: Thank you, Mr. Jorgenson. That is all.

JUDGE: Cross-examination, Mr. Usussis?

PLAINTIFF: No cross-examination, your honor. I would like to compliment the witness on his fair testimony to this illusion.

JUDGE: I'm sure the witness is gratified. You may step down, Mr. Jorgenson. Any more witnesses, Mr. Paulson?

DEFENDANT: Your honor, at this point I would like to call myself as a witness—that is, I would like to make a statement for the record and the information of the court.

JUDGE: Is there no other way of bringing this information out, Mr. Paulson? Can't you put someone else on the stand who was present and elicit the information by questioning?

DEFENDANT: Unfortunately not, your honor. I was alone at the time in question.

JUDGE: I am against it. This sort of thing simplifies matters enormously and is against all legal tradition. However, if you must, I suppose you must. Go ahead.

DEFENDANT: On first discovering and experiencing Zeepsday for myself, I must admit I was overjoyed. Here was a boon for Earth, indeed. One extra day in the week —one extra day to get all those things done that people were never having the time to get done. One extra day for resting, for visiting, for reestablishing family ties. What could the human race not accomplish now? You all know our human record for rapid technological development—

(*Murmers of shocked protest from the courtroom audience*)

JUDGE (*sternly*): No propaganda, Mr. Paulson. I've already had to warn the plaintiff about that. I don't want to have to speak to either of you again in this regard.

DEFENDANT: Sorry, your honor—I got carried away. As I said, I thought of all the benefits Zeepsday could bring my world. I was enthusiastic. I went to bed that Thursday night happy, having arranged with the plaintiff—who by sheer chance happened to have a friend who is factory comptroller general back on Sloon—to sign a contract the following day for purchase of various useful Sloonian commodities. Such items as nine-day clocks, four hundred and seventeen day calendars, and other items, with last, but not least, the equipment to dilate time sufficiently to make Zeepsday planetwide on Earth. The next morning, however, I awoke with some doubt in my mind. I thought to myself, as I was brushing my teeth—

(*Wild screech from the back of the courtroom. General consternation as a Daffyd from Lyx is carried out, his petals stiff and rigid in a state of hysterical shock.*)

JUDGE (*pounding*):   Order! Order! This sort of occurrence is taking place far too frequently of late. The bailiff clearly announced at the beginning of this sitting that those who feared offense to personal and delicate sensibilities were warned to retire. The gentlebeing from Lyx saw with perfect clarity that the defendant in this case is of a dentate species, and should have foreseen that mention of teeth or chewing might very well enter the discussion. A mature entity should be responsible for his own emotional welfare, and not expect this court to shoulder that burden for him. . . . Continue.

DEFENDANT: As I say, the next morning I found myself, while not exactly at that time suspicious, somewhat more sober in my assessment of the good to come from Zeepsday on Earth. What, I asked myself, about the legal status of this new day? Should it be a holiday or a workday? What would Congress say? How would the labor unions react? What, in particular, would be the position taken by the powerful bloc represented by the votes of school-age children? Would Zeepsday, in short, really prove to be an unmixed blessing?

JUDGE (*graciously*): Your reflective caution does you credit, Mr. Paulson, if—

DEFENDANT (*with equal graciousness*): I thank your honor. Those were practically the words with which the plaintiff sought to reassure me later on that same day when we met for the signing of the contract.

JUDGE (*sternly*): —*if*, I was going to say, Mr. Paulson, before you interrupted me, it can be proved. While I, myself, would be inclined to give you the benefit of the doubt in this respect, this is after all a court of law; and we are concerned only with facts. For proper substantiation you should have a witness to your sensible thoughts.

DEFENDANT: As a matter of fact, I have, your honor. Shortly before the plaintiff arrived with his contract, I expressed these same doubts to my secretary. If you will allow me to put Miss Jolman back on the stand—

PLAINTIFF: Objection! The witness in question is in court and has just heard the defendant claim the attitude under scrutiny. How do we know that she will not confuse these recent statements with those the defendant may have made earlier—

(*Murmurs of protest from the audience. Cries of* Shame! *from a Tyrannosauroid Sapiens, who is ejected by the bailiff for disturbing the court.*)

JUDGE: The plaintiff has already been answered concerning the admissibility of the question of prejudice in a witness. May the bench add that it feels no doubt about the competence of this witness. Overruled. Miss Jolman, will you take the stand, please?

(*The witness ascends the stand.*)

JUDGE: Mr. Paulson—

DEFENDANT: Thank you, your honor. Marge—will you tell the court what I said to you?

WITNESS (*tremulously*): I'll never forget it.

DEFENDANT (*clearing throat noisily*): Just the facts, Marge.

WITNESS: I remember every word. "Marge, honey," you said to me, "I wonder if I'm really doing the right thing? You know you have to be tough to be a purchasing press agent, Marge, when billions of interstellar credits of currency depend on your unofficial decision. And I've always been tough. But now I'm starting to wonder. What sort of a world is it going to be for humans here on Earth —for you and me—us, Marge, if this deal goes through? What kind of a world for future generations, with a Zeepsday in it? All of a sudden, that's important to me—" and then you took me in your arms—

DEFENDANT: Please, Marge, just the facts.

WITNESS: "—because of you, Marge," you said, "because I love you." (Witness is suddenly afflicted by a rush of circulatory fluid to the face similar to that which affected a previous witness.) And I said, "I love you, too—" and then you asked me to marry you and we talked for a while; and after a while I said, about Zeepsday—you ought to do what you thought was right and then things would be sure to turn out for the best.

DEFENDANT (*mopping brow*): Thank you, Marge. That's all.

(*Spontaneous applause as the witness leaves the stand, quelled by the Judge pounding for order and interrupted by cries of* Objection! *from the Plaintiff*)

JUDGE: Yes, Mr. Usussis?

PLAINTIFF: I demand to know whether the defendant is to be allowed to sway the court by these unfair emotional appeals. I demand—

JUDGE: The bench is *not* swayed. (*adds, sternly*): And I warn you against imputing such a weakness to the bench under pain of being held in contempt of this court. Now, do you wish to examine the witness?

PLAINTIFF: I have no interest in this witness whatsoever.

JUDGE: Yes—or no?

PLAINTIFF (*more subdued*): No, your honor.

JUDGE: Very well. Mr. Paulson?

DEFENDANT: It only remains for me to state that my misgivings were well founded. Shortly after signing the contract, I was to discover that the Zeepsday Mr. Jorgenson and I had been taken to visit was not native Earth time at all, but a deliberately contrived intrusion of Sloonian time into our Earth week—

(*Pandemonium in the courtroom. Cries of* Objection! *from the plaintiff's compound.*)

JUDGE: Order! *Order!* Mr. Usussis, what is it this time?

PLAINTIFF (*excitedly*): The defendant's statement is unsubstantiated, unfair, and unprovable.

DEFENDANT: But it's the truth.

PLAINTIFF: That is beside the point. We have agreed that everything you experienced was nothing more than an illusion. An illusion does not exist. Therefore whether it is truthful or not is irrelevant.

DEFENDANT (*turning to Judge*): And just there, exactly, is my point, your honor. The plaintiff has admitted that everything up to the signing of the contract was based on something that did not exist—

PLAINTIFF: Which does not render the contract null and void—"A commercial agreement shall be binding without respect to its relation to the real universe." Nuggle *vs.* Jwickx, Galactic Court Decision 1328474639475-635. You are legally committed to the purchase of twenty quintillions of galactic monetary units worth of goods from Sloon.

DEFENDANT: That I admit, provided the plaintiff wishes to enforce the contract. My point is otherwise. The contract, being a real thing with a real existence in its own right, even though the basis of it was non-existent, is unchallengeable. However, the insult for which the plaintiff has brought suit against me, having no real existence of its own, merely a *reported* existence, to be real must have a basis in reality. Since the plaintiff denies the real basis of the insult—to wit, the situation and causes out of which it stemmed—and further denies any physical basis for the insult—that is, the plaintiff insists that he possesses only *three* tentacles—then the insult, having no real basis, has no real existence. In other words, not only was the original insult beyond the authority of this court to punish, but repetitions of this insult would likewise be so. I ask dismissal of the plaintiff's suit on the basis of non-existence of cause.

PLAINTIFF (*wildly*): This is barefaced robbery. He knows that I'd never be accepted by polite society on Sloon again if I permitted myself to be freely insulted.

Your honor, he's out to make me tear up the contract by forcing myself to deny having ever been associated with him or it. If you permit him to continue to insult me, I'll have no alternative. I—

JUDGE: Order! The plaintiff will restrain himself! (*Plaintiff subsides with twitching tentacles.*) Now, if the plaintiff wishes to rebut the defendant's contentions, he will do so in a legal manner.

PLAINTIFF (*shakily, but with growing strength and confidence*): Pardon me, your honor. I had forgotten that I had a legal answer at my disposal. The defendant forgets that an injunction need not necessarily show real cause to be granted. *Fear* of insult is sufficient reason for an injunction to be granted enjoining restraint upon one or more parties. Then, if insult occurs and witnesses to it can be found, no further proof is needed. Twingo *vs.* ¼Kud, Galactic Court Decision 19483738473645485937. I rest my case.

JUDGE: Any further comment, Mr. Paulson?

DEFENDANT: No, your honor, except to point out that the whole economic system of Earth trembles upon the outcome of this trial—

JUDGE: That has no bearing on this case, which is solely a question of manners and morals between two private parties, irrespective of race or residence. I see no reason to stretch out this hearing, if both parties have concluded their pleadings. It will not be necessary for me to retire to consider my decision, since the law in this case is perfectly clear and allows of only one interpretation and one conclusion. I myself am of course completely impartial and would have nothing but contempt for anyone who might pretend to see behind this trial a clever con game by an unscrupulous being who has seen an opportunity to take advantage of a particular current legal condition. But even if I were so uncontemptuous of such a point of view as to share it myself, it would remain my duty to render my decision with the same scrupulosity as if I were an outspoken adherent of that being, be he tentacled or be he not tentacled and regardless of the number of tentacles.

The defendant has presented an ingenious, and perhaps some of the prejudiced among the spectators might say, a gallant structure of logic to show cause why an injunction should not be issued restraining him from insulting the plaintiff in terms of the number of tentacles the plaintiff possesses. The court is forced to admit that he is perfectly correct in his contention that the original insult under the conditions alleged had no real existence. However, the plaintiff's contention that real cause is not necessary to an injunction is also correct. Consequently: Be it ordered by this court that Garth Paulson, Human presently residing on the planet Earth, be restrained from expressing an opinion about the number of tentacles possessed by Drang Usussis, Nesbler of the planet Sloon, where such expression may be construed to be damaging or injurious to the sensibilities of the said Drang Usussis, Nesbler of the planet Sloon. Further, if the said Garth Paulson shall, in defiance of the order of this court, so express such an opinion, be it ordered that he be visited by the full penalty of the law in such cases: to wit confinement for not less than two years in the place or places determined by a person to be appointed by this court, who shall have him in custody. Full expense of both prisoner and custodian to be borne by the plaintiff in this suit. Unka, a Bolver from Bol, decisioning. . . . Clerk, you will provide all interested parties with copies of his decision.

DEFENDANT (*shouting*): Your honor, don't leave the bench! Let go of me, Marge—I know what I'm doing! To hell with the penalty. Listen, Usussis! I don't care what they do to me. You've got four tentacles and you know it—

(*Bloodcurdling scream from the plaintiff. Uproar in the court.*)

DEFENDANT (*shouting more loudly*): —not three, *four!* Everybody knows it; and if you try to come to Earth and enforce that contract you swindled me out of, there isn't a red-blooded human that won't stand up to you, face to face, and point out that *fourth* tentacle. Listen, folks, do you know why he doesn't want to admit to that fourth tentacle?

(*Plaintiff fights furiously to reach defendant. Is restrained by well-wishers and the court bailiff.*)

DEFENDANT: Do you know what he uses it for? That fourth tentacle is the one he uses to zorrgle his grob! (*Plaintiff shrieks and faints.*) Didn't know I knew you were a grob-zorrgler, did you, Usussis? But I do. I—

JUDGE: Order! Order! Be silent, Mr. Paulson. Order in the court! Before I order it cleared!

(*The noise in the court gradually subsides, except in the compound of the plaintiff, where the plaintiff, now revived and convulsed with shame, is furiously gnashing his teeth and tearing up a contract-sized sheaf of legal papers.*)

JUDGE: Bailiff, apprehend the prisoner and bring him before me.

(*Bailiff does so.*)

JUDGE: Garth Paulson, you have just been witnessed in the flagrant act of violating an injunction issued by this court. Do you plead guilty or not guilty?

PRISONER: Guilty, your honor. And let me say that I would gladly do it again—and *will* do it again, if necessary.

JUDGE: Silence! The law is not to be flouted with impunity, whatever good motives the prisoner may conceive himself to have.

PRISONER: Give me liberty or give me death.

JUDGE: You are forbidden to attempt to instruct the court. I hereby sentence you to two years in terms of the time on your native world, in the custody of a person to be appointed by the court, who will determine the places and conditions of your confinement. And I appoint as custodian of this prisoner, the Human female Marge Jolman, provided that, the better to carry out the duties hereby imposed on her by the court, she submits to the mating ceremony with the prisoner without delay. Expenses of both prisoner and jailer to be borne by the plaintiff in this case for the duration of the sentence. That's all. Court concluded. Clear the room, Bailiff.

PRISONER: Thank you, Judge.

JUDGE (*with twinkles in his top dozen eyes*): Don't thank me, Mr. Paulson. It was a pleasure to put a spoke in the wheel of that sneaky Sloonian's finagling. Where will you children be going on this honeymoon of yours at Usussis' expense? May I recommend the resort areas on Elysia? Nothing but the best, there.

PRISONER: We'll think about it, Judge.

JUDGE: There's just one thing, though. How did you manage to discover that Usussis had actually salted your week with that fake Zeepsday made out of Sloonian time?

I've always understood it was almost impossible for even an expert to distinguish alien from natural time when it's been firmly intruded in the temporal structure.

PRISONER: Well, I know it's supposed to be—

CUSTODIAN OF THE PRISONER: It's just that Garth is so sensitive—

PRISONER: Let me tell him, Marge. You see, Judge, there was nothing you could put your finger on, at first. But the morning I signed the contract I had begun to itch; and shortly after I did sign the contract, I took a look at the wrist I was scratching; and the truth jumped at me.

JUDGE: Ah, yes, I remember something being said about that.

PRISONER: Exactly.

JUDGE: You saw on your wrist . . . ?

PRISONER: Hives. I was allergic to Sloonian time.

JUDGE: Marvelous! Truly virtue triumphs in the most unexpected—Clerk, what are you doing, putting all this down? The court has concluded. Close your record.

RECORD CLOSED.

TRANSCRIPT CONCLUDED.

THINGS WHICH ARE CAESAR'S

> *"I know you," Jamethon said. The dark*
> *skin of his face was like taut silk. "You are*
> *one of the Deniers of God."*
>
> *"An incorrect name for us," answered*
> *Padma. "All men deny and believe at the*
> *same time—and each builds to his own*
> *heaven."*
>
> Soldier, Ask Not (Childe Cycle: revised)

Men and women born of cities find it hard to realize how utter a dark can come, outdoors, when the last of the sunset goes and the moon is not yet up. For a long hour of gradually fading twilight, the meadow between the road and the lower woods had been almost as visible as in full daylight. Now, suddenly, it was all dark as an unlit cave. The few people already camped in the meadow moved closer to their fires or lit lanterns inside their tents.

A few were caught away from the camping spaces they had rented, visiting either at the store trucks selling food and supplies alongside the road, or at one of the temporary chemical toilets set up on the road's far side, where the ground lifted in a wooded slope to the near horizon of the hilltop. These stumbled and felt their way back to where they thought they should be, not helped much by the limited beams of flashlights, even if they were lucky enough to be carrying such.

The only one who did not fumble his way was Ranald. With neither sunset nor flashlight to help him, he kept moving at a normal pace over the now invisible ground. In the first breathing of the night wind his full, sandy beard blew back around his neck under his chin. He did not stumble over anyone, even those couples lying together in darkness. To his ears, each person there was a beacon of noise in the obscurity. Even those who were not talking, breathed, gurgled or rustled loudly enough to keep someone like himself from walking into them; and, even if they had not been so loud, he could smell each of them and their belongings from ten or fifteen feet away. Possessions or people, they all smelled, one way or another. Even those who thought of themselves as extremely clean stank of soap and dry-cleaning fluids and city smokes.

Ranald passed them by now; and he passed by their fires. Almost to a man or woman, these early-comers to the campground were loaded with outdoor gear of some sort or another. Most had brought food of their own, as well—the store trucks had barely begun to do the business their owners expected to do tomorrow or the next day. Ranald himself carried no camping equipment. But under each arm he had a chunk of log from a dry sugar maple. Behind him, now, he could hear some follower, someone heavy-footed and unsure, using him as a guide through the dark. Ranald grinned a little sadly in his beard and breathed deeply of the night breeze. Among and beyond the smells of the campers, he scented pine and spruce trees from downslope, swamp soil, and running river.

His searching gaze settled at last on one small fire and

his nose found the reek of it right. Turning to it, he detoured around four city-dressed adults who were lying, talking in the total dark like children backyard camping for the first time. He came up to the small fire. It was a narrow blaze, fed by the ends of five pieces of oak limb, pointing to the burning area like wagon spokes to a hub. Just beyond the flames was a lean man, himself the color of peeled, old oak, dressed in Levi's and a red-and-white-checked wool shirt. He sat on an unrolled sleeping bag with a poncho staked at a rain slope above it.

He and Ranald looked at each other like strange dogs across the plains.

"Hard maple," said Ranald, dropping his two pieces of wood beside the fire. "Burns slow."

The other man stared for a moment at the chunks of wood, then reached off into the darkness behind him with his right hand and came back holding an aluminum coffeepot with its base blackened from the fire. "Tea?" he asked.

"I thank you," said Ranald. He sat down cross-legged himself; and he and the man behind the fire regarded each other in its light. The man who owned the fire was easily a foot taller than Ranald and looked competent. But Ranald, under his thin, worn leather jacket, was oddly wide across the shoulders and heavy-headed under a mass of sand-colored hair and beard, so that in a strange way he looked even more competent than the man with the fire.

"Dave Wilober's my name," said the man with the fire.

"Ranald," said Ranald.

The distance separating them across the flickering red flames was too far to reach across easily for the shaking of hands. Neither man tried.

"Pleased to meet you," said Dave Wilober. His accent was Southern and twangy. Ranald spoke almost like a Midwesterner, except for a slight rhythm to his phrasing—not the singsong of someone with a Scandinavian inheritance of speech, but a patterning of words and emphasis that was almost Irish. The two looked at each other examiningly.

"And you," said Ranald.

The coffeepot on the white-glowing wood coals in the fire's center was beginning to sing already. Dave reached out and turned the pot to expose the curve of its other side to the greatest heat.

"I was thinking I'd probably sit by myself here," he said, half to Ranald, half to the fire. "Didn't guess anyone neighborly might come by."

"There'll be others," Ranald said. He frowned at the fire, with his beard blowing about his face in the night breeze. In the unrelieved darkness behind him, he heard an uncertain shuffling of heavy hiking boots, and there was the sound of embarrassed breathing.

"Others?" Dave frowned a little. "Don't know about that. I'm not great for company."

"There'll be others," Ranald repeated. "There were the first time."

"The first time?" Dave raised an eyebrow and lifted the coffeepot off the coals. Inside it now, they could both hear the boiling water hammering at the metal sides. "There been a Sign in the Heavens before this? When?"

"Far back," said Ranald. He was tempted to say more, but the years had made him taciturn. "Long since."

Dave watched him for a moment. Ranald only gazed back.

"Any case," said Dave, taking the top off the hot pot

with a quick, clever snatch of his fingers, and dropping it inside-up on the ground beside him. He poured some tea leaves from a bag into the pot. "Likely most anybody coming to something like this'd be churchy. I'm not."

He paused to glance at Ranald again.

"You neither?" he asked.

"That's right," said Ranald, softly. "There's nothing for me in god-houses."

Dave nodded.

"Not natural," he said, "going into a box—for something like that."

He half rose, to turn and produce a couple of plastic cups before sitting down again. As he did so, a small chinking noise came from him—so slight a noise that only ears like Ranald's could have caught it. Ranald cocked his head on one side like an interested bird, staring at the lower half of Dave's body, then raised his gaze to find Dave's eyes steady and unmoving upon him.

"Brother," said Ranald, peacefully, "you go your way, I go mine. Isn't that so?"

Dave's gaze fell away, back to the fire.

"Fair enough—" he began and broke off, turning his head to the right to look off into darkness. From the direction in which he stared came plainly now the noise of two pairs of feet, two breathing bodies, heavily approaching. After a moment a pair of people loomed into the illumination of the fire and halted, staring down at the seated men.

They were male and female—both young. The man was only slightly taller than Ranald, and slighter of build. Like Ranald, he was bearded; but the dark-brown hair on his face was sparse and fine, so that with the wind blowing it this way and that it seemed as if he were only

bearded in patches. Above the beard and narrow cheekbones his brown eyes had the dark openness of a suffer-
ing, newborn animal. Below the beard, his narrow body
was thickened by layers of clothing. He walked unsurely.
Beside him, the girl also was swollen with clothes. She
was smaller than he, with long, straight-hanging blond
hair, and a mere nub of a nose in a plate-round face that
would not have looked old on a girl of twelve. But her
arm was tightly around his waist. It was she who was
holding him up—and she was the one who spoke.

"We've got to get warm," she said; and her tone of
voice left no choice in the matter. "We've got to sit down
by your fire."

Ranald glanced across at Dave. In the flickering
firelight Dave's features were like a face carved in bas-
relief on some ancient panel of dark wood. He hesitated,
but only for a moment.

"Sit," he said. He reached behind himself once more
and came back this time with two more plastic cups and
an unopened can of vegetable beef soup.

The girl and the young man dropped clumsily down
before the fire. Seated now, and clearly shown in the red
light, the man was shivering. The girl knelt beside him
in her baggy, several layers of slacks; and placed the palm
of her small, plump hand flat on his forehead. Her nails
were top-edged in black; and to Ranald's nose she, like
the young man, reeked of old dirt and sweat.

"He's got a fever," she said.

They were both wearing packs of a sort, his hardly
more than a knapsack, hers sagging, heavy and large, with
a blanket roll below the sack. She helped him off with his,
then shrugged out of the straps that bound her, and
opened up the blanket roll. A moment later she had him

wrapped with a number of thin, dark-blue blankets, most of them ragged along their edges, as if something had chewed them.

Dave had opened the can of soup and emptied it into a pan on the fire. He rinsed out the can with water from a white plastic jug, then filled the can and the three cups with tea from the coffeepot. He handed the cups to Ranald and the other two, keeping the can for himself.

The girl's eyes had gone to Ranald as the cups were passed out. She had put her own cup down; and it was cooling beside her as she continued to urge tea into the young man. Ranald gazed back at her without particular expression, all the time Dave had been in constant activity.

"He's sick," the girl said to Ranald.

Ranald only continued to watch her, without moving.

Behind him, there was a sudden rush. The hiking boots that had followed him here, and which had been fidgeting in the background since, came forward with a rush, carrying a man in his mid-to-late thirties into the firelight. The light of the flames played on the boots, which were new-looking, with speed lacings, fastened tight to the tops of the thick corduroy pants above them with leather straps around the pant cuffs. He was zipped up in a plaid jacket, with a large back pack of yellow plastic strapped to an aluminum pack frame that glinted brilliantly in the firelight.

He smiled eagerly at them, turning his head to include everybody. His face was softened and his waist thick with perhaps thirty pounds of unnecessary fat. His hair was receding, but what was left was black and curly. Only his long sideburns were touched with gray. He ended his smile upon the girl and squatted down beside her, getting out of his pack.

"I've got some antibiotics here . . ." he chattered, digging into the pack. "I couldn't help hearing you say your friend was sick. Here . . . oh, yes . . ."

He brought his fist out with a tube of bicolored capsules, red and black in the firelight. The eyes of both the young man and the girl jumped for a moment at the sight of the capsule-shapes, then settled back to quiet watching again.

"What's that?" asked the girl sharply.

"Ampicillin." The man in boots tilted one of the capsules out of the tube into the palm of his left hand, offering it to the girl. "Very good . . ."

She took the capsule and pushed it between the lips of the young man.

"Take it with the tea," she told him. He swallowed.

"That's right. And keep him warm—" the man in boots started to hand the tube of capsules to the girl, whose back was turned. He hesitated, then put the tube back in his pack. "Every six hours. We'll give him one. . . ."

He looked across at Dave and ducked his gaze away as Dave looked back. He glanced at Ranald, and looked away from Ranald back to Dave, almost immediately.

"My name's Strauben," he said. "Walt Strauben."

"Dave Wilober," said Dave.

"Ranald," said Ranald from the other side of the fire. Walt Strauben turned his face to the young man and the girl, expectantly.

"Letty," said the girl, shortly. "He's Rob."

"Rob, Letty, Dave . . . Ranald. Myself . . ." said Walt, busily digging into his pack. He came up with a heavy black thermos bottle and held it up. "Anyone care for some coffee—"

"Thanks," said Dave. "We've got tea."

"Of course. That's right. Well, I'll have some myself." Walt unscrewed the cap of the thermos and poured the cap half full of cream-brown liquid, closed the bottle again and put it away in his pack. He dug into his pack and came out with a folded newspaper. "Did you see to-day's paper? They're camping out all over the world just like us, waiting. Listen— *'The promise of a Sign from some supernatural power on the day of the vernal equinox has already, today, sent literally millions of people out into the fields all over the world to await the evidence of faith that rumor has promised for tomorrow. Expectation of some sort of miracle to celebrate the Christian year 2000, or simply to reward those who've been steadfast in their beliefs in any faith, continued to mount through the morning. All over the globe ordinary business is effectively at a standstill. . . .'"*

"That's all right," said Dave.

Walt stopped reading, lowered the paper and stared at Dave. The paper trembled a little in his hand. His heavy lower lip trembled a little as well.

"No need to read," said Dave. "You're welcome—for now."

"Oh all right. I just thought . . ." Walt cleared his throat and refolded the newspaper. Its pages crackled in the stillness as he thrust it back into his pack.

"Thank you," he said, speaking more into the packsack than in any other direction. "I appreciate . . ."

The girl, Letty, had been staring at him. Now, nostrils spread, she turned sharply to Dave as if to say something.

Dave's eyes met her, still and steady. She turned back to Rob without speaking.

"Is that soup ready yet?" asked Rob. He had a sharp, high-pitched voice, with a ring to it that sounded just on the edge of excitement or anger.

"Soon, baby," said Letty to him, in a different voice. "Soon."

Dave sat drinking his tea from the soup can. Walt worked with his pack, unfolding an air mattress, blowing it up and unrolling a sleeping bag upon it. After a little while Dave took the pot holding the soup off the coals. Letty passed over the cup from which Rob had been drinking tea and Dave emptied the last of the liquid in it on the fire. It hissed and disappeared. Dave filled the cup with soup and handed it back to Letty.

"Thanks," she said, briefly, and held the cup for Rob. He sucked at it, not shivering visibly anymore.

". . . All the same," said Walt, now lying on his sleeping bag and beginning to talk so quietly that his voice came at the rest of them unexpectedly, "it's an amazing thing, all the same. Even if no miracle happens, even if no Sign is shown, everybody coming out to watch for it, like this, all over the world, has to count for something more than just hysteria. . . ."

Neither Dave nor Letty nor Rob answered him. Ranald watched him unmovingly, listening; but Walt, as he talked, avoided Ranald's eyes.

". . . So many people of different religions and cultures, getting together like this everywhere, has to be a Sign in itself," said Walt. "Spiritual values are beside the point. Personal weakness hasn't anything to do with it. We've all been *called* here when you think about it, in a sense. . . ."

Ranald's head lifted and his head turned. He listened and sniffed at the darkness behind him. After a second he got up and moved off away from the firelight so quietly that not even Dave's head turned to see him go.

Once he was well away from the fire, the pastureland between the road and the woods took shadowy form in his eyes. The moon was barely up above the hill, now—a fairly respectable three-quarters moon, but blurred by a high, thin cloud layer. Through this layer it spread enough cold light to show the upright objects in the pastureland as silhouettes, but left the ground surface still deep in obscurity.

Over this obscurity Ranald followed his nose and ears to a scent of perfume like lilacs, and an almost voiceless sound of crying. He came at last to a shape huddled on the ground, away from any fire or tent. Nose and ears filled in what his eyes could not see in the little light there was. Seated alone was another young woman or girl, tall, wearing shoes with heels made for hard cement rather than soft earth, a dress thin and tight for indoors, instead of out, and a coat cut for fashion, not warmth. Besides these things, she had nothing with her—no pack, no blankets, no lantern or shelter materials.

She sat, simply hunched up on the open ground, arms around her legs, face in her knees, crying. The crying was a private, internal thing, like the weeping of a lost child who has given up hope any adult will hear. No ears but Ranald's could have found her from more than six feet away; no other nose could have located her, huddled there in the darkness of the ground.

Ranald did not touch her. He sank down silently into a cross-legged sitting position, facing and watching her.

After a while, the girl stopped crying and lifted her head, staring blindly in his direction.

"Who's there?" Her whisper was shaky.

"Ranald," said Ranald, softly.

"Ranald who?" she asked.

He did not answer. She sat staring toward him without seeing him in the darkness, as seconds slipped away. Gradually the tension of fear leaked away and she slumped back into the position in which he had found her.

"It doesn't matter," she said, to the darkness and to him.

"It always matters," said Ranald; but not as if he were answering her. He spoke out loud but absently, to himself, as if her words had pressed a button in him. "Every spring it matters fresh. Every fall it begins to matter all over again. Otherwise, I'd have given up a long time ago. But each time, every time, it starts all over again; and I start with it. Now and now."

"Who *are* you?" she asked, peering through the darkness without success.

"Ranald," he said.

He got softly to his feet, turned, and started back toward Dave Wilober's fire. Behind him, after a few steps, he heard her rise and follow the moon-limned silhouette of his body. He went with deliberate slowness back to Dave's fire, and all the way he heard her following. But after he had sat down he heard her come only to the edge of the thick shadow his own body cast from the fire flares. Having come that far she sat down, also, still slumped but no longer weeping.

". . . What does someone like you know about it?" Rob was saying sharply to Walt. "What do you understand?"

Rob had straightened up and even thrown off most of his blankets. His face was damp and pink now above the beard, and the beard itself clung damply to his upper cheeks under the brown, yellow-lit eyes.

"Very little, very little. That's true. . . ." Walt shook his head.

"You talk about how fine it is, everyone getting together out here, and every place. But what do you really know about it? What makes you think you know anything about why people are here? You don't know why Letty and I are here!"

"No, that's true. I don't deny it," said Walt. "Who can know? No one knows—"

"Not 'no one'! You!" said Rob. "*You* don't know. You and the rest of the dudes. You don't know anything and you're scared to find out; so you go around making it big about nobody at all knowing. But that's a lie. I know. And Letty knows. Tell him, Letty."

"I know," said Letty to Walt.

"I believe you. I really believe you," said Walt. "But don't you see, even if you think you're positive about something, you've got a duty to question yourself, anyway. You have to consider the chance you're wrong. Just to make sure—isn't that so?"

"Hell it is!" said Rob. "It's just a lot of junk you pile up to hide the fact you haven't got guts enough to face life the way it really is. Not other people. *You*—"

He broke off. Another pair of booted feet that Ranald had already heard coming toward the fire from the nearest fire downslope stepped into the firelight, and the flames showed them.

"No. That's a mistake, of course," Walt was saying in a voice that shook a little but was calm. He folded his

hands together and closed his teeth gently on the middle
knuckle of the first finger. "You don't—"

He caught sight of the boots and broke off in turn, raising his gaze to the man who had just joined them.

"All right, all of you. Let's see your permits."

As the firelight painted him standing there against the
black frame of the darkness, the lawman now looming
over them was shiny with leather. He was agleam with
white motorcycle helmet, brown boots, and black jacket,
unzipped in front to show the straps of a Sam Browne
belt supporting a holstered revolver, glittering handcuffs
and the dark, bloodsucker shape of a black leather sap.
He had a heavy-boned, middle-twenties face with a short-
bristled, full moustache, so light-colored of hair it was almost invisible in spite of its thickness.

"I said, permits," he repeated. His voice was a flat
tenor.

Without saying anything, Dave reached behind himself
once more and brought out a piece of printed blue paper.
The man took it, looked at it, and handed it back. He took
a similar paper from Walt Strauben, read it, and gave it
back. His eyes slid along to Ranald, who had not moved,
neither to produce a paper nor anything else. Eyes still
locked with Ranald, the lawman reached down to take
the piece of paper upheld by Letty. With a sudden effort,
then, he broke his gaze from Ranald's and looked down at
Letty's permit.

He handed it back to Letty and looked at Rob.

"All right," he said to Rob. "Where's yours?"

"We're together," said Rob. His voice had thinned from
the note it had held talking to Walt. The yellow glint was
out of his brown eyes, leaving them dark and flat.

"He's my guest," snapped Letty. "The permit's good

for a space ten feet by ten feet. That's all we take up, together."

"One person only to every ten-by-ten plot." The lawman turned back to her. "This isn't one of your garbage-heap camping grounds. The place is clean—it's going to keep clean. If your friend wants to stay, he'll have to get another permit."

"Who're you?" said Rob. His face seemed narrower now. It was pale and damp with sweat; and his voice was still thin. "This is private property."

"Pig," said Letty, strongly. She got to her feet. Standing, she looked no more than half the size of the lawman. "It's nothing to do with you. We'll talk it over with the owner."

"Now if you want trouble," said the lawman, answering her without lifting his voice, "you just keep on. There's deputies enough of us here on special duty from the county sheriff's office to keep things orderly. I'm not going to waste time arguing. You can buy another camping permit for twenty-five dollars; or one of you is going to have to clear out."

He stood, still holding the paper Letty had given him. "Make your mind up," he said.

"He's sick, you bastard!" snarled Letty. "Sick, don't you understand? He can't clear out."

"All right," said the deputy, in the same tones. "Then we'll give him a ride into the hospital in Medora. If he's sick, they'll take care of him there. But nobody camps here without buying a permit."

"Do you buy and sell people the chance to know God exists?" asked Walt. But his voice trembled a little and was so low-pitched that what he said went ignored by both Letty and the deputy.

"What about *him?*" Rob said suddenly, nodding in the direction of Ranald. "Why just us? You aren't giving him a hard time for his permit!"

Ranald did not move. The deputy's eyes flicked a little in his direction, but not far enough for their gazes to lock together again.

"Never mind anyone else here," he said to Rob. "I'm talking to you. Get a permit to stay, or get on your feet and get moving."

He stepped forward and reached down as if to pull Rob to his feet out of the cone of blankets that swathed him.

"Wait! No, wait . . ." The words came tumbling out of Walt. "Here, officer. I'll take care of the permits. Just a minute now . . . wait. . . ."

He was digging into a side pocket of his corduroy pants. He came up with a wallet and thumbed out bills, which he handed up to the deputy.

"I'll take two of them," Walt said. "Fifty dollars—that's right?"

"Two." The deputy, still holding the bills, took out a pad of blue papers and a pen, scribbled a date and initials on two of the papers and tore them from the pack. He handed both to Walt, who passed one over to Letty and held out the other to Ranald.

"All right," said the deputy, putting money and pad of permits away. "Remember to keep the grounds clean. Pick up your own trash. And the comfort stations are across the road. Use them. That permit doesn't entitle you to make a nuisance of yourself. Any trouble by anyone and you'll still go out."

He stepped back into darkness and everyone there heard his boots going away.

Ranald reached out to take the permit Walt was still

holding. He examined it for a moment and then turned to hand it to the girl he had found crying, and who all this while had hidden, crouched behind him.

"Who's that?" demanded Walt, twisting to stare at her.

"I'm . . . Maybeth Zolovsky," the girl said. Her voice was thin, as Rob's had been.

Walt opened his mouth and saw Ranald mildly watching him. Walt's eyes shifted; he closed his mouth and turned back to find himself facing the round, childish, hard features of Letty.

"The world's as much ours as anyone else's," she said. "He's got no inherent right to keep us off any part of it, when we aren't doing any harm, any more than we've got a right to keep him off."

Rob said something inarticulate, endorsing. Walt shook his head and looked away from them down into the flames of the fire.

"*You* thank him, if you want," said Rob, turning to Ranald. He added, "But I guess you don't need to. You weren't going to get asked for a permit anyway, were you? How come? Why didn't he ask you?"

Ranald looked back at him silently, the night breeze blowing in his beard.

"Don't want to tell us?" said Rob. "All right. But I'd like to know. What makes you a special case?—You don't want to tell me, is that it?"

Dave snorted a little, filling his soup-can cup again from the coffeepot. Rob looked back across the fire at him.

"Now you're laughing," Rob said. "How about letting the rest of us in on the joke?"

Dave lifted his soup can, drank some hot tea, and looked across the rim of the container at the younger man.

"You want to know why that deputy didn't ask a man like him for a permit?" Dave said. "Whyn't you find out for yourself? He gave the permit away to the young lady there. Whyn't you just go try to take it back from her?"

Rob stared at Dave.

"What?" he said, after a moment.

"I said," Dave went on, "you want to know why the deputy done what he done, you go do something like it. Go take the permit back from"—he hesitated, looking at the dark-haired girl—"Maybeth?"

She nodded back at him, only half-sheltered now behind Ranald.

"Take it away—" Rob's voice cracked. "What do you think I am? Why'd I want to do something like that?"

"To learn," said Dave.

"Learn? You mean learn how to be like that?"

"No." Dave looked directly at him. "Learn why you'd never try to do it, even if you wanted to—no more than that deputy'd try it. Look at him—." Dave's voice went a little harsh. "I say, look at *him!*"

Rob turned and stared again at Ranald. Ranald gazed back, sitting quietly bathed by the moving firelight. In its red and yellow light he was a short man in a thin leather jacket; but he was strangely wide across the shoulders and heavy-headed under his mass of sand-colored hair and beard. His blue eyes watched Rob without blinking.

For several seconds Rob looked at him in silence. Then he gave something like a start and a shudder combined, and jerked his gaze back to the fire. He sat hunched toward the flames and muttered something under his breath.

Letty lifted one of the dropped blankets to wrap about

him, again, meanwhile throwing a brief, fierce glance first
at Ranald and the dark-haired girl, then at Dave. She
tucked the blanket about Rob's huddled shape.

"Baby . . . ?" she murmured, feeling his forehead once
more. Rob pulled his head back from her touch.

"Never mind!" he said. "I tell you, never mind!"

"You see?" said Dave, from across the fire. "It'd have
been more trouble to a man, than it was worth—for that
deputy to mess with Ranald—or for you to."

"Or for you," muttered Rob to the flames.

Dave looked down at his tin-can cup for a second without speaking.

"Could be," he said, quietly.

A silence came down on them all, which lasted several
minutes. Then Walt Strauben stirred. He turned to his
pack and dug out a blue-and-white blanket three times
the thickness of any of the dark blankets wrapping Rob.
He held the blanket out to Maybeth Zolovsky.

"Come in next to the fire?" he said.

Maybeth hesitated, glancing at Ranald. But he looked
back at her with no particular expression. She got up and
came forward to sit down beside Walt, wrapping the
blanket around her, hugging it to her.

"Thanks," she whispered.

From across the fire, Letty gave her a grim glance.

"Coffee?" Walt said, pouring from his thermos.

"Thank you," she said. She turned to Dave. "Thank
you."

"Welcome," said Dave.

"You must have made up your mind to come out here
on the spur of the moment . . ." Walt said to her.

They fell into low-voiced conversation. Dave let them
talk, only feeding the fire from time to time. Ranald sat

back in silence, listening to other sounds of the evening.
After a while, Letty began to rearrange the blankets
enclosing Rob, until she and he were wrapped up together in a sort of cloth cocoon that was bed and tent in
one for them both. A little after that, Walt produced another blue-and-white blanket and made up a bed of sorts
for himself, turning his own sleeping bag over to Maybeth. The three-quarters moon traveled upward, burning
its way slowly through the low-lying cloud layer and
climbing at last into a star-clear sky, so that the pastureland with its people and tents and pinpoints of fire or
lanternlight showed up like the negative of a photograph
taken by daylight.

When the moon was almost straight overhead, Dave
stirred from where he had sat feeding the fire all this
time, reached back behind him to come up with some
middle-sized, dark object, and rose to his feet. He went
off toward the woods at the lower end of the pasture.

Ranald silently got up and followed the taller man.

The moon was bright enough now so that Dave walked
almost as surely as Ranald had walked earlier in full darkness. Dave threaded his way between the fires, and to
anyone's hearing but Ranald's, his going was utterly silent. But to Ranald's ears, each stride of the taller man
produced the same faint chinking noise Ranald had heard
earlier by the fire.

Dave went downslope across the pastureland to its
lower edge and moved in among the trees. He went some
little distance, until the ground under its layer of dead
grass and leaves began to feel soft—if not yet damp. The
sound of the running river was close, now. In a little open
space, in the moonlight, Dave sat down on a dead and
fallen tree trunk. For a second or two he simply sat; not

exactly slumped, but with his back gently curved like the back of a man who has been carrying a heavy pack through a long day. Then he stirred, lifted the shape he had carried away from the campground, and unscrewed the top of it.

The moonlight showed the shape of a large bottle in black silhouette against the stars as he drank. He lowered the bottle, sat again for a moment, then recapped it and put it aside. Leaning forward, he began to rake together some of the ground trash and fallen twigs before him. Once or twice Ranald heard the small snap of a dead branch, breaking.

In a pool of moon-shadow cast by a twisted oak-trunk, Ranald sank into a squatting position on his heels. The darkness around him hid him utterly as he watched Dave's hands, like independent small creatures squirrel-busy at some instinctive task, glean the makings of a fire from ground that hardly appeared to bear anything worth burning. Once, Dave stopped to drink again from his bottle, but otherwise the craft of his hands seemed a reflexive, automatic thing—as if wherever he went, there had to be fire.

After a little, he finished. A match scratched and spurted yellow light in the darkness. The flame caught among the twigs and other stuff of the little conical pile of twigs before the log on which he sat. The flame spread and rose. In its new light, Dave got up briefly to go a few steps aside for larger pieces of dead branch, which he returned and fed into the fire, end-on, as he had done with the fire above in the pasture.

This was a smaller fire, however, than that earlier one. A private fire. Still, its light pushed back the shadows; and, as Dave lifted the bottle to drink a third time, the flickering of the flame illuminated Ranald, squatting at the base of the oak.

Dave drank and lowered the bottle.

"You?" he said. "I came here to get away from the crowd."

Ranald said nothing.

"True," said Dave, "you're not like the rest. Come to the fire."

Ranald rose, approached the other side of the flames and squatted again. There was a naturalness and ease about the way he sat on his heels, as if he could remain that way for hours with as much comfort as another man in an armchair.

"Drink?" said Dave. He held out the bottle.

"I thank you," said Ranald. He lifted the bottle and swallowed. Its contents was store-sold bourbon. Not the best, perhaps, but store-sold and distillery-made, a half-gallon bottle heavy against the firelight.

He handed the bottle back to Dave, who drank again.

"It's happened before," Dave said, setting the open bottle down to one side of the fire, but equidistant between them. "You said that. You told me there'd been a Sign in the Heavens before. Long ago. How long? Fifty years?"

"Longer," said Ranald.

"A hundred? Five hundred? A thousand—"

"About that," said Ranald.

"But you remember it?" Dave gestured to the bottle. "Help yourself."

Ranald reached for the bottle, drank and replaced it exactly where it had sat a moment before.

"You remember?" repeated Dave.

"I remember," Ranald answered.

"Could be," said Dave, looking at him across the fire. "Could be—anything. But here you are with the rest of us; and you said there was nothing for you in godhouses."

"I've found nothing there. That's true," answered Ranald. "But there's no telling. Maybe I'll go to a god-house in the end, to die."

"Maybe they'll bury me out of a church someday, too," said Dave, thoughtfully. "Maybe . . . And here we are, all of us sitting out here, waiting for a great Sign of Faith. God, his own self, is going to come down and walk among us in glory, amen. Tonight, maybe, or tomorrow. All over the world at once, there's going to be proof it's been true, all this time and—then what?"

"I don't know," said Ranald.

"But you've seen it once before, you said." Dave made a motion toward the bottle. "Drink. Drink when you feel like it. I can't go drinking myself, with you waiting for an invite each time."

Ranald reached out and drank.

"All these people," said Dave, drinking after him. "That Letty and Rob. That Walt Strauben. That deputy even, and that Maybeth girl you pulled out of a hip pocket—that deputy sure didn't want to make trouble with you, now, did he? Mighty queer how a man can get to be the way you are, and another man just know it without being told. No one ever monkeys with you, do they?"

"Odin," said Ranald, "had one eye."

"Odin?"

"Another god," said Ranald. "He gave his eye for wisdom, they said. But any man who wants to give the price for anything, can buy, like that. Having bought, it shows

on him. And so it goes. Each buys his own want and pays
the price. That part never changes."

"What changes, then?" asked Dave. His tongue stumbled a little on the *ch* sound.

Ranald shook his head.

"I don't know," he said. "Every season, every year, the
thought of living comes fresh and new to me. Fresh and
new—and I go on again. But nothing changes. Over a
thousand years, now." He looked across the fire to Dave.
"Why do I keep on starting and starting again, if there's
no change? If you can, tell me; and I can rest."

"Nothing I can tell you. Take a drink," said Dave. "It'll
help you think."

Ranald drank.

"Thanks," he said, "I give you thanks." His tongue had
not thickened as had Dave's; but there was a different
note, of something like an echo chamber's echo of melancholy in his voice.

"Welcome, brother," said Dave, lifting the bottle himself. "Welcome and rest yourself. Tomorrow the Sign
comes, the papers say—and the world changes. We'll all
change—"

He put down the bottle and began to sing, a little
hoarsely but in key with a light baritone voice.

"There was a rich man and he lived in Jerusalem.
  Glory, Hallelujah, hi-ro-de-rum!
He wore a top hat and his clothes were very spruce-ium.
  Glory, Hallelujah, hi-ro-de-rum!

Hi-ro-de-rum, hi-ro-de-rum!
Skinna-ma-rinky doodle-doo, skinna-ma-rinky doodle-doo,
  Glory, Hallelujah, hi-ro-de-rum!

Now, outside his gate there sat a human wreckium.
  Glory, Hallelujah, hi-ro-de-rum!
He wore a bowler hat in a ring around his neckium.
  Glory, Hallelujah . . ."

"Sing!" Dave interrupted himself to say to Ranald. Ranald cocked his head on one side, listening, as Dave started a new verse.

"*. . . Now the poor man he asked for a piece of bread*
  and cheesium—"

"*Glory, Hallelujah, hi-ro-de-rum!"* sang Ranald along with him. Dave nodded. "*. . . The rich man said, I'll call for the police-ium,"* Dave went on. "*Glory, Hallelujah, hi-ro-de-rum!"* They sang together:

"*Hi-ro-de-rum, hi-ro-de-rum!*
Skinna-ma-rinky-doodle-doo, skinna-ma-rinky-doodle-doo!
  Glory, Hallelujah, hi-ro-de-rum! . . ."

The singing, the firelight, the bottle passing back and forth, made something like a private room for them in the midst of the darkness. They went on through other verses of the same song and other songs after that, while the fire burned down toward the coals and they came back to talking again. Or rather, Dave came back to talking.

". . . that Walt," he was saying, no longer stumble-tongued, but with a deliberate slowness of pronunciation. "I smell preacher on him. Maybe not now he's a preacher, but he's been one. So, that's why he'd be here. He'd come to see a Sign because he needed one to preach. But that Letty and Rob—what do they want with a proof of God?"

"To know, perhaps," said Ranald.

"To know?"

"To find out what actually is.—For themselves, as men and women always do each generation, over and over again."

"And Maybeth? What do you say for that Maybeth girl?"

"Lost," said Ranald, "with nowhere else to go. Maybe she came here, hoping."

"Hoping?" Dave said. "Come here praying, you mean. Praying for a miracle, to set everything right for her without her having even to lift a finger for herself."

"A broken finger," Ranald looked across the dying flames at him, talking in a voice that showed no trace of effect from the liquor, "lifts hard. Broken legs don't run easy nor broken wings fly, brother."

"Can't fly or run, you can walk. Can't walk, can crawl. I been there. I know."

"You know," said Ranald, softly. "But do you know all there is to know?"

"Enough," said Dave. "Been there, I say. Could have given up anytime. Never did. You know why? Even with everything else gone, broke or rotted—there was still air, dirt, and water. Air to breathe, dirt to grow in, water to wash life down into the dirt. Running water. Rain. Black dirt. Green stuff. Trees."

"Yes," said Ranald, his eyes going past the fire and Dave for a moment. "New and new—each fresh season. I know that part, too."

"And I damn near lost it all," said Dave. "Things nearly turned me away from that part of it." He lifted the bottle to his lips, but it was empty. He stared at it for a moment, then set it down carefully. "Three sisters of

mine, four brothers, all died before they were old enough
to go to school. My daddy died. I got born last, after he
was put in the ground."

"A sickness?" Ranald said.

"Yes. No. Killed." Dave stared hard across the fire coals
at Ranald. "Worked too hard, they said. Mine—coal mine
and then fieldwork. No. People killed him. Other people
killed him, taking him away from dirt and water, and
air. . . ."

> *"—Down in the mountain, in a fall of the coal,*
> *Buried in the mountain is O'Shaunessy's soul . . ."*

"—they buried my daddy aboveground, but his soul was
buried down in the mine like O'Shaunessy's, just the
same. All the people of the world, with their mines, their
coal, their things—they put my dad down in a mine to kill
and bury him; and when I asked why, they sent me to
church for answer. Church!"

The breath of his last word fanned the red coals of the
fire momentarily white.

"Looky here," said Dave. He bent forward and rolled
up his right pants-leg, uncovering what looked like a
bulky white bandage covering his leg from the ankle to
low on the calf. "I was the last alive of the children. Ma
near on frantic to keep me from the chance of dying too
and making it all for nothing—babies and husband, all in
the grave. Now, she was one believed what people told
her. She asked around and they said, 'Take the boy to
church. Take him to the preacher. Ask help of the Lord.'
So she took me."

Dave started to reach for the now-empty bottle,

checked his hand halfway there and let it drop back on his knee.

"She took me to a preacher and he prayed over me," Dave went on. "Middle of the week too. Just into May; apple blossoms, peach blossoms on the trees, and all. No one in the church, but we three went and knelt there before the altar with the windows open and the bird noise sounding all around outside. 'Guard this boy, Lord. The last of the flock. . . .' And then we all waited for an answer on our knees, with the preacher's eyes closed, Ma's eyes closed—mine supposed to be, too, but I got tired holding them shut. . . ."

Dave's voice ran down. Ranald sat perfectly still, watching him and listening—not just like someone who is merely attentive, but like someone waiting, and who has been waiting a long time for an answer.

"Preacher opened his eyes, at last," Dave went on, suddenly. "I got mine closed again just in time. 'God has answered,' he told Ma and me. 'There's a way to make this boy of yours safe, but only one way. Straight and narrow is the road to the gate. Straight the road he must walk. You got to give him to the Lord; and he must know the Lord is with him, the hand of the Lord is on him, guiding him, night and day. . . .' And Ma believed him; and—looky here."

Dave reached down and began to unwind the cloth around his leg and ankle. It fell away, so that Ranald saw a section of limb just above the ankle that looked blackened and crusted—as it might have been by dirt, but was not. The darkness and the ribbed skin were the markings of calluses and old scars, very nearly solid callus and scar tissue for six inches from the ankle upward. And what had caused this still circled the ankle—a loose loop of tractor chain with two-inch links, shiny with age and rubbing against itself and the leg it encircled.

Dave turned his ankle to the firelight and the chain slipped, chinking as Ranald had heard it chink earlier.

"It would come off," said Ranald, looking at the chain. "A hacksaw, a file—even a good knife. It wouldn't be hard to take off."

Dave laughed. It was only the second time he had laughed in Ranald's hearing.

"Oh, I had it off," Dave said. "Ma died when I was sixteen; and I took out for other places. First night away from home, I had it off me. Crowbar and hatchet. Stuck a crowbar end through a link, chopped the link open with a hatchet, then buried the chain in some woods. Five years I walked around with no weight on my ankle."

"Then what?"

"No 'then what,'" answered Dave. "Bit by bit it come back on me. I moved around; but everywhere I went—city, town, farm or backwoods—there wasn't no notch, no wrinkle, no fold, no place for me to back myself into like everybody else was backed into and settled. Bit by bit, then, I come to understand. That chain hadn't been just something I could chop off and throw away. It was part of a deal my ma had made for me with someone that wasn't there, far as I was concerned. But the fact that someone wasn't there for me, though, didn't make no difference. Takes two to make a bargain; and there had been a bargain made. Only I hadn't kept my end."

"Odin gave his eye," said Ranald.

"Like that. I'd taken, but I hadn't given. My not believing didn't matter, long as I wore the chain; because the chain stood for what I hadn't got to give—that believing I couldn't do, no matter how much my ma wanted me to. But when I took the chain off . . ."

Dave sighed.

"So," he said, "I put it back on, without nobody telling me to. Just like you see now. And then things began to straighten out for me. I found my way back to my own country; and I found out how it was I had to live. Alone with the fields, the barns, and all; and got along with neighbors all right, long as we didn't visit together too much. But I had my honest dirt, water, and plain air—and peace out of it all."

He stopped talking. For nearly a minute the silence filled the moment between the little cracklings of the dying fire.

"Now, it was *my* mother," murmured Ranald, looking at the red and white wood coals, "said I would never find my way home again, if I went. But our ships sailed out that spring; and I was twelve. I went with them; in time, to many places. But, when years later I sailed north again, I could not find where I'd been born. It had been a small place always; and maybe some other ships had put in to raid and burn there, killing or making slaves of all—and afterwards it went back to forest. Or maybe it was only that all the old people I'd known there were dead; and I did not recognize the place when I saw it again, remembering it only the way a boy remembers things, bigger than they are. But my mother was right. I'd gone, and after that I could never find home again."

He hesitated, gazing at what was left of the fire.

"That's when I first thought I would die, because there was no reason for me to live longer," he said, softly. "But I found I could not bring myself to it; and since, I go on and on."

He raised his head from its tilt toward the cooling embers and looked across at Dave. Sometime since, Dave had slid from his seat on the log to a seat on the ground, with his back against the thick round of the log from the dead and fallen tree. Now his hands were limp, palms-upward on his thighs. His chin was down on his chest and his eyes were closed.

Ranald lifted his head and sniffed the night air. The moon was low on the far horizon, and the breeze blew from a different direction, bringing a chill with it. Ranald made no attempt to build up the fire, but lay down on his side and drew his arms and legs in toward his body, curling up animal-fashion. Like Dave, he slept.

Dawn woke them both. They rose without conversation, left the dead, small fire, and went back to the campground. There, Dave silently revived the earlier fire he had left unattended and cooked them both a breakfast of bacon and pancakes. As they were finishing this, the others—Maybeth, Letty, and Rob—began to wake and stir in their various bed-shelters. These looked with attention at the remains of breakfast; but Dave made no move to invite them to eat. It was Walt, struggling out of his blankets with a stubble of a twenty-four-hour beard gray on his face and underchin, who finally produced a small Coleman stove, cookware, and breakfast materials for himself and the other three.

As the morning warmed, the pastureland rapidly began to fill. There was a steadily growing feeling-in-common above the tents and shelter-halves and groundsheets that blossomed all about. A feeling like excitement, but not like a holiday sort of excitement. A tense thread of apprehension laced like a red vein through the body of eager expectancy that enclosed them all, there between the comfort stations and the woods stretching below down to swamp and river. It was a cloudless day, promising to become hot.

As it warmed and grew close to noon, the pressure of the tensions in the people increased; as if they were all under water that was becoming steadily deeper. By eleven o'clock it was hard to believe that any space in the pasture remained unsold; and there were a number of deputies of the local county sheriff to be seen, sweating under their equipment and uniforms. The particular deputy who had checked those around Dave's fire for permits the night before now passed by frequently, as if their space were within an area he had to patrol. In the daylight he looked much younger than he had the night before; and it was possible to see that he wore not only a star-shaped gold badge, but a nameplate below it with white block letters spelling out TOM RATHKENNY on a blue background.

In the daylight, some of the certainty he had shown during the dark hours earlier was missing. He no longer stood out among the crowd of people who had bought space in the pastureland, but seemed more to fit in among them—a little shorter and less heavily-boned, a little more of flesh and less of leather. Sweat gleamed on his chin in the sunlight and his glance shifted more frequently from person to person as he walked past.

Just past eleven thirty, the pressure broke. The universal oceanwash of voices was interrupted by a moving wave of silence that traveled across the pasture and, on the heels of that moving silence, a man walked among them.

". . . him"—the word erupted everywhere in the crowd as the man passed—". . . him . . . him . . . him . . ."

He went by not fifteen feet from Dave's fire, walking swiftly and apparently alone; a thin, brown-faced man, beardless, with shaven head and eyes spaced widely above sharp cheekbones. He was barefoot and wearing what seemed to be only a loose gown of coarse and heavy brown cloth, the skirt of which rippled with the length of his strides. Beneath the hem of that skirt, his feet were mottled with dirt.

". . . *him*," echoed Walt as the voices took up after the man had passed. "The prophet. The one who promised the world a Sign. But what brings him here, out of everywhere else on the Earth? Why to this one little place? Him . . ."

"Him . . . him . . ." said Letty and Rob and Maybeth, and all the other people crowding in the wake of the one who had passed. "Here . . . here of all places. *Him* . . ."

Dave had gotten to his feet with the rest. Now he sat down again to face Ranald, who had not risen.

"Why's he here?" Dave asked. "Is there something special here?" He looked steadily at Ranald. "It's not because of you?"

Ranald shook his head.

"Was he really here?" said Ranald. "Perhaps they're seeing him everyplace where people have gotten together to wait for the Sign."

"What're you talking about?" Walt turned suddenly to stand above Ranald. "He was here. I saw him. We all saw him. Didn't you?"

Ranald shook his head again.

"I saw, but that was all. I heard no one passing. I smelled no one," he said.

"Heard?" echoed Rob. "Smelled? In this crowd? Who could hear or smell anyone in a crush like this?"

Ranald glanced at the younger man.

"In any case," Ranald said, "he would only be a messenger."

"You can't know that," Letty said. "He could be the Sign, himself. Maybe that's what he was."

Ranald looked at her, almost mildly.

"When Signs come," he said, "there's no question."

And there was none. Just at noon, just as Ranald remembered from the time before, there was a shock that went through everyone and everything. A shock like that of a great gong being struck in a place where no sound was permitted—so that the effect was not heard, but felt, in great shudders that passed through all living and nonliving things like light through clear water. And when the shock had passed, a knowledge of sorts came into them all, as if a part of their minds which had been asleep until this moment had now been awakened to report what it witnessed. Above them, the sun had ceased apparent movement. They felt the fact that it no longer moved. It stood still in a sky without clouds.

Earth, also, stood still under their feet. They could feel its new lack of motion, as well. The laws of the universe were no longer touching sun, or Earth, or people. Something like a hand was now holding them apart from such things.

In the pasture, the crowd too was stilled. No one moved or spoke. In the woods downslope no birds sang, no insects hummed. Even to the ears of Ranald, the river seemed to have ceased its murmur. Matters were as he remembered them happening that earlier time, before he had learned that he could never find his way home again —back when he had been already far from home. He sighed silently inside himself, now, lowering his head and closing his eyes; and, sharp as a burn, fresh-branded on his inner eyelids, was suddenly the image of that home as he remembered it in the moment just before he sailed. The shore, the ships, the log buildings in the green clearing by the sea came back to him across more than a thousand years, with such immediate pain that he could almost believe he might open his eyes to see it there after all, alive again instead of lost forever.

He got to his feet, still holding his eyes tightly closed to keep the picture to him. Moving by sense of hearing and smell alone, like a blind man with radar, he drifted through the silent, unstirring crowd toward the sanctuary of the woods. It was not until he had left the crowd behind him and felt the shade of the trees on his face and his exposed lower arms and hands that he paid any attention to the fact that once more boots had followed him, familiar boots.

This time, however, they caught up with him.

"Forgive me . . ." said the voice of Walt, trembling and a little breathless behind him. "But I have to talk to you. You *knew*, didn't you? You're a Messenger yourself, aren't you—or something more than mortal?"

Ranald stopped. The picture on the inner surface of his eyelids was already fading. His shoulders sagged. He opened his eyes.

"No," he said.

"Oh, but I know you are.—Aren't you?" Walt came walking around to face him. They stood, surrounded by thick oaks, dappled themselves with oak shade in the hot, still air. "I mean—if you are, I don't want to intrude. I don't want to pry. If you don't want to say anything about yourself, that's all right. But I have to talk to you about myself. I have to explain to . . . a part of God, anyway, to some man who's part of God Eternal."

Ranald shook his head again.

"I'm no god, nor god-man," he said.

"But I was," said Walt eagerly. "I was a God-man—or at least, a man of God. That's what makes talking to you now important. It's as if this has all happened just between God and me. Do you understand what I'm saying?"

Ranald sat down wearily cross-legged on the ground with his back against an oak trunk.

"Yes," he said.

"Then you can see what it means—." Walt squatted also, facing Ranald, but found the position awkward and ended up sitting down clumsily with an unsuccessful effort to cross his legs as easily as Ranald had, "—means to me. And if it means that much to me, what it must mean to the whole world. I don't flatter myself it was just for me, of course. But that's the essence of miracle, that it works for everyone as if it were just for him, alone. Isn't it?"

Ranald shook his head, without answering. Walt made a wide gesture at the sky and the unmoving noontide sky overhead.

"Now we've had the Sign," Walt went on. "Now we'll never be the same again—each of us, as individuals, never the same again. Now all our doubts are answered, finally and completely. And now that my own doubts, my special doubts, have been answered, I can see how little, how shameful, how sinful they were. Do you know what my particular sin and crime was? Doubt itself. Not just plain doubt—simple doubt—but doubt for doubt's sake. Can you imagine that?"

Ranald nodded.

"Yes," said Walt, his face pink-brown in the pinto shade-and-sunlight. "I played a game with the Creator. Even my choosing religion as a lifework was part of that game. I knelt and prayed '*I believe, Lord,*' but the words were a lie. What I meant was '*Prove to me that I should believe, Lord.*'"

He paused, looking at Ranald; but Ranald only sat watching.

"You understand?" said Walt. "I had to be continually testing God. Not only God directly, but God as He was made manifest in the world—in other men and women, in the things man had built, in nature itself. *Render unto*— do you know the verse from Matthew, Chapter twenty-two, Verse twenty-one—"

"Yes," said Ranald. "I was a slave in a monastery for a while, and I served the tables while they ate and one read to the others."

"There were no slaves in monasteries," said Walt. "Matthew twenty-two, twenty-one has to do with the questioners that the Pharisees sent to test Jesus. What do you think their question was?"

"Whether it was lawful to give tribute to Caesar or not," said Ranald.

"They asked Him whether it was lawful to give tribute to Caesar or not," said Walt. "And you know what He answered? '*Why tempt me, ye hypocrites?*' He made them show Him the tribute money with the image of Caesar on it, and told them, '*Render unto Caesar the things which are Caesar's—*'"

"Render *therefore* unto Caesar—" murmured Ranald.

"'—*And unto God the things that are God's,*'" continued Walt. "Two thousand years ago He said those words; but all down those millenniums this has been our major confusion. We confuse our duties to Caesar with our duties to God. In essence, we tend to think of God as just another Caesar—to be paid tribute, if necessary, but also to be questioned. This has been my sin, in particular; a sin which men like you and Dave, gifted with a simple response to nature, have learned instinctively to avoid. Now, you two are naturally free in this respect, so free neither of you even suspected I had something like that in me. But that young man Rob did. You remember how he kept saying it was *my* particular fault, my own lack, that I saw in the world and other people.—You remember that, yesterday?"

"Yes."

"Well," said Walt, slapping the pants-cloth stretched tightly over his bent right knee, "he was right! Absolutely right. That's been my missing part all along, a lack of simple faith. Faith like you have, and Dave Wilober has. But now I have it, like everybody else; and now that I *know* this, I can do something about it, I can learn—from people like you and Dave."

He leaned forward, eagerly, his heavy shirt creasing over his belly.

"Talk to me," he said. "Tell me how you see the world."

He stayed leaning forward, waiting. Ranald gazed at him for a long moment, then shook his head.

"No," he said, getting to his feet.

"Wait . . ." Walt began to scramble to his own feet. "What do you mean—'No'?"

"It's no use," said Ranald.

He turned and went off through the woods. Behind him, he heard Walt calling him by name and trying to follow, but the other man crashed noisily among the trees, tripping over roots and blundering into bushes; and Ranald soon left him behind.

Once he was free again, Ranald turned and went back to the pasture. On the way, he met others of the campers, wandering under the unmoving sun, as if the suspension of physical laws had suspended all responsibility as well; and there was no longer any requirement upon them but to follow the whim of each second, through a noonday pause that was unending.

The sound of a steady metal-on-metal hammering drew him back to the campfire he had shared with Dave and the others. Dave was seated on his bedroll, singing to himself, cutting with a chisel and hammer through a link of his ankle chain, laid upon a hatchet-blade for support. Maybeth was half seated, half kneeling beside him, watching. Across the now small fire, with flames nearly invisible in the bright sunlight, were three people close together. The deputy, Tom Rathkenny, was huddled up on the ground with his head in Letty's lap. She was stroking his short, pale-blond hair soothingly; and the new-softened weapon of her gaze was turned on him, rather than Rob, who was standing, looking down at the two of them.

". . . The whole world's changed," Rob was saying to Letty. She did not look up at him.

". . . *Now the poor man died,*" sang Dave in tune to the clink of his hammer on the head of the chisel. . . .

> ". . . *and his soul went to Heavenium.*
> *Glory, Hallelujah, hi-ro-de-rum!*"

"Are you listening to me, Letty?" demanded Rob.

". . . *He danced with the angels till a quarter past elevenium . . .*"

"—I said, are you listening?"

But Letty did not answer him. Her head was bent forward, her hair falling over the head in her lap.

"Poor baby," she was murmuring. "All right, baby. All right. I'm here . . ." She interrupted herself to speak briefly to Rob. "Go to hell! Can't you see I'm busy?"

"*Skinna-ma-rinky doodle doo! Skinna-ma-rinky doodle doo!*
Glory, Hallelujah, hi-ro-de-rum . . ."

"All right," said Rob.

He straightened up. In the noonday heat, he had shed more of his layers of clothing. The antibiotics seemed to have conquered his illness and his fever. With his beard no longer plastered to his face by the wind and his face no longer damp with sweat he looked slim, but supple and strong, in both determination and body. He turned and walked over to stand above Maybeth, who looked away from Dave and up at him.

"Come on," said Rob to her.

She hesitated and looked back at Dave. But Dave was occupied only with his chiseling and his singing.

". . . *Now the rich man died, and he didn't fare so wellium . . .*"

"I said, come on!" repeated Rob.

Maybeth looked at him again, and from him to Ranald. Ranald met and returned her gaze with the same open, uncommenting stare with which he had dealt with her from the beginning.

"It's happened, don't you understand?" said Rob to her. "It's the New Age. We've had the Sign and it'll never be the same again. Now, everyone *knows;* and the world's going to be completely different. Don't you understand? Some of us don't want to face that. Letty there, she doesn't—and look at that mess over there in her lap, scared out of his wits because what really *is* has caught up with him. It's too much for him and her—but not for people like you and me. For us it's the New Age of Actuality; it's the Garden of Eden really for the first time. Come on! What're you waiting for? You don't belong here with a couple of failures, and two old men."

Maybeth looked down at the ground before her. Slowly she got to her feet without looking again at Dave or Ranald. She went off with Rob and they disappeared among the moving figures of the crowd that was still in the pasture.

". . . *couldn't go to Heaven, so he had to go to Hellium. Glory, Hallelujah—*"

With a final *clink* the chisel cut through the link on which it had been biting; and Dave broke off his song. The chain parted and slithered snakelike from around Dave's scarred and callused ankle to the hard, heel-beaten ground of the pasture. Dave picked up the links and laid them, with the hammer and chisel, carefully back into his pack behind his sleeping bag. He looked up at Ranald and laughed.

"Sing!" he said. "I got me religion at last. Don't need no chain anymore to stand for no faith I never had. All it took the Lord was a little old stopping of the sun at mid-day to set me free—from that, anyhow. Now I can give to folks without thinking I'm paying back for something."

"You always could," said Ranald. "And did." His mind was half lost in time.

Dave frowned for a second.

"What?"

"*'For owre ioye and owre hele. Iesu Cryst of hevene,'*" said Ranald, "*'In a pore mannes apparaille pursueth us evere . . .'*"

"What?" repeated Dave. "Say it again?"

"It's part of a poem," said Ranald, "that the priests used to use for a text in sermons. All week long, up and down hall, the priest was nothing to the gentles. But on Sunday all the good families around would come into chapel and the priest could say his sermon with a god's voice, paying them all back. And so he would tell them how Piers the plowman was closer to God than they. And those listening used to weep to hear it—people do not believe that now, but all were more open with weeping in those days. They wept, knights, ladies, all matter of warm-dressed folk. But later, after chapel, it made no difference you could see."

Dave fingered his chin, which was now lightly shadowed by twenty-four hours of beard.

"I've plowed," he said. "But I'm no 'pears-to-be-a-plowman.' I'm Dave Wilober."

"That, and more too," said Ranald. "But all of us are something more, with the sun straight overhead the way it is now."

Dave glanced briefly at the unmoving daystar above them.

"Could be. Could well be," he said. He laughed again. "Never mind, I'm free."

"Let's go get something to drink, come back and talk."

Tom Rathkenny lifted a crumpled face from Letty's knees.

"There's no alcoholic beverages out here," he said in a choked voice. "Every truck's been told . . ."

"Still, always something around," said Dave. He jerked his head at Ranald. "Come on, brother."

They went off to the line of trucks by the road; and, the third truck they came to was occupied by a drunken driver-owner who first tried to share his own half-empty bottle; then offered to give them an unopened one, but only if they would take it for nothing. Quietly telling the man that he took things for nothing only from neighbors or friends, Dave tucked bills unnoticed into the pocket of the driver's shirt and accepted the fresh bottle.

He and Ranald went back to their camping place. Letty and Tom Rathkenny were gone, now. Rob, Maybeth, and Walt had none of them returned. Ranald and Dave sat down on opposite sides of the fire with the bottle to one side of them, uncapped. But although Dave poured cups half full of the tepid, blended whisky, neither of them drank. It was hot and the air was without movement. They forgot the liquor and became lost in talk; which went down mines, up mountains, and from the California shore to the Ob River half a world away. Their words swung them through all sorts of places and seasons; from winter through summer and fall and back to winter again. Meanwhile, the sun stayed in place above them and the hours without time went by.

". . . A knife like that with a deer-antler handle," Dave heard himself saying at one moment. "I had a knife like that, and lost it commercial fishing—handlining sharks at the mouth of the Tampico River down in Mexico."

"Sharkskin soon spoils any knife edge," said Ranald. "Sponge-dredging off the Libya coast . . ."

Unremarked, alone, Maybeth crept quietly back to join them, sitting down back a little from the fire and listening. She nodded after a while, lay down with her head just on a corner of the foot of Dave's sleeping bag, and fell asleep.

Later, yet, Rob came back by himself. He glanced at the sleeping Maybeth without smiling and then lay down on the pile of blankets he and Letty had occupied the night before. Shortly, he began a light, easy snoring.

It was some hours later that Letty returned with Tom Rathkenny. The former deputy now wore only shirt, motorcycle breeches, and boots, and the shirt was open at the neck. While the shadow of beard on Dave's lean face stood out darkly in the sunlight, Tom's blond features looked as clean-shaven as they had the night before. Letty took one of the thin blankets not pinned to the earth by the weight of Rob's sleeping body and, with Tom helping, set it up on two sticks as a sloping sunshade to keep the eternal noontide glare out of their eyes. In the shadow of this, they both also lay down and slept.

Similar things were happening all about the pasture. People were yielding everywhere to the weariness of the unchanging noon day. Like wilting flowers, they were returning back to the earth beneath them and falling into deep, unmoving slumber. The sound of the voices of those left awake slowed, diminished, and fell silent at last; and that same silence crept in the end even between Dave and Ranald.

"Me, too," said Dave, at last looking around at the pasture full of unconscious figures. "Whatever comes next, for now there's got to be some time to rest." He glanced back at Ranald. "How about you?"

"Soon," said Ranald.

Dave picked up his untouched cup and poured the liquor in it back into the bottle without spilling a drop. Ranald picked up the cup from which he himself had not drunk and began to pour its contents back as well.

"You don't have to do that," said Dave. "Keep the bottle with you."

"Later," said Ranald. "Now's no drinking time."

"Maybe right," Dave answered. He turned, saw the head of Maybeth on the corner of his sleeping bag and carefully stretched himself out on it without disturbing the girl. He put his hand up to his face to shield his eyes from the sunlight. "Talk to you later, then."

"Yes," said Ranald.

Ranald closed his eyes. Smoke-thin across the inner lids, misty and unsubstantial, drifted the vision of home that had been so clear to him before. The heat of the sunlight beat on his closed eyes like the silent shout of a god demanding to be heard. He dozed.

—And woke, with animal instinct, a second before her hand touched him. Maybeth had crept close until she was seated just beside him and her fingers were inches from the fingers of his right hand. At the sight of him, awake, she drew back and looked down away from his pale-blue gaze.

"I'm sorry . . ." she whispered.

"There's no magic in me," said Ranald. "Touch me if you like, but nothing will change."

Her head bent lower on her neck until she looked only at the earth.

"Why won't you like me?" she said, barely above her earlier whisper.

"There's no magic in that, either," said Ranald. "In time, even love and hate wear out. Not all the way out . . . each new season a little comes back again. But near out. Your god has spoken above you. Turn to him for magic."

She lifted her face to him at that.

"But He's your God, too," she said. "Now that He's proved Himself. Isn't He?"

"No god have I," said Ranald.

"But He's stopped the sun at noon. He's stopped the Earth."

"Yes," said Ranald. "But I neither thank nor curse him for it. It's long since I hardly remember giving up praying at every sound of thunder, or touch of the dry, hot wind that threatens drought. Gods may stop Earths and suns, but none of them can give me back my home again, or make me what I was—and it's I, not he or any other, that keeps me going on, and on, from season to season, when I see no sense in it any longer. I do that to myself, against myself, and don't know why. But no god has any hand in it."

She sat, staring at him.

"You aren't afraid—" she began.

But at that moment Walt Strauben came back to them. He was flushed and panting, barefoot now and stripped to the waist, the hair on his head and the rolls of fat on his chest and belly grayed and darkened with what looked like dirt. Trickles of sweat had cut streaks of meandering cleanliness down his upper body. In his right hand he carried a cardboard sign nailed to the neck of a cross made of two pieces of lath; and on the sign in

grocer's crayon was written "RENDER UNTO CAESAR . . ."
In his left hand he carried a newspaper which he threw
down between Ranald and Maybeth as he collapsed,
panting, into a sitting position on the ground beside them.

"Look—" he gasped.

They looked. Two words filled the upper half of the
front page of the paper—SUN EVERYWHERE. Below that
headline, the page was black with type with no pictures
showing.

"Everywhere!" said Walt. "The sun's at noon everywhere around the world. Every place there were people
gathered together, they saw the Messenger, just the way
we did here. The sun's stopped at noon all over the
Earth."

"Everywhere?" asked Dave. He had woken up and
now lay propped on one elbow, watching them. "Don't
make sense. Earth's round, isn't it? Has to be dark on one
side."

"Can you ask a question like that after what you've
seen happen here?" Walt turned on him. "If it's true here,
why not everywhere? Why not anything? Why not?"

"Have to show me something more than a newspaper,"
said Dave. He shut his eyes and lay down again.

"There'll be some lacking enough faith—even now,"
said Walt, turning back to Ranald and Maybeth. "But
read the paper. Read it. A few people stayed with their
jobs to make sure it was printed; and because of that we
know that God has indeed touched this Earth with a Sign
of His power. Not just for our few numbers here in this
meadow—but for everyone, everywhere."

He reached out clumsily to the edge of the dead fire
and scraped up a handful of ashes, which he added to
what was already thickening his disordered hair.

"Glory, glory!" A good share of the ashes he had scraped up had clung to the palm of his sweaty hand instead of falling on his head. He wiped the hand clumsily on the hard ground beside him. "I'm my God's man now, truly, at last!"

He met Ranald's eyes directly for the first time, with a glint of defiance.

"This was all it took, this news about the sun everywhere," he said, "it cleared up my last shred of doubt."

Ranald looked back at him without answering.

"But not people like Dave! Not you—" Walt's voice rose. "You don't believe in Him, do you? Even now, you don't believe He exists!"

"I believe," said Ranald.

"It's a lie! You—"

"It's not a lie," said Maybeth, out of nowhere. "Of course he believes. It's just that he doesn't have to be jolted, or shook up, or frightened, like we do. He just takes God for granted."

"Sin—sin! Blasphemy!" shouted Walt, pounding the butt end of his sign's post on the ground. "To take God for granted—"

"Walt," said Ranald.

Walt looked defiantly back at him; and this time Ranald caught and held the other man's eyes with his own.

"Walt," he said, "look around. All these people here are tired. So are you. You need sleep. Sleep now."

He held Walt's eyes unmovingly with his own.

"I . . ." Walt began, and broke off as his mouth, opened to speak, opened wider and wider into an enormous yawn. "I said . . . I . . ."

His eyelids fluttered and closed. He leaned sideways to the ground and half curled up there, hugging his sign to him. Within five breaths he was inhaling and exhaling deeply in slumber.

"We need sleep, too," said Ranald.

He lay down and closed his eyes once more against the sunlight. He heard Maybeth lie down near him; and a second later he felt the touch of her hand creeping into his.

"If you don't mind," he heard her murmur, "I'll hold on, anyway."

This time Ranald fell into full sleep.

He woke, briefly and instinctively, some time later. His body had felt a sudden cutting off of the sun's heat, and he opened his eyes to look up into a night sky full of stars. Once again, from the woods and the river he heard bird and water sounds, and the whisper of a breeze. He went back to sleep.

The next day found the people in the meadow more normal after their night's sleep, but still under the influence of the timeless noontide that had held them awake to the point of exhaustion. They were like people who had been stunned, and were now conscious again, but unsure of themselves, as if at any moment dizziness might make the ground rock beneath their feet. In the meadow, this unsureness showed itself in the reluctance of those there to leave their encampment and go back to whatever place it was from which they had come.

—And there were other aftereffects.

Walt was not the only one with something like ashes in his hair and a sign or cross or other symbol in hand. There were a number like him; and they were mostly busy speaking either to small groups in near-privacy, or from stumps or boxes to any who would listen. Many listened, others had withdrawn into meditation or trance, ignoring

the noise around them. There were those who sang and
prayed together; and those who sang and prayed alone.
There were those in the store trucks parked along the
roadway who had given away all their goods, and those
like the driver-owner from whom Dave had bought drink
the day before, who still sat numb with drink or drugs in
their vehicles and indifferent to anyone who wanted to
help himself to what was there.

Letty and Tom Rathkenny had gone off once more by
themselves early. Walt, still holding his sign and smeared
with the dirt of ashes, was wildly preaching to a group
farther down the meadow. Rob, either high on something
obtained from one of the trucks or self-hypnotized into a
near-trance state, was engaged in a meditative process,
seated cross-legged on the ground by himself, staring at
the few grass blades upon the trodden earth between his
knees.

"This is too much holy for me," said Dave finally, when
a natural noon sun had passed its high point in the sky.
He looked around the meadow and back at Ranald and
Maybeth. "Far as I'm concerned, a hallelujah or two in
the morning ought to take care of it, and then a man
could get down to other things. I'm going to walk off a
piece. How about you two?"

Ranald got to his feet and Maybeth followed. The three
of them wove their way through the crowd downslope,
into the trees and away through the trees, skirting the
soggier spots until they came to a firm bank opening between trees on the clear-running water of the river. It was
a middle-sized stream, perhaps two hundred feet across at
this point, and shallow with midsummer dryness so that
the pebble shoals could be seen under the clear water
reaching out for some distance from the bank. They came

to a halt there and stood watching the running water. Insects buzzed by their ears; and now and then a bird call sounded not far from them. It was cooler here, down by the river and under the thick-leaved branches.

"Never stops running, does it?" said Dave, after a while. "Somewhere, always, there's water running downhill to the sea."

"I think it may have stopped yesterday," said Ranald. "When everything else was stopped, too. I didn't hear it."

"Held up a bit was all, probably," said Dave. There was almost a loving note in his voice as he spoke about the moving river. He bent, picked up a pebble and threw it far out to midstream. The pebble made a single neat hole in the water, going in, and then there was no sign it had ever fallen. "Stopped for good is dead. Like with that shark-fishing, down in Mexico. *Finito*, and you're through for the day; *acabo*, and the sharks got you. This river just got finitoed along with everything else, for a little while. That was all."

"You're not afraid of things, either of you, are you?" said Maybeth, unexpectedly. "I've always been afraid. I tried to pretend I wasn't for sixteen years, and then, when I got away from home, I didn't have to pretend any more and I faced it."

"If you faced it, what's the difference?" said Dave. "I can get scared like anybody."

He looked over at Ranald. But Ranald shook his head.

"Not often for me, any more," he said. "I was telling her—things wear out. Love, hate . . . also fear."

"You don't understand, either of you," said Maybeth. "I'm always afraid. Of everything. It's a terrible feeling. I keep hunting for something to stop it. I thought this would, but it didn't. Even stopping the sun didn't do it.

I'm just as afraid as ever. What if there is a God? He doesn't really care about me."

"Nobody used to expect gods to care without reason," said Ranald. "It's only the last few hundred years—" He stopped speaking rather abruptly. Something or someone was crashing through the underbrush in their direction. Ranald stepped forward to the riverbank, bent down and picked up a handful of sandy soil. As he straightened up, Tom Rathkenny, carrying a revolver, burst through the leaves of the brush behind them to join them.

"What'd you do with her?" the young deputy sheriff shouted, pointing the revolver at them. "Where'd you—"

At this point, he saw the handful of sand, which Ranald had already flung, coming at him through the air like a swarm of midges. The flung soil fell well short, but Tom ducked instinctively and the revolver went off, pointing at the sky.

Before he could pull its muzzle and his gaze back to earth again, Ranald had reached him—running very quickly but effortlessly with what looked like abnormally long strides—and as Tom tried once more to aim the revolver, Ranald hit him. It was a blow with clenched fist, but as odd in its way as Ranald's method of running. The fist came up backhand from the region of Ranald's belt level in a sweep to the side of the other man's jaw. It snapped Tom's head around sideways; and he took a step backward, fell, and lay apparently unconscious. Dave, who had come up meanwhile, reached down and picked up the revolver.

"What got into him?" asked Dave. He squatted down comfortably on his heels beside Tom, holding the gun loosely on one knee with his right hand and waiting for Tom to come to.

"Letty," said Maybeth. "Maybe he thought she was with you instead of me."

Tom opened his eyes, blinked stupidly at them all, and tried to sit up, reaching for the revolver. Dave pushed him back to the ground.

"Can't go shooting around like that," Dave said. "Lay there for a minute and cool off. Then maybe you can tell us what got you worked up."

"She isn't here?" Tom said. "Letty isn't?"

"Last I saw of her she was with you," Dave said.

Tom let himself go limp. His head rolled back on his neck so that he stared bitterly at the sky. He lay for a moment.

"She went off," he said, then. "She expects me to read her mind. For God's sake, I don't know what she's thinking!"

Dave, Ranald, and Maybeth watched him.

"She got mad," Tom said to the sky. "She wants me to change; but she's got all these crazy ideas of what I am. And I'm not. How can I change from something I'm not? How can I tell what she's thinking when she doesn't tell me?"

He waited, as if for an answer. None of them offered any.

"Guess you can get up," said Dave, getting to his own feet. Tom scrambled upright. His eyes went to his gun, now tucked into the belt of Dave's Levi's.

"That's mine," he said hoarsely. "Give it back."

"Guess I will," said Dave, "when I figure you can be trusted with it again."

"That's stealing," said Tom. "I could arrest you for that."

"You still a sheriff's man?" Dave said. "You don't look

it much, right now. Anyway, how do you know there's
still a sheriff?"

He stood. Tom leaned forward a little as if he might try
to take the revolver back, but kept his arms down. He
turned, suddenly, and plowed off into the brush.

"We'll just hold on to this for now," said Dave, patting
the revolver butt fondly. "He'll be all right once he gets
his head clear. How if we move on down the river?"

He turned and led the way along the bank, downstream. Ranald and Maybeth went with him.

"She's like you two," said Maybeth, a little bleakly as
they went. "She's not afraid of anything. That's why it always happens to people like her."

But as they moved on beside the river, her mood im-
proved. Some time later, the two men even heard her
humming almost inaudibly to herself. They followed the
curving stream until the bank began to rise and they
found themselves at last on what was actually a small
bluff, looking through a screen of birch and maple trees
down a vertical drop of perhaps eighty feet to a small
open area like a valley. There a road emerged on the right
below the bluff to run straight ahead, until the trees of a
wooded slope to its right seemed to move in and swallow
it up in the distance; and the river emerged on the left to
run right beside the road with only a small strip of bank
between them.

"That'll be the farther part of the road from back
where we're camped," Dave said. "This way must be the
way to Medford. Let's go back. Thought I saw a pool up a
ways with some fish in it."

They went back the way they had come for perhaps an
eighth of a mile to the pool Dave had seen. He produced
a fishing handline and hooks from a leather folder in his

right hip pocket and discovered some earthworms under a log. He turned the line and worms over to Ranald and went to build one of his reflexive fires. By the time he had it going and burned down to a useful set of coals, Ranald had, in fact, caught four middling-sized brook trout.

"Let me do that," said Maybeth, when the fish were cleaned and spitted on twigs over the coals.

There was actually nothing more for her to do but watch the fish and turn them occasionally. But she sat keeping an intent watch on them and the two men heard her humming once more to herself.

When the fish were done, they ate the flaky, delicate flesh with their fingers, using some salt Dave produced in a fold of wax paper from the same leather folder that had contained, and now contained again, the fishline and hooks. The four trout made next to nothing of a lunch for three people, but by this time the day had heated up to noon temperature and none of them were very hungry. After eating, they put the fire to rest with river water and walked back upstream.

It was quite warm. Maybeth took off the sweater Walt had lent her and carried it. Dave took off his jacket, folded it, and tucked it under the belt of his Levi's, in back. Only Ranald stayed dressed as he was, indifferent to the temperature.

They passed the spot where they had first come upon the riverbank and Tom had burst out on them with his revolver. They went on up the river's edge, detouring only here and there when some small bay or close stand of brush barred the direct route. Returning from one of these small detours, they heard ahead, through a stand of young oak and elm trees, a sound of voices in relaxed and comfortable argument.

"That's Rob and her, now," said Maybeth.

They came up through the stand of young trees and looked out on a wide, shallow stretch of the river. Letty and Rob were there in the water, naked in the sunlight. Rob was seated on a fallen log that had its upper edge barely out of the river's surface; and Letty, standing behind him, was washing his hair. Up to her knees in water, she worked her fingers industriously and had succeeded in raising a good lather. The sun gleamed on her pale, compact back and firm buttocks; and wads of lather dripped from Rob's narrow and bent, but sinewy, shoulders to float off like foam flecks on the current downstream.

". . . that's your trouble," Rob was saying, "you always want to run things."

"Like hell I do," she answered.

"The hell you don't."

"The hell I do—sit still, you son of a bitch," said Letty. "Anyway, hold your head still."

"This log . . ." said Rob, shifting his weight uncomfortably.

Dave laughed softly.

"Just as well I kept that Tom's gun," he said, low-voiced. He turned away. They went off from there without any further words.

"I think I'll go back," said Maybeth unexpectedly, when they were once more out of sound of the voices from the two in the river. She was not humming now, and her face had gone back to its old expression. She turned, and stopped. "Which way is it?"

Ranald pointed through the woods.

"Just keep the sun at your back," said Dave. "If you

don't hit the meadow, you'll run into the road. If it's the road, turn left and the meadow'll be down a ways, only."

She left.

"Well, now," said Dave, looking after her. "And I was just about figuring she'd come out of it."

"Nothing changes," said Ranald. "As I said."

Dave glanced at him.

"You really hold to that," Dave said.

"I'd like to believe it's not so," said Ranald. "But it's what I've learned. All that's left to know is why I go on, knowing it, getting a new start each time spring turns to summer, summer to fall—to winter—to spring again."

"Go on because you're wrong," said Dave. They were walking on together, once more, following the riverbank upstream. He pointed to the moving water. "See there? Riverbed's changing all the time. No spring's like any other spring. No two trees alike. That tree there"—he pointed to a young birch—"there never was one like it before. After it's grown big and died and fallen, never be another like it. There never was another like it, from the beginning of the world until now. Same with people. Anyone, he dies, no one just like him's ever going to come again."

"What profit in that?" Ranald said, "—if all he does is what men have always done—no more, no less. What gain is there in his special differences if he comes from nowhere just to walk the same treadmill in one spot before going back into nowhere again?"

"Why bother to argue it with me if you think that's so?" said Dave. "If you're so sure of it and we're just saying what's been argued all out, time and again, before?"

"Because I wish you were right and I was wrong. Still," said Ranald, "that's the one thing I can't understand.

Why I go on, why I still hope.—Also, you aren't like most men, brother."

"That's a kind word," said Dave. "Well, listen to my side of it, then. You're wrong thinking people never get nowhere. We've come a long ways. Apes once, wasn't we?"

"Or something like that. What of it?" said Ranald. "As apes we walked in the woods like this and the sun made us hot, like this. Where are you and I different, now? What difference Rob and Letty, naked in the river? They were naked there as apes, also."

"Not washing hair."

"Grooming each other. As apes and monkeys do, today."

Dave laughed.

"Might be right about that," he said. "But even if you're winning the argument, you're still not changing my mind. I still feel you're wrong—know you're wrong."

"You have your god," said Ranald. "That may be the difference."

"Have Him?" Dave said. "I believe He's there, sure enough. I can't hardly say no to that after seeing the sun stopped over my head the way it was. But *have* God? No more than I ever had when He was just a chain around my ankle."

"He'll be a chain around your ankle again," said Ranald. "Nothing changes."

"What it is I believe in, that says you're wrong," said Dave, "that's not God or religion. That's what I got from what I've seen—everything I seen all my life long. I tell you a tree lives and dies and there never was nothing like it before, nor can't anything ever be like it again—nor it don't make sense things ever be the same after it's once lived and died. Trees, everything's that way. People can't be any different—and they're not. I know it by feel, inside me."

"I felt like that once—now only my foolish self goes on acting as if I did," said Ranald. "*'Render therefore unto Caesar the things which are Caesar's.'* That's the verse Walt's taken for his text. *'—and unto God the things that are God's.'* Meaning that when all the dues of the world are paid, faith remains. But what if one pays all dues and then finds no faith, nothing left over?"

They walked on a little way without talking, their feet finding level and uncluttered space without conscious thought on either man's part.

"You told me you went through this once before," said Dave. "The sun stopped—"

"No," said Ranald. "That time it was a matter of darkness at midday. A hand held the light of the sun away from the Earth."

"Eclipse, maybe?" suggested Dave.

Ranald shook his head.

"A hand," he said. "We were made to know it. The sun was there, unmoving as it was this time. We could see it. But a hand held its light from reaching us and the other things of Earth. And so matters stayed for some time, for about as long as it happened in the meadow to you and me and the rest. But afterward, there was no difference. Just as there was no difference a little later after the gentlefolk had wept at chapel at hearing that Piers Plowman was closer to God than they. Soon afterward, no man or woman stayed changed."

"Everyone's been changed this time, far as I can see."

"At first. It seemed all those there were changed, too, that earlier time. But it was like in the chapel, for a small time only. Very soon after the hand was gone, any difference it had made was gone from those who had seen it."

"Maybe," said Dave. "Got to see it myself to believe it. Got to see it *in* myself, to believe it."

They went on a few more miles up the river, then turned and came back to the meadow in the midafternoon. Maybeth was not by the dead ashes of their campfire, nor Letty, Rob, or Tom. But Walt was there, no longer preaching, sitting on his sleeping bag, still dirty and shirtless with his sign face down on the ground by him. Newspapers were spread around him; and he pushed front pages from these into the hands of Dave and Ranald as they came up.

"Read!" he said. "The counterattack of those who hate God. The lies of the atheists."

Headlines on the sheet in Ranald's hand took up nearly half the available white space there.

ACT OF GOD
OR
ACT OF NATURE?

The paper Dave had been given had smaller headlines.

MIRACLE MAY BE AN ILLUSION

"Not all," said Walt, "could testify to the truth. There had to be those few who had to try to tear it down." He waved his hand at the snowdrift of other newspapers scattered around him. "All these other papers are honest, reporting the new era as it is." His voice trembled a little. "But among the sheep there have to be a few goats—a few wolves, wolves would be a better name for them; and they're tearing at the truth, trying to tear it down. Pity them, as I do. Pity them!"

"Says here," said Dave, bending his head over the newssheet he held, "the whole thing could have been the result of massive autohypnosis. Guess not. I don't hypnotize well. Man tried it once on me some years back, then said I kept fighting him. I wasn't fighting; just sitting there waiting to see what it felt like. He said that was the same thing as fighting."

Ranald was reading below the headlines on the page in his hand. . . .

"We owe at least this much to nearly three millennia of scientific thought and work," Nobel Prize winner Nils Hjemstrand said today, *"not to throw out all possibility of a natural explanation for this apparent miracle before a thorough investigation is made by competent physicists, astronomers, and students of any other scientific disciplines which might have been involved in what seemed to happen. . . ."*

"Their investigation won't work," said Walt, looking up at Ranald's face. "They'll learn that."

Ranald handed the paper back down to him and looked over at Dave.

"Tomorrow you'll begin to see it for yourself," he said to Dave. "It'll begin."

"Fools," muttered Walt, staring down at the paper Ranald had just given back to him, "doubting fools, clinging to a superstition called science. . . ."

That night Maybeth rejoined them, and the praying and the singing of religious songs was louder in the meadow than it had ever been. But at dawn there were gaps among the line of store trucks parked along the road and the number of campers in the meadow was noticeably less. During the morning, Walt washed himself, put on a clean shirt, and gathered an audience around him. Standing on a wooden egg crate, he lectured his listeners earnestly on the chance, now, to form a new society, a new world. Maybeth stood in the audience with Walt's other listeners for perhaps an hour, then she left and came back to the campsite where Dave and Ranald, Rob and Letty were turning a loaf of bread and two cans of corned beef into lunch.

She sat down, but made no move to reach for the bread and meat. Her shoulders were curved and she stared down at the gray-black ashes where the fire of last night had glowed.

"Walt's right," she said, without looking at any one of them in particular. "It shouldn't be lost, what we all know happened here. The people who went through it ought to get together and change things."

"Not his way," said Rob. "People tried it his way for hundreds of years—and look what it led to. He just wants to set up more of the same. But that won't work— anymore."

Maybeth looked at him as if she would argue, then gazed back at the ashes without saying anything.

"You don't believe me?" Rob got to his feet. "I'll prove it to you—it's not going to work."

He went off toward the road and the store trucks. Letty started to rise and follow him, then sat back down again. She looked for a moment hard at Maybeth, but Maybeth was still staring at the fire's dead ashes.

It was over an hour before Rob returned; but when he came he brought with him almost as many newspapers as Walt had surrounded himself with the day before. They were a new day's editions, and he dumped them on the ground before the seated Maybeth.

"Read those," he said. "Half of them, anyway, have already switched over. Half of them don't believe any more it was a miracle. They're full of articles by scientists saying how it could have happened without anything supernatural about it."

"But there was!" Maybeth said. "Don't you remember? It wasn't just the sun stopping, it was what we all felt. Remember? We all *knew* it was God doing it, then."

"What if we did? What if it was?" Rob said. "What matters isn't what happened, but what people are going to think happened, a year from now."

"Oh, no!" said Maybeth.

"Oh, yes," he said. "You damn right, yes. That's how things happen. You just have to face it."

She looked hopefully at Dave and Ranald. Dave, however, was occupied in using a wire pad to clean fire-black from the bottom of his soup pan, and did not even see the glance she gave him. Ranald met her eyes in open, unresponsive silence.

She looked down again at the headlines on the newspapers before her.

"I'm no good arguing," she said. "Walt'll answer you. Why don't you try to make him believe it's going like that?"

"That's what I'm sitting around here waiting for," said Rob, the yellow glints showing in his eyes. "Just that."

It was early afternoon before Walt gave up his efforts long enough to come back to the place where the rest of them were, to make himself a sandwich and a cup of coffee. All the others, though they had strayed some little distance away from time to time since Rob and Maybeth had talked, came drifting back to their common campsite when Walt sat down with his coffee cup and a pressed-ham sandwich.

He ate and drank hungrily, saying nothing. Rob spoke to him.

"It's not working, is it?" Rob said.

Walt looked at him and bit into the sandwich without answering.

"It isn't, is it?" said Rob. "I mean, you talking to them. It's not doing any good, not keeping them from changing their minds?"

Walt swallowed the last of his sandwich. His back was bent as Maybeth's shoulders had been bent, earlier.

"Forgive me," he said. "I'm all talked out for the moment."

"Are you? Are you?" Rob, who had been sitting down, got to his knees and walked several steps on his knees clumsily to bring himself right in front of Walt and only half a body's length away. "You sure it's not just you don't want to discuss it—I mean, really discuss it, not just stand up there and shout while people pretend to listen?"

"I think," said Walt, holding his voice very even, "some at least were listening."

"The ones who want to be brainwashed, you mean?" Rob said. "Look around, for Christ's sake. This place hasn't got half the people it had yesterday, or when it happened."

"Then you admit it happened," said Walt heavily.

"Happened? Happened? It happened, all right," said Rob, leaning forward. "But what's 'happened' mean? According to you it's supposed to mean something great, is that it? Well, it doesn't. *Nothing*—that's what it means!"

"You don't believe in God," said Walt. "That's what makes you talk this way."

"Believe? I don't not-believe and I don't believe. I don't give a damn one way or another. Because it doesn't *matter*—don't you understand? Haven't you seen these latest papers?"

"I looked," said Walt, not looking at them. "There's nothing new there. A few dissenters—"

"Not a few," said Rob. "A lot. Half of them, at least. And even the ones who're still shouting miracle are starting to tone down and go cautious on it—keeping an open mind, that's how they put it. But toning down, all the same!"

"I repeat," said Walt, slowly and deliberately, "you don't believe in God. If you believed in Him, then what you saw here would have been a revelation for you, too."

"Revelation!" Rob laughed. "Do you know what it was to me? You never saw anything like the sun stand still in the sky before. That was really something for you, wasn't it? And so you think it had to be really something for everybody else, too. Well," Rob leaned even closer, "I'm telling you now, it wasn't; no matter what people like you want to make out of it. I'll tell you what it was. An experience—that's all. A trip, man! And you never had one before, so you thought it was something to turn everybody in the world inside out."

Walt shook his head and turned to face away from Rob. Rob scrambled around on his knees to keep them nose to nose.

"You think that's the first time I saw something like the sun standing still?" Rob demanded. "I've seen lots of things—things you couldn't even dream up; and not just from being high, either. A trip, that's all it was; and there's all kinds of trips. I don't care where this one came from. It was a trip, that's all. Just that and nothing else."

"The two things," said Walt, staring at him now, "don't compare in any way. What you're talking about is subjective. What we all saw here was objective."

"All right, call it objective. You think that makes any difference? God exists and He made the sun stand still," said Rob. "You think that impresses me with Him? If He wanted to get to me, why didn't He feed a million people that are starving right now in the world? Now, that's something I've never seen done. Why didn't He clean all the smog out of the air everywhere and make it that there couldn't be any more? Why didn't He stop the wars and the killing and heal everybody in the hospitals and out of the hospitals who're sick or hurt?"

"These are our own sins," said Walt, heavily. "We have to cure them ourselves."

"But we're already curing them, old man." Rob sat back on his heels. "We. Us.—Not you. We're already not making smog, or polluting, or killing people. It's people like you who keep on doing that, talking one thing and doing another. You and your '*Render unto Caesar*—' How'd you like your own quotations to turn around and bite you? What was it Jesus was supposed to say when they came to ask him that question about what was Caesar's and what was God's? '. . . *Why tempt ye me, ye hypocrites?*' Wasn't that it? Who do you suppose the hypocrites are now, with this miracle business—Us? Or you people?"

Walt jerked the last coffee in his cup out onto the dead ashes, staining the gray dust black. He put the empty cup in his packsack and got to his feet.

"You're twisting things," he said, "and you know it.

You're doing it quite deliberately. I think you know you're not being fair or honest."

He walked away. From the other side of the campfire ashes, Letty looked at Rob.

"You stink, every so often," she said. "You know that?"

Rob did not look back at her. He had picked up a small stick and was digging one sharp end of it furiously into the ground before him, watching the dirt break and move.

"Shut up," he said. "Will you just for once shut up?"

That night, though at least half of the original crowd had gone, the singing and praying in the meadow was as loud as it had been the night before. If anything, the prayers were more sonorous and the songs more shouted. There were also more intoxicants in evidence. Several times during the early evening, when all the campfires were alight, fights broke out and there were men and women to be seen staggering about, or lying sprawled and thickly breathing in unlikely or inconvenient places.

The late editions of the newspapers, when they reached the meadow, contained many stories that backed off even farther from putting the name of miracle to what had happened. Now, less than a third of the press took for granted that a Sign of some kind had been given to the people of the Earth. And there were news stories in opposition to the idea of miracle that used words like "gullible" and "frenzied" in their descriptions of those who might still be wholeheartedly believing.

Meanwhile, as the evening grew, Dave had been sitting by the evening fire, seeming to become bonier of jaw and more bleak of eye as the noise and activities in the meadow increased. Now, a few hours after full dark, he rose suddenly and disappeared into blackness in the direc-

tion of the woods lower down. This time Ranald did not
go after him. Instead, he stayed by the fire with Maybeth,
who was the only other person still there. When Dave left
she moved closer to Ranald, who sat cross-legged now, in
the midst of the meadowful of noisy people, with the light
of the flames playing yellow variations on the rusty colors
of his beard, like a magician surrounded by the demons
and other dark figures of his conjurations.

"This is going to be the last night here, isn't it?" she
asked him.

He did not answer.

"You know," she said, after a little while, "I think I really have been changed."

His face lifted then, and he turned his head to look at
her. His gaze was completely unblinking and the firelight
reflected from his eyes as if they had themselves caught
fire. She had never faced such a brilliant and piercing
look in her life; and after a second she looked away from
him, down at the ground.

"Never mind," he said. "You meant well. But after
these many years I've learned the ways people look when
they lie."

"I—" She had intended to speak out loud, but her
throat hurt so from tears she did not dare let loose, that
her voice could only come out in a whisper. "—just
wanted to give you something."

"I know," he said. "And you have, as much as anyone
can. But no one person's changing can be an answer to
my trouble. The answer I need has to be one that fits everybody. If I can know why I want to go on living, then
I'll know why the whole race wants to keep on living
when it rejects all gods and keeps trying the impossible as
if it were possible."

"But maybe it *isn't* impossible," she said. "Maybe it's possible and you just can't see it."

"I?" he asked; and the single questioning syllable tore to dust rags the fine fabric of the argument she was forming in her mind. Without an argument and without hope, she went on talking, anyway.

"It could be because you're different," she said. "After all, you're immortal."

"No," he answered. "I've only lived a long—a very long time. And that's the problem of it. I'm mortal, all men and women are mortal, the human race is mortal. That's why it makes no sense. An immortal would want to keep the eternal life he had. But people are like climbers on a cliff too high even to imagine. Each knows he can struggle up only a little distance before he dies and drops off and another climber takes his place.—Still, when a god comes winging close like some great bird, ready to carry at least some of them toward the top, they reject him—turn their heads away and insist they're alone on the cliff."

"But, as you say," she said, "you've lived so long. Maybe it looks different to you from how it really is for the rest of us."

"No, it doesn't look different," he said, staring at the flames, "and I'm no different. I turn my back on gods, just like the rest. I want to climb, too."

"Instinct," she said.

He shook his head.

"Instinct's to find a safe notch in the cliff face and stay there. To climb goes against that."

"Maybe, then," she said, "that's what they mean by 'soul.'"

"A soul is a god-thing," he replied. "A soul would reach for the god who comes swooping by just like the instinct-part would try to find a safe spot and live there without pain and effort. But in spite of soul and instinct, the climbing goes on."

He rocked a little on his hips. It was the first physical sign of emotion she had ever seen in him.

"And still I keep going on," he said. "And on. And on."

Two dark figures broke from the clutter of the crowd in the darkness downslope and came running toward their fire, a larger shape chasing a smaller. As they broke into the firelight the pursuer grabbed for the smaller figure, which dodged with the easy smoothness of much faster reflexes and cut around the fire to stand behind Ranald and Maybeth. Panting on the other side of the fire, the pursuer showed himself to be Tom Rathkenny.

"Yellow—" he gasped. "Why don't you stand still? You, doing all that talking about not being afraid of anything—anybody."

"Who's—afraid?" said the voice of Rob, behind Ranald and Maybeth. "You just want me to give you all the advantages. If I weighed forty more pounds, I'd stand still. So, I don't. So, let's see you catch up with me."

"I'll kill you," panted Tom.

"Sure—you will." Rob was getting to be breathing almost normally. "That's all you can do. You can't win the argument, so you'll kill me. You can't catch me, so you'll kill me. Sure, pig, come kill me!"

"Yug—" It was a sound without words. Tom started straight ahead through the fire at the two seated people and in the direction of Rob's voice.

Ranald got to his feet without touching his hands to the ground, so suddenly that his appearance in Tom's path was almost like a stage trick.

Tom checked, the flames licking about his boot tops.

The heavy-boned young man swayed on his feet for a second like an animal caught in a trap. Then he turned and plunged off down the slope into the darkness and the crowd. From behind Ranald and Maybeth came a long, slightly shuddering outbreath.

"Woo," said Rob, gustily. He came around and dropped down at the fire in a sitting position facing them. Ranald reseated himself.

"I'm not afraid of him," said Rob, in a calm voice. "Not afraid of him at all. That's something somebody like him can't understand. I'm not afraid of"—he glanced at Ranald, then hesitated slightly and looked back at the fire—"hardly anything."

"You shouldn't drive him crazy like that, anyway," said Maybeth.

Rob looked at her.

"Well," he said. "The great silent one speaks."

"I'm just telling you," said Maybeth. "It's dangerous to get anybody—anybody, even—that mad at you. If people get mad enough they don't care what they do." He grinned and she turned to Ranald. "You tell him."

Ranald looked at her and at Rob, but said nothing.

"Please," she said. "Tell him. He'll believe you.—And shouldn't someone tell him?"

Ranald looked directly at Rob.

"He'll kill you," Ranald said.

"Kill me?" said Rob; but, eye to eye with Ranald, he did not grin. "Maybe he might even try it, at that. But he'd have to catch me first."

"I did not say what he might do," said Ranald. "I said what he will do."

Rob stared at him. Face to face across the fire, both short and wiry, silky beard and high white forehead facing full beard and brown skin faintly wrinkled about the eyes, the flames made them look for a moment like older and younger brothers. Then Rob jerked his head aside and scrambled to his feet.

"No," he said, "you don't—"

He broke off. Letty was coming upslope into the firelight to join them. She stopped in front of Rob.

"I got him to promise to stay away from you," Letty said, flatly. "And you're going to stay right here the rest of the night. I promised him that."

"You, too?" said Rob. "Oh, Mama!"

He sat down again with a thump, as if all his muscles had given way at once. Letty knelt beside him and put an arm around his shoulders.

"You can't help being a bastard," she said tenderly. "I know you can't. But he's a straight. He doesn't understand; and he could hurt you."

"Mama, Mama," said Rob. "No—*Aunt* Letty." He looked across the fire. "Mama Maybeth. Daddy Ranald."

"Will you stop it?" said Letty. She put her other arm around him and tried to pull him over backwards. After a second he gave in and they both fell back on the ground intertwined. The firelight played on the soles of their boots, but the upper parts of their bodies were in shadow. Rob laughed and muttered unintelligibly.

"Who cares?" said Letty, indifferently.

Maybeth looked sideways at Ranald. But Ranald's gaze went through and beyond the two on the other side of the fire as indifferently as if they had been half-sketched figures in some old drawing that familiarity had made practically invisible.

His face had shown little but calmness in the time she had known him; and there were no explicit lines of emotion on it now. But a shadow of sadness seemed to have appeared like a visor over his eyes; and he stared off into the distance at nothing, or at least nothing she could see. Timidly she rested a hand on his arm; but he neither moved nor spoke to her. It was like touching a carving in wood.

The fire burned down to red coals and Dave did not return. But close to midnight, Walt came heavily back to join them and dropped into a sitting position on his sleeping bag. After a minute, he reached out for some of the thicker pieces of dead oak limbs Dave had collected in a neat pile nearby, and put them on the coals. Little flames licked up immediately, feeding on the loose bark but leaving the heavy center wood no more than darkened.

"How many did you convert tonight?" Rob asked, from across the fire.

Walt ignored him, staring at the pieces of oak branch with the little flames feeding with temporary ease on the rough bark.

"Didn't hear me?" said Rob, raising his voice. "I asked you—"

"I heard you," said Walt. He sagged, a roll of belly bulging his shirt out above his belt as he sat on the sleeping bag. He still did not look up; and his voice was hollowed by weariness. In the new light of the little flames, his eyes showed bloodshot.

"But you didn't answer me."

"If you don't mind," Walt said with great effort, still not looking up, "I'm not in much shape to talk, right now."

"Hey, that's too bad," said Rob.

Walt sat silent and unmoving.

"I said," said Rob, "that's too bad." He raised his voice again. "Too bad—I said."

"Why don't you quit talking?" said Letty.

"Yes, that's a shame," said Rob. "Shows how little real faith there is in people. God says one thing and the newspapers say another; so naturally, they take the word of the newspapers. Here, instead of the converted growing in numbers, they've been staying just the same.—Or maybe they've even been falling off the bandwagon. Is that right?"

He paused; but Walt still did not respond.

"Come to think of it, it seemed to me there were fewer people standing around listening to you and the rest preach tonight, than there were earlier today.—To say nothing of last night. The congregations've been getting smaller and smaller all along, here. In fact, haven't the people been peeling off until there wasn't anyone left for you to talk to at all?—Walt?"

Walt stirred. He did not look up from the pieces of oak limbs which were now beginning to catch fire in the true sense and to grow rows of little flames flickering and running along their undersides. But he shifted his weight on the sleeping bag and the ground on which the bag was lying.

"God is not mocked," he said.

"No, of course not," said Rob.

Maybeth, still seated beside Ranald, tugged a little at his arm.

"Ranald . . ." she whispered.

Ranald's full attention came back slowly, as if from a thousand miles and a thousand years, away. He looked at her, and around the fire at Walt, Rob, and Letty, and back to her again. Then he went away once more into distance and time.

Maybeth dropped her hand strengthlessly to her lap.

"God can't be mocked," Rob was saying, "because that wouldn't be right. Or do I mean 'righteous'? That's right, I mean righteous. It wouldn't be righteous for God to be mocked; the way He is here when people begin to decide they don't believe in Him even after His stunt with the sun—"

"They believed," said Walt in a near whisper, staring at the fire.

"Of course they believed," said Rob. "After all, it happened, didn't it? And they should have gone on believing. You ought to have made sure they go on believing. After all, that was your job, wasn't it?"

"Please," said Walt, staring at the fire. "If you don't mind . . ."

"But I mean that really hurts me, those people who listened to you acting like this," said Rob. "They should have gone off in every direction after hearing you, like a batch of disciples, to spread the faith. And here they do just the opposite. They back off from the faith themselves, dropping away one by one until you haven't got anyone there listening to you. How could that happen? How could you let it happen?"

Walt was no longer looking even at the fire. His head hung down now, so that he stared directly at the barren, heel-trampled earth between his thighs.

"Leave him alone," said Letty, getting to her feet. "Come on."

"No," said Rob, not looking around at her, watching and speaking only to Walt, "I can't let something like that happen without trying to understand it. Something that rotten can't happen without a reason, some big reason. I mean—something besides the newspapers must have been working on those people listening to you, to drive every one—every single one of them—away from you, like that."

Walt shuddered a little, but he still sat without answering, staring at the ground.

"Rob," said Letty.

"Be with you in a minute, Let," said Rob, not moving from the ground. "I just want to find out how anybody could have a hundred percent failure, like that. Even the law of averages ought to give one or two converts, shouldn't it? Here now, it's almost as if Walt had been preaching against their believing in the miracle, instead of for it. Hey, do you suppose a man actually could do something like that? I mean, subconsciously? Say one thing, but say it so the people listening realized he was really lying to them? Like, for example, he would be saying out loud to them, 'Abandon doubt, believe and enter the kingdom of heaven . . .' but at the same time the way he'd say it he'd actually be telling them that even if they thought they were positive about something, they had a duty to question themselves about it anyway.—As if he was telling them sort of behind his words that they really had to consider the chance they were wrong. As if they ought to try doubt on for size, just to make sure—"

Walt made a choking sound. Then another. It was suddenly clear that he was sobbing, crying where he sat, making no effort to move or wipe away the tears.

"After all," said Rob, raising his voice a little over the sounds Walt was making, "it's true enough.—I don't see how any thinking person can deny it. You've got a duty to keep an open mind, no matter how much faith you have. That's the only good way, the enlightened way—"

"LEAVE HIM ALONE!"

The fury of Letty's scream was incandescent. Like a sudden eruption of white light in darkness, it left them all momentarily numb and dazzled; and it silenced not only Rob, but everyone in the meadow for fifty yards in all directions. Having exploded, Letty said nothing more, but stood waiting until Rob, after a moment, scrambled to his feet. Then she turned and stalked away. He went after her.

Walt looked after them, then turned to Maybeth and Ranald with a face in which the lines seemed to have deepened like the eroded gullies in some dry desert riverbed.

"He's right," Walt said. "I preached doubt to them. I preached my own doubt, after all. From the second day— right after those newspapers began to doubt, I began to doubt again, too."

"You shouldn't care," said Maybeth. "You did it in spite of what you were thinking. That's harder than doing it with no doubts at all. Doing something in spite of yourself is the hardest thing there is."

He shook his head and went back to looking down at the earth. She looked bleakly at the ground, herself. It had been no use, like throwing a kiss to a starving man; but it was all she knew to say to him.

The noise dwindled in the meadow and at last, with the moon small and high overhead and the fires low, there was silence. It was then that Dave came back and found all of them asleep but Ranald, who was still sitting as he had been.

"Two bells, and all's well," said Dave, sitting down and

tossing one of the oak limbs on the once more nearly dead fire. A scent of whisky came across the fire with his words to Ranald. Just as in the woods, only a deliberateness about Dave's speech backed up the evidence reaching Ranald's nose.

"Party's over, I take it?" asked Dave.

Ranald stirred and came back, as he had briefly for Maybeth earlier, from the distance of his mind.

"Tomorrow everyone will go," Ranald said. His eyes went to the bottom pants leg covering that ankle of Dave's he had seen dark with scar and calluses.

"No," said Dave, following the direction of Ranald's gaze, "I didn't put it back on. Don't intend to, either; but I don't know as it makes any difference. Turned out the covenant between me and the Lord wasn't something you could put on and off like a chain, anyhow."

"So," said Ranald, almost to himself, "like the gentle-folk leaving chapel, like these around us here, there's to be no change for you either, brother?"

Dave frowned.

"Don't know," he said. "I won't know until I get the sight and stink of this place out of my eyes and nose." He reached into his pocket and pulled out the cut chain. It glittered like a living metal thing in his grasp. "The day comes I can throw this away, I'll know I found something here—found it for good."

He turned, unzipped his sleeping bag and opened it. He lay down in it, throwing the unzipped top flap loosely over him.

"Paying Caesar never really worried me none," he said, looking up at the night sky. "It was paying God. Actually, a man ought to be able to pay them both off—and be free.

I'll see about that after I'm clear of this place. Well, party's over. Night."

"Farewell," said Ranald.

In a moment Dave was asleep and the meadow held only one waking mind under the moon and the stars.

Dawn rose on a meadow empty of more than nine tenths of the crowd that had filled it when it was most full. And these that were left now went about the business of leaving, themselves. Even before the sun was above the hill beyond the road where the trucks had lined up, most of the last few campers were gone or on their way; and, now that the meadow was clearing, it was possible to see the signs they had left behind them.

The crowd had been good about collecting their litter and trash in the beginning. But the last couple of days, all order had begun to disintegrate. Now that the surface of the meadow was no longer hidden by people, it showed all sorts of discarded material, as if the ground had sickened with a disease called humanity; and the illness showed now in a rash of useless items. Torn newspapers, unclean plastic and paper plates, empty cans, abandoned, punctured air mattresses in various gaudy colors, bits of tents and clothing, shoes and garbage, all blotched the gentle slope where sparse but tough green grass had covered loose, brown soil. Above, the morning sky was high and blue with clouds as fluffy and clean as if they had just been born out of the pure upper air. It was cool, with a fair, small wind blowing from the northwest, from the hill down toward the unseen river.

Around Dave's campfire, they were also getting ready to leave, packing up along with the two dozen or so other people remaining in the meadow. There were two of the sheriff's deputies in uniform going from group to group.

One of these was Tom Rathkenny. He came up to the fire with a paper in his hand, as shiny in leather helmet, boots, and Sam Browne belt as he had been the first time they had seen him. Only the holster at his belt was empty, though the fact that the holster flap was closed and buttoned down helped to disguise its emptiness.

"I'll take my gun back," he said to Dave, holding out his free hand.

Dave, seated as he filled his pack, looked at the hand for a second, then reached into the pack, pulled out the revolver and handed it up. Tom unbuttoned his holster and put the weapon into it; but he did not button down the flap again. He held the paper up.

"This is a legal notice," he said. "Your license to camp here has expired and the county court orders you to vacate the premises, after cleaning up any litter you have left, repairing any damage you have done, and returning the area you have occupied to the condition it enjoyed before you occupied it."

"I never was much for being able to grow grass in one day," said Dave.

The younger man ignored him. Tom was looking at Rob only, and running the thumbnail of his right hand back and forth along the top curve of his unbuttoned holster flap. Rob, busy packing the tattered blankets he owned with Letty, ignored the attention he was getting. Ranald, the only one of them unmoving, still seated as if he had not even shifted once from his position the night before, watched both of the younger men.

"Yang and Yin," said Ranald to Tom, without warning, "love and hate. '*Abou Ben Adhem, may his tribe increase, awoke one night from a great dream of peace; and saw within the moonlight of his room—*'"

It was a moment before they all realized he was reciting verse; and, when they did realize, they continued to listen—for the moment all stopped from what they were doing—as if caught by the magic of primitive people listening to an incantation.

"*Making it rich,*" Ranald went on, as if no one but Tom were there.

"*. . . and like a lily in bloom,*
  An angel writing in a book of gold.
Exceeding peace had made Ben Adhem bold;
  And to the presence in the room he said,
'What writest thou?' The Vision raised his head;
  And with a look made of all sweet accord,
Answered, 'The names of those who love the Lord.'
  'And is mine one?' asked Abou. 'Nay, not so,'
Replied the Angel. Abou spake more low,
  But cheerily still, and said, 'I pray thee, then,
Write me as one that loves his fellow men.'
  The Angel wrote and vanished. The next night,
He came again with a great wakening light;
  And showed the names whom love of God
    had bless'd;
And lo! Ben Adhem's name led all the rest."

"*. . . and there are others,*" Ranald said, without pause or change in his voice. '*Le temps a laissé son manteau, De vent, de froidure, et de pluie . . .*' Also, '*He prayeth well who loveth well both man and bird and beast . . .*' But it doesn't matter. I was too young the first time this happened. Each one must build or break his own god.—And I, like all . . ."

Then, as they still watched and waited, his attention

went away off from them again into time and space, as it
had the day before. They sat or stood, still without speaking—there was something in the air, something fearful
promised to whoever might break the silence first.

"What was that about?" asked Dave.

He asked the question of Ranald, but Ranald did not
answer and he looked around at the others.

"That . . . that last bit about praying was from
Coleridge—'The Ancient Mariner,'" said Walt, unsurely,
staring at Ranald. "The French bit was from the four-
teenth-fifteenth century—a poem about how wonderful
spring was, written by a man who'd been locked in prison
for years, I think . . . Charles d'Orléans. That first verse
is by some nineteenth-century poet." He looked at Maybeth and Letty and Rob in turn. "I can't remember who.
Do you know?"

They stared at him, and shook their heads.

"All three things he quoted have something to do with
loving—people or things . . ." Walt said. "I . . . don't understand."

Dave looked at Tom Rathkenny. Tom's features were
pale and tight. It was impossible to tell whether his expression was one of fear, or rage, or only of simple embar-
rassment. He wore a statue's or an idol's face; and, as
Dave's eyes hit him now, Tom turned and plunged away,
off down the slope of the meadow toward another group
of late departees.

Rob looked after him for a moment, then turned back
to stuff the last blanket into the pack he, himself, would
be carrying, and buckled it closed. Getting to his feet, he
put the pack on. Letty already bore hers.

"Well," said Rob, half turned to go. He hesitated, looking at Maybeth and Walt. "We've got the promise of a

ride in the last panel truck down there. The driver wants somebody along to help him change tires. He could take some more people besides us."

Walt got slowly to his feet, then shook his head.

"No," he said. "I've got to be alone—a while."

He snatched up his pack and went off away from the road, downslope, but not in the direction Tom had taken, until he disappeared into the woods between meadow and river. They watched him go; and neither Tom nor the other sheriff's deputy was watching as he went.

"Well," said Rob, after he had gone, "anyone who wants a ride better come along in a hurry. That trucker's ready to pull out."

He and Letty took their gear and went toward the road. Maybeth looked after them, hesitated, and looked back at Dave and Ranald.

Ranald's eyes, once more lost on the view of his inner vision, looked through and past her. Dave returned her look.

"Better go," Dave said.

"I can't stay with you," she said, "even a little longer?"

Dave shook his head slowly.

"Not me," he answered. "Someday, maybe, if it turns out this changed things, I may want a woman around steady, neighbors in to dinner, and all the rest of it. But that's someday."

He buckled tight the last buckle of his pack on its packframe and stood up, sliding his arms through the straps. Maybeth looked at Ranald.

"Good-bye, Ranald," she said.

He came a little way back from where he had gone, to speak to her.

"Go with a god," he said. "Your god, if may be. But any god will do."

She turned abruptly and almost ran after Rob and Letty, who were now standing talking to a short, brown-shirted man beside the left front door of a somewhat battered blue panel truck—the only vehicle left in the meadow except for two motorcycles of the sheriff's deputies. Dave looked after her for a moment as she joined them, and they all got into the truck. It pulled away, back down the route up which they had all come.

"The other way, for me," said Dave, "up that road alongside the river we saw, into Medora or whatever they call it. A day or so's walking'll clear my head."

He looked back at Ranald.

"So long, then," Dave said. "Maybe we'll run into each other again."

"I don't think so," said Ranald. His voice and eyes were a little strange because of his being only partway back. "I will turn away a little, then turn back and find you are dust. Unless . . ."

"Unless?" Dave stared at him curiously.

"Unless . . ." said Ranald, still from the in-between of two places, "you turn away, then turn back to find me dust. I was too young the first time I saw this."

"You figuring on dying?" said Dave, bluntly.

"No. Yes—eventually. Maybe, soon . . ." Ranald came almost all the way back and looked up at Dave with strangely clear eyes. "I do not know if I want to. I do not know if I should. I don't know if I will."

Dave stared at him.

"What makes you so sure anything'll happen?" he asked.

"Always," said Ranald. "People always do the same

things. A curse makes a blow—makes—wounding—makes a killing."

Dave grunted slightly under his breath.

"Man ought to know what's he doing."

"I belong to no god," said Ranald. "And no more do I belong to any people, so that their ways are a law to me. I belong, though, to myself—to Ranald; and I do not know what Ranald is going to do. It's a little thing to die after three score years and ten. To die after much longer is a hard problem. How can I be sure this moment is so worthwhile? Will it be worth all those other times before when I refused death, fought it off and said—'Not yet'?"

Dave hesitated. Then he took a step closer and held out his hand.

"Luck," he said.

Ranald reached up and took hold; but with his hand grasping Dave's forearm above the wrist, so that Dave had no choice but to fold his own fingers around Ranald's forearm in return. They let go.

"If I'm to die soon," said Ranald, "I'd like to see you free first, Brother Piers." He added, almost muttering under his breath, "'Cessez, cessez, gens d'armes et piétons —de piller et manger le bonhomme . . .'"

"You're full up with poems, today," said Dave.

"It's Walt and his question about Caesar that opened my memory to them," said Ranald. "Walt was right. His question is the question, after all. . . ."

He stopped talking as if he had run down.

"As I say, luck, then," said Dave after a second. But this time Ranald did not answer. Dave shook his head, turned, and went off with a loose, swinging stride toward the far end of the meadow where the trees came together, hiding the road to Medora.

Near the middle of the road beside the openness of the meadow, the two deputies watched him go. Then they turned back. Ranald was the last left amidst the litter of the open space, sitting cross-legged and unmoving. One of the deputies started toward him; but the other, who walked like Tom Rathkenny, caught the first by the arm and turned him around. They went to their motorcycles, the other got on his and left in the opposite direction Dave had taken, back toward the city. Tom started his own bike after a minute and slowly followed. Ranald was alone in the meadow.

Now that there was no human activity around to retreat from, he came all the way back into the present, opening all his senses to the land around him and its inhabitants. Already half a mile distant, the other sheriff's deputy droned on his motorcycle back toward his headquarters. Tom Rathkenny, just out of sight beyond the meadow, had pulled his machine off the road behind a willow clump and stopped. He put the kickstand down carefully and got off.

A few hundred yards beyond and out of sight on the winding road from Tom, the panel truck had stopped with a flat tire, which Rob was just now replacing with a spare from inside the truck, while the driver stood by and watched.

In the opposite direction, already out of sight beyond the meadow, Dave swung along the people-empty route to Medora, the sound of his bootsoles in the loose gravel on the shoulder of the roadway noisy in the noon silence. Down beside the river, beyond the woods and not moving —possibly on his knees—Walt was praying out loud.

". . . I'm this way because this is the way You made me, Lord," he was praying. "No, I don't mean to put all the responsibility on You; but You ought to share in what I am. . . ."

All these things—the rushing of the river, the rustling of tree leaves, the drone of a nearby wasp—came clearly and unavoidably to Ranald's acute hearing. There was a flutter of wings, and a male Western song sparrow came to a perch on the end of a leaning tent-pole near Ranald, a tent-pole abandoned, but still stuck in the earth and semi-upright. The song sparrow threw back his head and sang, and Ranald understood. Like the intentions of humans, the messages of birds and animals had become clear to him through long time and familiarity. But he had never understood a bird as clearly as this one, at this moment.

"*I am me!*" cried the song sparrow. "*Me! Me! And this meadow is mine! Mine—and no other's! Mine—and no other's!*"

". . . Lord," Walt was praying to a God in whom he had no trust, no hope, "You should help me. . . ."

". . . All right," Rob was saying to the driver of the panel truck, "suppose you get something into your head. We came along to *help* with your flat tires; not do all the work while you stand around juicing! The next tire that goes flat, you're going to do as much fixing as we do!"

"That's what you get for trying to do favors," said the driver, climbing back into the front seat of the truck. "To hell with you. Just to hell with you! You can walk into town!"

He closed the door of the truck, started the panel up and drove off.

"Wait—" Maybeth called after him.

"Let him go," said Rob. "They're all alike. I ought to've known."

Dave had begun to whistle as he strode along. Walt was still praying. Tom Rathkenny had left his motorcycle and was walking down the curve of the wooded road toward Rob and the others, although he could not yet be close enough for them to see him. The breeze blowing against the left side of Ranald's face ceased for a moment. Abruptly, he sprang upright; and headed down the road in the direction everyone but Dave and Walt had taken, breaking into a run.

He ran with some oddly long strides he had used down by the river when he had taken the gun from Tom. His running was effortlessly swift, so that he seemed to soar slightly with each step, the way a deer soars with each bound. He crossed the road and headed on a direct line through the trees, toward that spot beside the road where Rob and Letty were dividing up some of the load in their packs, so that Maybeth could help them carry it on foot back into town.

Ranald ran. Up ahead of him, out of sight beyond the trees, Tom Rathkenny came around a curve and walked up to the three as they were redistributing the load they had to pack.

"So, you're still here," said Tom.

Rob's answer was lost to Ranald. He was in full stride, now. He coursed the woods like a wild animal, hurdling fallen logs and small bushes in his path as if some instinct deep within him told him when to go over, and when around. The slope of the hillside and its sun-dappled tree trunks swam around him; and the late morning breeze was cold on face and neck where he had begun to sweat. Ahead, talk between Tom and the others had become some kind of an argument between Tom and Rob; and as Ranald rocketed down the wooded slope, close to the thers now, Rob's voice reached clearly through the eaves and pine needles.

"You and Letty?" Rob was saying. "Oh, sure . . . You know what she does? She collects cats, man; and squirrels; and birds with half a leg missing. But she doesn't keep them."

They were all right ahead of Ranald now, although the trees still hid them. He burst through that last screen and came out only a few running steps from them. Maybeth and Letty stood back by the side of the road with the opened packs, and one blanket that had been tied up to make it into a sort of packsack. Between the girls and the trees Tom stood facing Rob with perhaps eight feet of space between them. Rob's back was arched; the narrow, tight muscles of his shoulders under their shirt were thrust forward. Tom was stiffly upright and pale, with the sweat rolling down his face. In his hand he held his revolver, pointed at Rob.

"Go ahead," Rob said. "Let's see you shoot me. You've been talking about it long enough—"

Running at full speed, Ranald came between them, turning his upper body toward Tom just as the revolver went off. The battering-ram impact of the heavy revolver slug high on his left side spun him around. He tried to carry the spin on around in a full circle and stay on his feet. But his legs staggered and dropped him. He lay on his back on the soft roadside earth, looking at the clouds.

The blow of the bullet had left him without breath to speak. There were voices above him, and faces, looking down—Letty and Maybeth, particularly Maybeth. His eyes met hers. He could not remember a woman who had looked at him so.

Both she and Letty were kneeling over him, one on

each side. Letty ripped his jacket and shirt open, poppin
buttons as if they had been sewn with paper.

"It's down there," said Letty, staring at his bare ches
"He needs a doctor. He's got to have a doctor, quick."

"I didn't," Tom was saying. "I didn't pull the trigger.
wasn't going to hurt anyone. It just went off. It-
exploded. By itself. I wasn't going to shoot anyone. . . .

"God . . ." Rob said. His voice was like the thick voic
of a drunk. "God, you bastard . . ."

"We've got to get help," said Maybeth, looking up. "A
ambulance!"

"Where's his motorcycle?" Letty asked. She had tor
off a portion of Ranald's shirt and wadded it up. She wa
holding this against the bullet hole in his chest. "It
hardly bleeding at all. Maybe he's bleeding inside."

"Please . . ." said Maybeth, almost crying. She ha
lifted Ranald's head softly onto her knee and was tryin
to wipe dry his forehead with the edge of her skir
"Please, will somebody please go get an ambulance?"

"It just went off," Tom said. "I was holding it like th
—I didn't even have my finger—"

"Where's your cycle?" Letty asked over her shoulde
"Get on it and get going. Can't you see we need som
help?"

"You don't understand. It's not supposed to go off ur
less it's cocked," said Tom. "Well, I mean you can pu
the trigger, but unless it's cocked . . . I didn't have
cocked. I don't think I—"

"That iron's got to be back where we were camped. H
walked here just now." Rob's voice was still thick, but ser
sible. "I'll go find it. I'll ride the thing."

"No, I'll go . . . I'll go," said Tom's voice, movin

away. "It's just back around the curve, there. I'll ride up the other way to Medora. That's where the hospital is."

"You'll go someplace else . . ." said Rob, thickly. "You'll let him die—we all saw it, how you shot him!"

"No—I'm going . . ." There was a sound of boots running off. Tom's voice floated back. "Over the hill, there—down a ways—a farm. Maybe you can get to their phone before—"

He did not finish, running off.

"The farm—you go, Rob!" said Letty. "You—" Her face jerked for Maybeth. "Run back to the camp. Maybe there's somebody still there, or still near, who can help. Get going, damn it, will you both?"

Rob turned and went running into the trees up the hillside.

"No," said Maybeth, not moving, "I won't leave him. You go. Hurry!"

Letty lifted the wadded shirtcloth from the wound. It had all but stopped bleeding. For a second it looked as if she were about to hit Maybeth with the fist holding the cloth. Then she shoved the cloth instead into Maybeth's hand.

"Watch him!" Letty said, and scrambled to her feet. She started off at a trot back toward the meadow.

Left alone with Ranald, Maybeth pressed the cloth gently against the hole in his chest and let her head drop until her face was hidden by the long mass of hair that spilled forward like a dark wave onto the leather-brown skin of his lean chest. He had recovered his breath now; and he felt only something like an emptiness, a heavy emptiness, where the bullet had gone in and stopped.

"Do not mourn," he said to her, a little faintly, "this is

a great moment. I'm like the rest of them, after all. I did what any one of them would do."

She lifted her head and shook her hair back so that she could see his face, and he, hers. Her face was simply a face, now, but very still. She, who had been able to cry so easily, could make no tears in this moment.

"You'll be all right," she said. "Don't talk."

"I am all right," he said. "And why not talk? I came here knowing what would happen. Men and women do always the same things. It happened; and I will fall from the cliff now, leaving some other climber my handholds and my footholds."

"Don't talk like, that," she whispered, as if her throat were raw. "As if it was nothing—as if you were just being wasted."

"That is man," he said, "who can waste himself. It's a gift. The small birds and all other creatures don't know how."

She twisted as if a bullet had just entered her own body.

"No!" she said. "Don't agree with me like that. You saved Rob's life with your own, and he isn't worth it!"

"There is no worth," he said. "What is paid to God, or paid to Caesar, has only the value the giver gives it. A man must choose which one to pay, though, even though he's like me and needs neither of them. I was wrong about that. I had to choose; and I chose to pay the least foolish of the two."

"No!" she said. "No—you saved someone's life. You threw away your life after all this time to save somebody else. Because you love people, you really do. You just won't admit it."

"Do I?" he asked. "Even if I do, it doesn't matter. Man

loves man. They love each other—that's the important thing, even when they don't know it. Look at them; they love each other even when they hurt and kill each other. It's their pride. Which is why they will accept no god-help." .

She shook her head.

"All this," she said, "just to satisfy yourself! All this!"

"No, no," he said. "To find home, again. I was a wanderer and I've discovered my own place, again. I was a stranger and I've found my people. You—and Dave, and Rob and Letty and Tom and all the others."

He closed his eyes for a second, looking for the image of the green clearing and the log houses, but they were gone for good. He felt Maybeth's hands, suddenly frantic on his face.

"No," she was saying. "Don't . . . hold on. . . . They'll have help here in just a minute. . . ."

He opened his eyes.

"I'll have to be going now," he said. "Walt is down by the river. Go to him."

"Walt!" She went suddenly from her knees to a squatting position with her feet under her, ready to rise. "He's probably got things in his pack. Maybe he knows—where is he?"

"You remember where Dave and you and I came first to the edge of the river," he said. "Close to there. Go there and call him. He'll hear you."

"Oh, yes—" She started to rise, then stopped. "But I can't leave you."

"It makes no difference whether you leave me or not," he said.

"It does! But—" She looked back toward the meadow and the woods. "If Walt can help . . . I've got to go.

Maybe he knows something about medicine, or he was a medic in the army once, or something. Don't move, I'll be right back—"

She started to rise. He caught her arm with surprising strength for a wounded man and held her for a moment while he spoke.

"I'll lie still awhile," he said. "But things don't hurt me easily. It takes more to kill me than most imagine. If we don't speak again, remember to trust yourself as you would have trusted me."

"Don't talk like that!" She pulled away and he let her go, to her feet and running back toward the meadow. He lay still for a little, listening until the intervening trees softened the sound of her footfalls.

The sun was warm upon him, the heavy emptiness was only a little larger within him. He rose on his left elbow, rolled to his side, and climbed to his feet. For a moment he swayed and tottered, a little off balance. Then he put out one foot before the other and began to walk.

He went in the same direction in which Maybeth had left, running. But once more, his path was a straight line, and soon it took him away from the road and back into the trees of the hillside. He walked more surely now, and faster. Soon, he began to run—at first only at a slow trot, staggering a little, but then with more speed and balance.

Still, it was a slow and clumsy pace he made, compared to his earlier soaring run. The easiness was gone from his coursing. His legs, which had been weightless and instinctive, now were heavy and needed to be driven, one past the other, by the push of his will. At the same time, it was not all work and weakness. The sun flicked at him through the treetops, the breeze cooled his face, and the woods gathered around him as he went. He passed through the trees above the road by the meadow, hearing

Maybeth, now out of sight toward the river, calling for Walt, and Walt answering.

He ran on, leaving the meadow and the two of them together, behind. A Western song sparrow flew past him, perched on a low-swung sugar maple limb and watched him pass, cocking its head at him.

He ran on. Angling downslope now—until the straight line he followed once more intersected the road, so that he crossed it and went on into the woods on that same side as the meadow had lain, a way back. He could hear the river growing louder, now, as it swung in toward the road and him; and the angle of the ground on which he ran bent into an upslope, for he was coming close now to that point of land from which he and Maybeth and Dave had looked beyond to river and road running side by side toward Medora.

The heaviness was larger in him now; but now it made no difference. He had had some doubts earlier, but now he knew that even the stubborn will to live could be slain. He ran now almost as he had run before, not as lightly but nearly as fast as he had run to meet the slug from Tom Rathkenny's revolver. The woods swam past him and the song sparrow flew steadily to keep up with him.

Now, the meadow was more than a short distance behind and the heaviness in his chest was grown large enough to make him stagger again for all the length of his strides and his speed. It was done now. To stop would end it. He could hear not only the river loudly now but, even more loudly, Dave, whom he had caught up with and was now passing, above, and out of sight among the trees.

He passed Dave and saw the end of the woods, the edge of the cliff overlooking the partnering of river and road. His head spun, and his chest felt as heavy as if it contained a cannonball. He staggered to a stop and dropped to his knees at the edge of the cliff, looking out through a screen of low bushes and popple saplings at the road below. Dave, below and a little behind him now, had begun to sing:

> *"There was a rich man and he lived in Jerusalem.*
> *Glory, Hallelujah, hi-ro-de-rum."*

He seized the pencil-thin stem of one of the saplings to hold himself upright on his knees. For a moment doubt chilled him with something like terror; but his body cried the truth to reassure him. It was a hard body to kill; but there was a limit to any flesh and bone and the cunning toughness of a thousand years. This last run had finished what the revolver bullet had started; and the cliff that only he could see was growing misty and insubstantial before his inner vision, as the life-hold of his will upon its craggy surface slackened.

He swayed on his knees, still managing to stay upright; and caught hold of another popple stem with his other hand to support himself. The song sparrow perched on a narrow young limb not a foot from his eyes.

"Gods," he said, "I am overdue, long overdue, but I won't disappoint you. Watch me fall, like the others."

". . . *Now the poor man died,*" Dave was singing as he strode along the road down below, his voice growing stronger as he drew level with the high point where Ranald knelt above him, "*and his soul went to Heavenium.*"

> *"Glory, Hallelujah, hi-ro-de-rum.*
> *He danced with the angels till a quarter past elevenium.*
> *Glory, Hallelujah, hi-ro-de-rum."*

"Gods," murmured Ranald, "mourn that you can only fly; and were not born a human who knows what it is to climb."

He swayed, almost going down, but held up by his grip on the saplings. Dave was almost in sight now; and as Ranald held grimly on, the foreshortened, pack-laden figure came into view below, emerging by the river, singing . . .

"Now the rich man died and he didn't fare so wellium.
  Glory, Hallelujah, hi-ro-de-rum.
He couldn't go to Heaven, so he had to go to Hellium
  Glory . . ."

Ranald held to the saplings, watching Dave move off along the road, singing. A little way farther on he stopped, abruptly, both singing and walking, and stepped over to look down into the waters of the river by the bank.

"Now," said Ranald to himself, but unheard to Dave as well; "all men and women do the same things, time after time—only perhaps, just once, my brother . . ."

Dave started to turn back to the road, taking up his song again. But he broke off and swung once more to face the water. His hand went into the right-hand pocket of his Levi's and came out with something which he threw, arcing, out into the middle of the stream. It twisted and glittered like a metal snake as it flew; and a fraction of a second after it had entered the water there was no sign it had ever existed.

Ranald let all the breath out of himself in a deep sigh. He loosened his grip on the popples, and his cupped palms slid down their lengths, roughened and stained by sap from the young torn bark, as he fell forward onto the ground between them. With a last effort, he rolled over on his back to hear Dave's song more clearly as it moved off in the distance.

"Gods . . ." Ranald said; but that was all.

Above him the song sparrow looked down at him, then threw back his head, exposing the white blaze on its chest like a star of great worth, a medal of immeasurable honor, to the hot midday sun.

"*God is Man and Man is God,*" sang the song sparrow above Ranald, "*and I am a Bird!*"

Far and farther away, as the world closed in about Ranald, so that the sun was very close above his head and the song sparrow perched almost on the threshold of his mind, the last of Dave's song chanted faintly to his hearing.

"*Now, the moral of this story is riches are no jokium.*
  Glory, Hallelujah, hi-ro-de-rum!
We all will go to Heaven for we all are stony brokium.
  Glory, Hallelujah, hi-ro-de-rum . . ."

—And farther, fainter yet, but invincible still, as Ranald let go his last hold on the cliff and began to fall, the closing chorus followed him down. . . .

"*Hi-ro-de-rum! hi-ro-de-rum!*
Skinna-ma-rinky-doodle-doo!   Skinna-ma-rinky-doodle-doo!
  Glory, Hallelujah. . . ."